TREASURE COAST
Promise

EMERALD BAY
BOOK 2

LEIGH DUNCAN

Treasure Coast Promise
Emerald Bay, Book #2

Copyright ©2023 by Leigh D. Duncan

Digital ISBN: 978-1-944258-36-8
Print ISBN: 978-1-944258-37-5
Gardenia Street Publishing

Published in the United States of America

Welcome to Emerald Bay!

After a lifetime of running the finest inn in Emerald Bay, Margaret Clayton has to make a decision…sell the Dane Crown Inn to a stranger or put her hopes for the future in her family's hands. For most people, the choice would be simple. But nothing about her family is simple…especially not with her daughter and four nieces whose help Margaret needs now more than ever.

The five cousins know the inn as well as Margaret does. As young girls and teenagers, they spent every summer keeping the cottages and suites spotless, and enjoying the gorgeous beach as a tight knit family. Thirty years later, though, these five women have complicated, important, distant, and utterly packed lives. The last thing any of them can do is drop everything and save the inn. But, when it comes to family, the last thing is sometimes the *only* thing.

As the once-close cousins come together on the glorious shores of Florida's Treasure Coast, they learn that some things never change, but others can never be the same. And the only thing that matters is family which, like the Dane Crown Inn, is forever.

Treasure Coast Homecoming, Book 1
Treasure Coast Promise, Book 2
Treasure Coast Christmas, Book 3
Treasure Coast Revival, Book 4
Treasure Coast Discovery, Book 5
Treasure Coast Legacy, Book 6

To get the most enjoyment from the Emerald Bay series, start with *Treasure Coast Homecoming* and read the books in order.

One

Amy

A warm breeze rustled the ragged tips of the arborvitae planted around the deck where Amy and the others had gathered to discuss their Aunt Margaret's earth-shattering news. With her arm in a cast, the result of a recent fall, the matriarch of the family had announced her plan to sell the Dane Crown Inn, the only home she'd ever known. All she'd asked in return was to host one last family reunion at the inn.

Not that finding a buyer would be an easy task. Aunt Margaret refused to sell to just anyone. The stubborn senior citizen had her own way of doing things, and selling to the highest bidder would be way too simple. Instead, she'd insisted that any potential buyer must agree to keep the inn open, to continue the Dane family tradition of providing lodging for visitors to the Sunshine State.

Nostalgia washed over Amy in waves. Some of her fondest memories came from the inn. Sliding across the dark hardwood floors in her stockinged feet. The crisp, clean scent of freshly washed linens as she helped make the beds or replace the towels in the guest suites. The clatter of plates when she and the other girls cleared the dining room table. The heavy clomp-clomp-clomp of suitcases and feet on the stairs whenever new arrivals checked in or others departed.

She'd lived and worked at the inn from birth through her teens, and the thought of someone other than a Dane standing at the registration desk made her throat ache with unshed tears. She couldn't imagine how difficult it had been for her 80-year-old aunt to decide to sell the place.

Wondering how they were taking the news, Amy studied the faces of the others. In her usual fashion, Amy's younger sister Diane ignored the entire situation by scrolling through messages on her cell phone. Meanwhile, their cousins, Belle and Kim, sat motionless on opposite sides of the glass-topped table, apparently stunned into silence by Aunt Margaret's announcement.

Now that the summer sun had finally dipped

beneath the horizon, a blend of evergreen, jasmine and honeysuckle scented the air. Amy gulped a steadying breath as she scanned the distant Intracoastal Waterway that ran along the western edge of the property. Above it, low clouds had turned the sky into a glorious display of pinks and golds. From the other side of the house came the ever-present sound of waves rolling onto the beach. With the Atlantic Ocean a mere stone's throw from the entrance and front-row seats to spectacular sunsets, no wonder the Dane Crown Inn had once been hailed as "the gem of Florida's Treasure Coast." These days, though, even she had to admit that the jewel had lost its shine. Everywhere Amy looked, signs of neglect marred the once pristine inn.

Her tummy rumbled, and she realized hours had passed since she'd last eaten. She eyed a water droplet that clung to the pitcher of fruity punch on the table in front of her. Mentally, she shook her head. Alcohol on an empty stomach was never a good idea.

While she waited for one of the others to voice an opinion, she snagged a cracker from the tray Kim had brought out from the kitchen. As tasty as the morsel was, the baker in Amy argued that it could still stand a little something. What harm would a smear of dip do, she wondered?

3

Maybe a tiny dab of comfort food. Or cheese. She'd settle for a bit of cheese.

Not that her still-bare cracker was anyone's fault but her own. After all, she'd spent the most time with Aunt Margaret lately, and not even she had imagined the octogenarian would wander the uneven paths around the inn on her own. Or that she'd fall and shatter her arm so badly she'd earn herself an ambulance ride, one that had been followed by surgery and a hospital stay. No, Amy wouldn't have imagined that any more than she'd have pictured Belle putting her career on hold or Diane taking time away from the office during the busy tax season to be at Margaret's bedside. One thing for certain, though, Amy had never dreamed they'd hear the family matriarch talk about selling the property that had been passed down from one Dane to another for more than five decades. But here they were at the end of a bright summer day, clustered around a table on the deck between the two-story inn and the six cottages that stood on twenty acres of prime real estate while they discussed the end of an era, the demise of a legacy.

Anxious to know Belle's reaction, Amy glanced across the table at her famous cousin. Did she consider the Dane Crown Inn a white elephant? Was she relieved at the possibility of selling her childhood home? Or was she as appalled as Amy by the decision?

The woman who'd literally charmed kings and queens, who'd performed before crowds of thousands, gave no indication of how she felt about the bomb her mother had dropped on them all. For that matter, the superstar looked decidedly put-together for someone who'd arrived in Emerald Bay a short time ago wearing the world's baggiest T-shirt and with a tattered NY Yankees baseball cap pulled low over her eyes. Amy supposed her cousin's glam probably had something to do with the special courier who'd shown up lugging several large suitcases. One of them had held more curling irons, makeup brushes and lotions than Amy had ever seen outside a beauty supply store. No wonder Belle looked like she'd just stepped off a magazine cover.

Well, except for her hair. Though Amy would never be the one to point it out, her cousin's red curls had frizzed in Florida's humidity. And she suspected that underneath those oversize sunglasses Belle dropped into place every time she stepped outside, a few new worry lines etched the skin around her wide green eyes. But with all they'd gone through the last couple of days, Belle probably wasn't the only one who sported a new wrinkle or two.

Unable to read her cousin's thoughts, Amy sought to make eye contact with her sister, but Diane merely met her glance with an arched brow that gave away nothing. Amy wondered what was really going on with Diane. Her sister had been quieter and more withdrawn than normal ever since she strode down the hospital corridor and demanded an update on her aunt's condition. Maybe there was more to her husband Tim's vacation than Diane wanted to let on? Was that the reason for her moodiness? Amy shook her head. There was no sense in trying to ferret it out. She could use a crowbar, and Diane still wouldn't spill the beans until she was good and ready. Whatever it was, Amy'd bet a dozen cupcakes she wouldn't like the rest of the story.

When Diane continued to ignore her, Amy shifted her focus to Kim, but her cousin only returned Amy's reassuring smile with a worried frown. And no wonder. Kim had every right to be concerned. She, more than the rest of them, had the most to lose. After all, Amy reminded herself, she had Sweet Cakes, the bakery she'd built from scratch in the heart of Emerald Bay. Where business was so good she'd hardly notice if her aunt stopped placing the inn's daily order.

As for her sister, not only did she have a great job in a big Tampa accounting firm, but Diane's husband owned a thriving dental practice. The couple was so well off that Diane could afford to handle the inn's books for free. And then there was Belle. A pop star in her twenties, she'd practically been rolling in money from the very beginning of her career. Now, thanks to thirty-plus years at the top of the charts, she lived a lavish lifestyle. Amy had never visited Belle's condo overlooking Central Park, but she'd devoured the spread *Architectural Digest* had done on the place and had whistled at the apartment's multimillion-dollar price tag.

So no, the three of them wouldn't suffer financially if the inn went under. Kim's situation, however, was altogether different.

From practically the moment she'd been born, the cards had been stacked against Kim. Amy had never understood how her mom's sister Shirley could show up without warning, dump Kim and her younger sister Jen on the inn's doorstep, and just take off. But she did it, over and over. Amy had to give her own mom and her Aunt Margaret credit—they'd never complained. Instead, they'd done their best to show their nieces what it was like to have a regular home life. Not that it ever lasted long.

About the time her cousins would settle in to their new routine, Aunt Shirley's car would rattle up the driveway. One day Amy and Kim would be changing the linens in the suites upstairs, the next Shirley would be shoving Kim and Jen into the back seat of a car and moving on. That had gone on until Kim was in high school, when Aunt Shirley had succumbed to lung cancer. After that, Aunt Margaret had tucked her nieces firmly under her wings and kept them there until the girls graduated from high school.

Jen, who'd idolized her mom, took off to see the world at her first opportunity. She'd barely kept in touch ever since. Even now, no one—not even Kim—knew how to contact her.

Unlike her sister, though, Kim had stayed put. She'd paid her way through college by working holidays and summers at the inn. A good job, marriage and two kids had quickly followed. In all of that, Kim had only made one mistake— she'd married Frank. Amy had pegged him for a loser from the start, but it had taken her cousin nearly two decades to see the man for the user he was and file for divorce. Now Kim had come back to Emerald Bay to get a fresh start. But if Aunt Margaret sold the inn, where would that leave her?

"So are we really going to do this?" Belle demanded.

"You mean, restore the inn to its former glory so Aunt Margaret can sell the place?" Diane asked.

Leave it to her sister to overstate the obvious.

"Yes, that." Amy nodded. Several developers were champing at the bit to get their hands on the land, but Aunt Margaret refused to consider their offers.

"Plus, there's the little matter of hosting one final Dane Family Reunion," Kim added. For years the entire family had converged on the inn for two weeks of fun in the Florida sunshine at the start of every summer, a tradition that had come to an abrupt halt after Uncle Eric suffered a fatal heart attack nearly a decade ago. Now Aunt Margaret had insisted on getting the family together one last time before she handed the keys to the inn to new owners.

"Oh, those were such good times," Amy exclaimed as memories flooded back. "All our cousins, our aunts and uncles. Friends and family we only saw once a year. It was the highlight of every summer. What was your favorite part?" She looked at Diane.

"Searching for buried treasure." Diane finally set her phone facedown on the table. "We'd borrow the map from the study, and before you knew it, the whole gang was marching across the dunes, searching for the place where X marked the spot."

Amy's mouth twitched. Diane had been obsessed with finding some of the gold and emeralds from a Spanish fleet that had shipwrecked off the coast in 1715. Despite all her efforts, she'd never found so much as a single piece of eight.

Diane's voice turned pensive. "I wonder whatever happened to that map."

"Aunt Margaret probably knows." Amy brightened at her sister's interest. "We can ask her."

"The treasure hunts were fun, but I enjoyed helping Aunt Liz in the kitchen," Kim said in turn. "I think I was ten the first time she let me make the 'secret sauce' for the sandwiches."

"Ah, the mystery goo," Diane mused. "What *was* in that stuff?"

"It was simple, really," Kim explained. "Lots of mayo, a little ketchup and a dab of mustard. When she wanted to fancy it up, Aunt Liz would add some pickle relish. We'd deal slices of white bread out on the counter like cards, slather each one with secret sauce, pile on some lunch meat and top it with a slice of plain bread. A piece of fruit and a handful of chips and voila, lunch."

"Which you either ate or went hungry." Belle's pouty lips widened into a smile.

"Lord help anyone who asked for something different," Amy reminded them. "Mom didn't put up with people who were too full of themselves." The inn's kitchen had been her mother's domain.

"You're talking about Frank, aren't you?" Kim sighed. "I'll never forget the time he turned up his nose at a bologna sandwich and demanded Aunt Liz fix him roast beef. I was so embarrassed."

Amy's eyes widened. "I can still see Mom now, standing in the kitchen shaking one finger at him and demanding, 'Do you see a menu? Does this look like a fancy restaurant to you?'" Behind the hand she clamped over her mouth, she grinned. If she had a nickel for every time she'd heard her mom say those words, she'd be a wealthy woman.

"It took a lot of work to feed the whole family during the reunions," Kim pointed out. "It seemed like we were always grating the cabbage for coleslaw or peeling potatoes for dinner."

"I skipped out on that as much as I could, but I loved helping Mom with the breakfast rolls and the desserts," Amy confessed. She was thankful every day for all she'd learned as she worked at her mom's elbow in the roomy kitchen.

"You were a baker at heart, even then." Diane tilted her head.

"My favorite part was the talent show on the last day of camp each year," Belle added.

"Of course it was. You were always the star." Diane's wistful smile took the sting out of her words.

"I see now why Mama wants to get the whole family together again," Belle said. "We all have some great memories of those reunions. It'd be nice to pass some of them on to another generation of Danes, wouldn't it?"

At Belle's searching look, Amy pressed a hand to her forehead. "You know we'd be committing to a ton of work. We could have as many as fifty mouths to feed. That's a huge task."

"There'll be events to organize. Invitations to issue. We'll have to figure out where everyone will stay," Diane agreed.

"To say nothing of the repairs we'll have to make," Kim pointed out.

Belle's eyebrows lifted. "Repairs? What kind of repairs?"

Amy shook her head. Had her cousin really been here for three full days without noticing how shabby things had gotten around the inn?

Though, when she thought about it a bit more, she wasn't surprised. Belle had gone straight from the airport to the hospital. For the next two days, she'd spent practically every waking moment beside her mother's hospital bed. Once Margaret had been discharged, they'd all focused on making the elderly woman as comfortable as possible. As far as Amy knew, she and Kim were the only ones who'd taken a good, hard look at the state of things around the old homestead. She drew in a steadying breath. It was time to bring the others up to speed.

"Let's start with the cottages." She swept an arm through the air. Three small houses stood on either side of the main house. Each one had been named after a Spanish treasure ship lost in 1715.

Belle's gaze drifted past the sand dunes to Regala, the cottage she'd shared with her parents throughout most of her childhood. "I'd love to see the inside. Do you know if anyone ever repainted my bedroom?"

"I can't say for sure," Amy responded, "but I can tell you it's the only cabin fit to live in right now. Helen March likes it there. She's rented it for the next six weeks." The author reserved the cottage whenever she was on deadline. "The rest of them are in various states of disrepair. San Roman and Trinidad have leaky roofs. There's a broken window in Carmen. La Popa's currently being used for storage. The gutters have fallen off Rosario."

At the mention of the last cabin, everyone fell silent. Aunt Margaret had fallen when she tried to repair one of its downspouts on her own.

"The main house isn't much better." Kim tsked.

Diane shuddered. "I don't know about y'all, but staying in the Opal Suite is the stuff nightmares are made of. The wallpaper is literally peeling off the walls. The paint around the windows and doors is chipped, and the linens—don't get me started."

"You should have seen the rooms when I got here." Kim chose a cashew from a bowl of nuts on the table and chewed thoughtfully. "None of the suites upstairs had been cleaned in ages. I found out Aunt Margaret had been sending the maids home early every afternoon so they could spend time with their children."

Irritation swirled across Diane's face. "How long has that been going on?" she demanded.

"For quite a while." Kim shrugged. "Why?"

"Because I've been paying their full salaries each week." A muscle in Diane's cheek ticked. "That's not right. You don't pay people not to work."

"Maybe we should get a time clock like I have at the bakery," Amy suggested. "All my staff punches in and out or they don't get paid."

Diane took a pad from her purse and jotted down a note. "Time clock. Got it."

"Do we have to make a big deal out of this?" Belle's plaintive question drew everyone's attention. "So the maids have taken a few hours off. You know Mama. Family always comes first with her."

When Diane's scowl deepened, Amy intervened before an argument broke out. "I'm all for family, too," she said with a nod to let Belle know she sympathized. "But we are paying them for an eight-hour day. Besides, Irene's kids are in college. Eunice's are in high school."

"Really?" Surprise lit Belle's green eyes. "Well, that certainly changes things." She hefted the pitcher of fruit punch from the table and dumped a small serving into her glass.

"I don't think Irene and Eunice are entirely to blame," Kim soothed. "Aunt Margaret's been doing the same thing with the gardeners—sending them home so the lawnmowers and the leaf blowers won't disturb the guests."

"But the inn sits on over twenty acres," Belle protested. "Grass grows fast in Florida. By the time the crew finishes mowing and weed-whacking and trimming, it's time to start over at the beginning."

"I can't believe one of the guests actually complained." Diane's eyes narrowed. "I mean, this isn't some magical kingdom where fairies descend at dusk and work through the night so our guests wake up to a freshly mowed lawn and neatly trimmed hedges. They have to realize how much work it takes to maintain a place like this."

"I'm not sure there actually were complaints," Kim said. A teasing glint darkened her eyes. "I think the mowers were disturbing Aunt Margaret's nap time."

Belle laughed. "I can totally see that happening. Mama loves her little lie-downs after lunch."

Kim's expression turned sheepish. "It probably wasn't my place, but I had a chat with Miguel and with Irene and Eunice. I made it perfectly clear that, from now on out, if they work a half day, they get paid for a half day."

"That works for me." Diane drew a line through the note she'd jotted about time clocks. When she finished, she looked straight at Kim. "I couldn't help but notice all the throw rugs," she said slowly.

"Yeah. I thought you were going to get rid of those." Belle swirled the liquid in her glass before setting it on the table without taking a sip. Just last week, she'd begged her cousin to help make the inn safer for her mom. Scatter rugs were infamous trip hazards. Removing them had been at the top of Kim's list of things to do.

"I tried. What's under them is even worse," Kim said with a long-suffering sigh. "The carpet is so old, it's threadbare in places."

"So you're saying the inn needs new carpet?"

When Kim hesitated, Amy prompted her cousin to continue. Before the others got the idea that sprucing up the inn, either for a reunion or to put it on the market, was a simple task, they needed to know the enormity of the situation they faced. Kim had only been at the inn for a short while, but she'd already compiled a long list of much-needed repairs.

"The carpets are just the beginning," Kim said at last. "The inn has beautiful hardwood floors, but they're so badly scuffed and scratched that they all need to be refinished. The rug by the front door covers a particularly deep gouge." She paused as if she was consulting a mental checklist before she plunged ahead. "There's wood rot in the eves, and the railings are so rickety I'm surprised they haven't collapsed. The entire place needs new paint, inside and out. As Diane already mentioned, all the linens in the guest rooms should probably be replaced. Some of the furniture needs to go, too. The cottages need serious work—we'll have to replace boarded-up windows and leaky roofs. Then there's the landscaping. Now that they're working full time again, Miguel and his crew have begun cutting back all the overgrown plants, but it'll take months for them to get caught up. Some of the shrubs around the house are so far gone they should be replaced."

Across the table, Diane scribbled furiously.

Belle's eyebrows lifted. "I guess it's all necessary if we're going to hold a reunion."

"Or find a buyer. This place needs to be in tip-top shape if we hope to attract someone who wants to keep the lights on." Kim stared into the distance.

"I hate to bring this up, but…" Amy hesitated.

"Go on," Belle prodded.

"I sank a lot of money into remodeling Sweet Cakes last year. The inn is much larger than the bakery, and it's going to take a lot more money to spruce up. Does Aunt Margaret have those kinds of resources?" Her attention shifted to Diane, who handled the inn's books. Her stomach plummeted when the accountant shook her head.

Diane glanced at Belle. "I've been meaning to talk to you about your mom's finances. But things have been so busy at work that I just hadn't gotten around to it."

"No need to apologize." Belle wiped imaginary sweat from her brow. "I understand perfectly. What's up?"

"Well, not your mom's bank balance. But then, you already know that." To the others, she explained, "Aunt Margaret asked me to copy Belle on all the quarterly reports."

"Uh, you know math's not my thing, right?" The two pink spots that bloomed on Belle's cheeks made her look like a little kid who'd been caught playing hooky. "I don't actually see those reports. My assistant opens most of my mail. I'm pretty sure your statements are all neatly filed away in my office."

"So you haven't even looked at them?" Diane's face bore a horrified expression.

"I guess I assumed if there was something I should know about, you'd call me," Belle said with wide-eyed innocence.

Diane's laughter carried a note of despair. Shaking her head, she brushed tears from her eyes. "That explains a lot. I kept expecting you to ask what on earth was going on. Do you want to talk about this now?" She tilted her head toward Kim and Amy. "Or should we wait until…"

A small smile tugged at Belle's lips. "No sense in keeping it secret. We're all family. This is going to affect all of us."

"Okay, then." Diane took a breath. "You know the inn has been losing money for years now." When Belle's face blanched, she immediately backtracked. "Sorry. If you'd seen the quarterly reports, you'd know the inn has been operating in the red practically since Uncle Eric—your dad—passed away. Reservations mostly provide enough income to meet the monthly expenses, but the last couple of years I've had to dip into savings to cover the property taxes and insurance. Aunt Margaret's reserves have gotten pretty low."

Amy winced. Before she'd opened Sweet Cakes, Diane had lectured her on the importance of maintaining a healthy savings account. "So how much is left?" she asked.

"Enough to keep the doors open for another two years. Maybe three, if Aunt Margaret is careful. Very careful."

Amy whistled softly. Now that she stopped to think about it, though, she had to admit she'd simply chosen to ignore the obvious. She only had to look as far as the ever-shrinking orders for the breakfast rolls and other baked goods she delivered from Sweet Cakes each morning to know that fewer and fewer people were staying at the inn that had once been *the only* place to stay on Florida's east coast. Whether the rooms were full or empty, though, the expenses mounted up. The air-conditioning still ran day and night. Salaries, utility bills, taxes and insurance still had to be paid.

The four of them had just gone over a lengthy list of expensive repairs that needed to be made before they could plan on having a reunion here. Much less put the place on the market. But could they, in good conscience, use what little money Aunt Margaret had left to refurbish the inn? What if their aunt changed her mind about listing the property for sale? Even if she did move forward with her promise to sell, the odds were against ever finding the right buyer, one who'd keep the inn open. In the end, she might not have a choice. She might have to sell the land to a developer.

Amy blinked back tears. Her aunt's heart wasn't the only one that would break if bulldozers knocked their childhood home to the ground and some developer built a high-rise in its place.

"Mama knows all this?" Belle asked, her voice barely above a whisper.

"Yeah." Diane nodded. "She kept telling me not to worry. That you'd take care of things."

To Amy's surprise, Belle only shook her head. "Don't look at me. I might be able to swing a new roof or pay for new carpets, but not much more." Belle's shoulders slumped. "I'm having a little cash-flow crisis of my own right now," she admitted.

Amy blinked. Her cousin's words certainly put a different slant on things. She'd always imagined that money simply dripped from the tips of Belle's elegantly manicured nails. It was oddly comforting to know that her cousin was forced to watch her pennies like the rest of them. None of which helped solve the problem of how they were going to pay for repairs around the inn. She shot her sister an inquiring look.

Diane only shook her head. "This isn't a good time for us, right now. Tim and I, we…" Her breath hitched suddenly, and she shifted her weight in her chair. "With Nick at Virginia Tech and Caitlyn due to graduate in a couple of years, we're putting every dime aside to pay for their college expenses."

Amy caught the false note in Diane's tone and wondered what her sister had been about to say before she decided better of it and made up that excuse about Nick and Caitlyn. Were her sister and brother-in-law having problems? That couldn't be right. Diane and Tim had been a team since the day they met. Together, they'd built the kind of life others only dreamed of living. They had two great kids, thriving careers and a beautiful home. The idea that there was trouble in paradise was ridiculous and she needed to forget it. Besides, there were other pressing matters to address right now.

Carefully, she considered her own finances. When she'd opened Sweet Cakes ten years ago, she'd done so on a shoestring budget and a prayer. For years, she'd scrimped and saved to remodel the forty-year-old building in the heart of Emerald Bay. When she'd finally taken the plunge, unforeseen problems had blown up her budget. In the end, she'd been forced to take out a loan to rewire and replumb the bakery. It had been worth it, though. Business at the bakery was better than ever. Even so, it'd be years before she was free and clear again.

Kim's gaze shifted to a cracked windowpane in the back door. "Can we DIY this?" she asked. "We all know how to wield a paintbrush, strip wallpaper and make minor repairs, don't we? Plus, there's a good handyman in town, isn't there?" She turned to Amy.

"Max," she replied as she recalled the tall, angular man who frequently stopped in at Sweet Cakes for coffee and a Danish on his way to a job site. "I've had him make a few repairs around the bakery. He does good work."

"We could handle a lot of the work ourselves and hire Max for some of the rest. Of course, we'd have to leave the new carpets and the roof repairs to the professionals."

"I'll help whenever I'm not needed in town," Amy volunteered. Relief swept through her. She'd comb through the books at Sweet Cakes, but unless she stumbled across some unknown cache of money, her contributions would be limited to what she could produce with her own two hands.

"Between Caitlyn's soccer schedule and my work, I'm swamped right now, but I can free up a couple of weeks later in the summer. Till then, I'll be here on weekends," Diane offered.

"I'm headed to Atlanta to clear out my apartment first thing tomorrow. That'll take the better part of a week." Kim shrugged. "After that, I've already agreed to help out with Aunt Margaret. At least until her arm heals."

"And Jen? Do you think she could help us?" Amy asked.

Kim slowly shook her head. "She probably

would, but I haven't spoken to her. With her late hours, we play a lot of phone tag." The cocktail waitress usually worked into the wee hours.

Amy turned to Belle. "What about you?"

Belle shoved a mass of red hair behind one ear. "I'm not sure how long I can stay. Through next weekend, for sure. Meantime, if you can give me a list of the big-ticket items like carpets and such—" She glanced pointedly at Diane's notepad—"I'll get bids on the things we can't do ourselves." She nibbled her lip. "And I'll talk to Mama. Ultimately, it's her decision whether we make the repairs or not." Belle's lips flattened. "I want to make sure she understands the risks."

The plan wasn't perfect, but at least they had one. That was more than they'd had when they sat down, Amy thought. Now it was time to nail down the specifics. "Assuming Aunt Margaret wants to go ahead with the reunion," she asked, "do you think we can hold it this winter?"

One by one, the others shook their heads. There was too much work to do. And besides, most people had already made their plans for the holidays. The foursome discussed other options without arriving at a consensus until, finally, Belle crossed her arms across her ample chest.

"Traditionally, we held the reunion just before Memorial Day. I think we should stick with that timeframe. Only, instead of two weeks, we'll limit it to a long weekend. Will that work?"

Diane hesitated only a moment before she nodded. "That gives everyone the better part of a year to arrange vacations and travel plans."

"And it gives us enough time to tackle the necessary repairs around here." Kim waved a hand at the main house.

"That works for me," Amy agreed. Business at Sweet Cakes usually slacked off at the start of the summer. It didn't pick up again until the busy bridal season kicked into high gear.

"I'm game," Kim said.

"Then it's settled. We'll hold one more Dane Family Reunion...for Mama's sake?" Belle wiped tears from her eyes when the rest agreed.

Kim refilled everyone's glasses from the pitcher on the table, and they raised their glasses in a toast to the future.

After she took a sip, Amy quietly mused. It was one thing to agree to help out, quite another when it came down to doing the actual work. How much time could she take away from Sweet Cakes before she jeopardized her own livelihood? Would Diane or Belle be willing or able to put their own busy lives on hold to help out around the inn? Just as important, where would they get the money they needed? New linens, carpets and furniture could cost a pretty penny. To say nothing of paint and countless other supplies.

She rubbed her forehead where a headache had taken hold. She was all for fulfilling her aunt's wishes, but if they weren't careful, they'd all end up worse off than when they started.

Two

Kim

Snatches of a muted conversation drifted from the kitchen as Kim pored over the dizzying array of forms spread across the dining room table. She tsked softly. Craig Morgan had probably meant well, but his suggestion that they put the Dane Crown Inn on the National Registry of Historic Places was proving far easier said than done. Far, far easier. Like, impossibly easier.

From what she could tell, it'd take degrees in history and architecture, plus an innate ability to interpret government legalese, in order to navigate all the necessary steps and jump through all the required hoops. And what good would it do? Sure, making the list might qualify the inn for federal funding. But grants were scarcer than hens' teeth, and low-interest loans were still loans than needed to be repaid with money her aunt didn't have.

She ran a hand through her hair. The scads and scads of paperwork sure seemed like a lot of work to do for little or no reward. But she'd promised Craig she'd look into it, and unlike her ex-husband, she always did her level best to keep her word.

The sound of dishes rattling in the kitchen told her Belle and Aunt Margaret had finished their tea and cookies. Smiling, Kim drained the last few drops from her own mug. Whenever they'd stayed at the inn as children, she and Jen had looked forward to the nightly ritual of drinking milky sweet tea and eating two vanilla wafers before bed. Kim had enjoyed the custom so much that she'd passed it down to her own children. While she had no idea whether Natalie or Josh still brewed themselves a cup now that they were grown and out on their own, she'd kept up the habit. Although, these days, she skipped the cookies, and she'd swapped her aunt's Earl Grey for sleep-inducing chamomile tea.

The thump-thump of Aunt Margaret's cane punctuated the sound of footsteps that originated in the kitchen and slowly moved down the hall. Nearly a minute passed before Kim spied movement in the doorway. She set her pen aside. Summoning a smile for Aunt Margaret and Belle, she quickly rose and pulled out a chair for her aunt.

"Why didn't you come and sit in the kitchen with us?" Margaret lowered herself onto the chair with an audible grunt. "We missed you."

Kim gestured at the array of papers and ledgers strewn across one end of a dining room table that could easily seat twenty. "I was trying to make some headway with this National Registry paperwork."

"Oh? Any luck?" While Belle settled onto a seat beside her, Margaret peered over the tops of her glasses at the forms.

"I managed to fill in the address." No small feat in itself. She'd had to search the county property records for the precise legal description of the twenty-acre plot.

Belle eyed the paperwork with obvious skepticism. "Remind me why you're doing this again?"

Kim shrugged. "Craig Morgan. Do you remember him?"

Belle's brow furrowed. "Tall? Good looking in a James Garner kind of way?"

"I suppose." Craig's wide smile reminded her

more of Tom Selleck, but she wouldn't argue the point. All three men were easy on the eyes.

"He's Kim's new beau," Margaret teased. The look she gave Kim was filled with challenge.

"Not hardly," Kim answered, hating the way her cheeks warmed at the mention of Craig's name. The man wasn't interested in her. He was merely looking out for Emerald Bay. Which was fine because her own life was far too messy for her to even consider starting a new relationship.

"Craig's the mayor of Emerald Bay now," she said, hurrying to correct any misconceptions before Belle, too, joined in a chorus of 'Kim's new beau.' "He suggested getting the inn on the registry as a way to qualify for federal grant money. You know, to pay for all those repairs we were talking about earlier." According to Craig, it was either that or take a wrecking ball to the place. But that opinion was one she didn't dare repeat within her aunt's earshot.

"That'd be great!" Interest sparkled in Belle's green eyes. She'd followed through on her promise to discuss the pros and cons with her mom. No one had been surprised when Aunt Margaret insisted on moving full steam ahead with the renovations.

"Don't get your hopes up," Kim warned. "From what I've read, the odds of winning a grant are not in our favor. But it definitely can't happen unless we're on the registry, so..." She let her voice trail off.

"So you're trying to get us on it."

"It's a long shot," she admitted. The inn was certainly old enough to qualify, but age wasn't the only criteria. It wasn't even the most important part. Plenty of older homes didn't make it. According to the guidelines, something of historical significance had to have happened at the inn before it could make the list. To determine that, she'd been searching through the old registration ledgers, newspaper articles and diaries scattered across the table. It'd probably take weeks to thoroughly search the records unless...

She cast a questioning look at her aunt.

"Aunt Margaret, do you remember anyone famous ever staying at the inn?" Beneath the tabletop, Kim crossed her fingers.

"You mean like Helen March?" Books by the author currently ensconced in the Regala cottage were featured prominently in stores across the nation.

"Ummm. More famous than that. The president. Or the vice president. Maybe a head of state?" Once lauded as the "gem of Florida's Treasure Coast," the inn would have attracted its fair share of the rich and famous, wouldn't it?

Aunt Margaret's features bunched, but after a few seconds, she shook her head. "No, dear. Several actors brought their families here back in the day, but none of them went on to fame and fortune. I doubt if anyone even remembers them now. No doubt, we've had a few people who would have made it to the *Forbes* list, if the magazine had been around back then. But presidents? Why, the whole town would have been in an uproar. To say nothing of the inn itself."

"Hmmm. Too bad," Kim murmured as disappointment coursed through her. Not that she'd expected anything else. If President Kennedy had once occupied the Diamond Suite, people in town would still be buzzing about the day he'd stopped in at the bookstore; they'd be bragging about the pillbox hat Jackie had picked up in the dress shop.

Moving on to the next item on the list, Kim asked, "What about significant events? Has anything special taken place here over the years?"

"We've hosted some lovely weddings in the front room," Margaret offered hopefully.

"Anyone important?" Belle asked.

Margaret's glasses slid down her nose. She peered at her daughter over the lenses.

"Everyone's important, dear," she said dryly.

Kim nearly chuckled when her famous cousin ducked her head and responded to her mother's reprimand with a quiet, "Yes, ma'am."

Margaret cleared her throat. "If you want to know did a senator or a billionaire get married here, I'm afraid not. If someone wanted a big, formal wedding, Momma or Daddy would send them to First Baptist or St. Helen's in Vero Beach." Both churches had been around for more than a hundred years. Each had hosted their fair share of celebrity weddings. "The inn has always aimed to give our guests a peaceful, quiet respite from all the hustle and bustle. Making the news wasn't exactly on our agenda."

Which was great, unless you were trying to save the inn from a demolition crew. Kim took a breath and tried again. A few buildings had made it onto the registry based on their innovative design alone. She closed her eyes and tried to picture the property the way a first-time visitor would see it. Immediately, she ruled out the cottages her Uncle Paul had built. He'd owned a contracting business, and while he'd been a first-class builder, he was no Frank Lloyd Wright.

But would the inn itself, with its wide, wrap-around porches, coquina driveway, white shutters and tin roof, make the list? She took a breath and faced her aunt. "Do you happen to remember who designed the main house? Or do you have the original blueprints?" Those would have the architect's signature on them.

The wrinkles above Margaret's eyes deepened. "Now what was the name of that man? Mr. Johnson, Charles Johnson?" She tapped her chin. "No. That's not quite right." She snapped the fingers of her good hand. "His first name was Gregory. Greg Johnson. That was it." She sighed happily. "He only visited us here once. Strange little man. He smoked cheap cigars. Momma had to air out his room each day to get rid of the smell."

Odd or not, Gregory Johnson had obviously been good at his job, considering the Dane Crown Inn had weathered more than a few hurricanes over the past sixty years. But had he made the Who's Who of Architects? Intending to check him out, Kim scribbled the name on a notepad.

"How did Grampa come to hire Mr. Johnson?" she asked.

"Daddy bought the plans from him through the mail. Later, when Erik and I were thinking of adding on, we tried to get in touch with Mr. Johnson, but his company had gone out of business. We heard later that he'd died of influenza in 1968."

Kim swallowed a bitter disappointment. So

much for tying the name of a famous architect to the inn. As for the final possibility—some significant detail about the land itself—Kim couldn't think of a thing. While it was true that the Dane Crown Inn faced the ocean, their stretch of white sandy beach was no different from, nor better than, countless other Florida beaches. Despite all the treasure hunts they'd gone on when they were kids, no one had ever discovered a cache of pirate's loot buried behind the dunes. No gold doubloons or emeralds had washed ashore from a ship lost at sea.

Thinking about gems and pieces of eight, though, reminded her of their earlier conversation with Diane. She turned to her aunt. "Aunt Margaret, do you know where that old treasure map ended up? The one we used when we were kids. Diane was asking about it earlier."

Margaret resettled her cast in its sling. "I was thinking about that myself not too long ago. I thought it might be nice to frame it and hang it in the entryway, but I have no idea where it is."

"We've lost it?" Belle asked.

Margaret sighed. "I wouldn't say lost, exactly. It's probably around here somewhere."

"Unless someone took it home with them and never brought it back." Belle puffed out a frustrated breath.

A sense of loss struck Kim harder than she expected. How many lazy summer afternoons had she and the others traced their fingers along the lines etched into the soft and supple leather? They'd spent hours arguing over possible starting points for their hunt, Diane insisting they begin at the waterline, while their cousin Scott maintained that any proper map began with a well-known landmark, like a boulder or a tree. She and Jen, Amy and Diane and even Belle had struggled to determine whether the squiggly line at the edge of the map was a stream or the beach, or if the lines that looked like steps were actually the rocky outcropping that led to the river.

Kim closed her eyes for a moment. She could practically feel the well-worn leather beneath her fingers. Inhaling, she imagined its earthy scent.

"I wish Uncle Paul were still around." Belle sighed. "We could ask him to make us a new one."

The remark put a frown on Margaret's face. "Why Paul?"

"He was a builder. He drew blueprints. I just assumed he made the map, too." Belle paused. "He didn't?"

Margaret laughed softly. "Honey, that map existed long before Liz and Paul met. My brother

Edward and all us girls used to search for buried treasure with it when we were children, just like you and your cousins did."

"Really?" Kim was surprised. Like Belle, she'd always assumed one of her uncles had created the map as something to keep the children entertained…and out of the adults' hair. "That makes it, what—at least sixty years old?"

Margaret brushed a hand over the rough surface of her cast. "There's no telling how old it really is. My daddy found it when he was clearing the land for the inn. He told us it was hidden under a pile of rocks."

"Like a cairn or something?" Belle asked. Throughout history, the carefully stacked rocks had identified everything from trails to boundaries, from graves to food caches and, yes, even treasure troves.

Could the old map have actually belonged to some long-ago pirate? Or would it lead to the place where the survivor of a shipwreck had stashed a few, precious belongings? Kim cleared her throat as a tiny frisson of excitement coursed through her. "Did Grampa ever say where, exactly, he found the rocks?"

"Let me think for a minute." Margaret's thin, white eyebrows drew together. Her body stilled until the only sound in the room was her quiet breathing. After a bit, her brows unraveled and she said, "I overheard him and Mama talking about it once. Papa had chosen the ideal spot to build the inn, only there was a dense cluster of old palm trees right where he wanted the front door. Thatch palms, he called them. Mama wanted him to leave the trees where they were and find a different spot, but Papa insisted. He spent days hacking away on them." She smiled as if lost in memories. "We slept in tents for six months while the workmen built the inn. We had an outdoor kitchen, and Papa used palm fronds to make a roof for it. They cut up his arms something fierce. Thatch palms don't have the same jagged edges as palmettos, but they're still plenty sharp."

"But the stones," Belle prompted when her mother once more fell silent.

Margaret started. "Papa said he found the stones stacked up between the palms. Like the trees had grown up around them."

"That would put it…" Belle's green eyes met Kim's.

"Right about where the front door is now," Margaret finished.

So much for discovering a chest of gold where X marked the spot, Kim thought. She didn't know much about construction, but she imagined that in the process of building the inn, bulldozers and heavy machinery had dug up the entire area. Surely they would have unearthed anything buried there.

Slowly, Kim blinked away the possibility that the map was real. Pirates and shipwreck survivors were the stuff of children's stories. It was far more likely that her grandfather had created the map himself, along with the story about finding it beneath a cairn. Especially since at least two generations of Dane children had followed the lines that meandered across its surface without discovering anything of value. Much less a chest full of gold and silver buried on their particular narrow spit of land.

Which was a pity. Uncovering even a little bit of treasure would go a long way towards paying for repairs around the inn. To say nothing of the historical significance of such a discovery. A find like that alone would qualify the inn for the National Registry.

So far, though, her study of the inn's history hadn't turned up anything special about it at all. Finding a long-lost stash of gold or silver was her last hope, and now that the map was missing—along with the cairn where it'd been hidden—there was little likelihood of that ever happening.

"Well, I guess that about wraps it up." Kim

swept the papers into a neat pile. Unless she could prove a president had spent the night at the inn or some important event had taken place on the grounds, filling out the paperwork was a complete waste of time. She'd already spent hours combing through the inn's ledgers and receipts. Aunt Margaret had only confirmed her own conclusion that the inn didn't qualify for the National Registry.

She stretched. "I probably ought to be thinking about packing. I'll have to leave around six tomorrow if I'm going to catch the shuttle to Melbourne."

"Do you need me to drive you?" Belle asked.

"Nah. I appreciate the offer, but Amy's going to pick me up when she drops off the morning delivery." Kim smiled at Aunt Margaret. "She said to tell you she's making lemon Danish." With homemade curd for a filling, the treat was their aunt's favorite.

"I hope she brings extras so I can save one for the next day." Margaret's wrinkled brow furrowed. "Speaking of good stuff, though, that broccoli salad you made tonight was excellent."

"To die for," Belle echoed.

"It was good, wasn't it?" Kim asked. They'd all had second helpings of the crisp-tender broccoli and cauliflower drenched in a sweet mayonnaise dressing and sprinkled with crumbled bacon.

"I haven't had that salad in so long." Memories flooded Margaret's voice. "My sister Liz used to make it, you know."

"I do." Kim touched her hand to her heart. An accomplished cook, her aunt had kept all her favorite recipes in a bright red binder. One Kim had found tucked away behind a row of cookbooks in the cupboard. "Aunt Liz used to cook for a crowd, didn't she?"

Margaret nodded. "We used to seat twenty, sometimes thirty people right in this very room." She gestured to the long sideboards where guests had once helped themselves from steaming bowls of mashed potatoes and pans filled with pork chops swimming in gravy.

"I thought so. Aunt Liz's recipe called for four heads of broccoli and two of cauliflower. I had to cut it down a good bit." She paused before grinning to add, "Otherwise we'd be eating nothing but broccoli salad for a month."

"That would make my nutritionist happy," Belle said with a wry smile. "But she'd be the only one."

"It'd make a good dish to take to the church potluck, though," Margaret suggested.

Kim blinked. In the chaos following her

aunt's fall and hospital stay, she'd completely forgotten the monthly get-together she'd planned to attend with Aunt Margaret. "We missed the potluck, didn't we?"

"There'll be others." Margaret played with the strap that helped support the heavy cast that ran from her upper arm past her wrist. "Maybe next month? If I'm out of this thing?" She scanned their faces with hope in her eyes.

Sorrow stained Belle's cheeks as she leaned forward to pat her mother's hand. "You'll probably still be wearing the cast…" she began.

"Honestly? You think so?" Margaret's expression sagged. "I was hoping to get it off in a couple of weeks."

"I'm afraid you're stuck with it for the time being. The doctor said you'll have to wear it at least a month and a half. Maybe longer."

"That long?"

Her aunt's disappointment brought tears to Kim's eyes. She swallowed hard. Despite the cane she relied on, her aunt prided herself on her independence. Now, with her poor broken arm, Margaret was forced to depend on others for help with the basic tasks of dressing and bathing. But that didn't mean she had to stay home all the time. "I bet you'll feel a whole lot stronger by the time I get back from Atlanta. As soon as you're up to it, we can plan some outings. We'll go to the beauty salon. The library. The grocery store. We can even go to the next potluck, if you want."

"And you'll bring the broccoli salad?"

"And I'll bring the broccoli salad," Kim confirmed.

She might as well, she supposed. Aware that anyone who attended was expected to bring a covered dish to share, she'd been searching through the cookbooks she'd found in the inn's kitchen ever since she'd agreed to take Margaret to the dinner. But she had a few constraints. First, considering the impoverished state of her checkbook, any recipe she chose couldn't cost an arm or a leg to make. Then, just in case people fell in love with the dish and wanted her to bring it the next time, and the time after that, the instructions had to be easy enough to follow with a minimum of fuss. On the other hand, they couldn't be so simple that she'd get bored fixing it after the first try. To make things even more challenging, she knew better than to step on anyone else's toes by bringing a dish that one of the regulars usually prepared. Which had ruled out all the old standards—the potato and macaroni salads, the deviled eggs and the green bean casseroles. She'd thought she'd have to work her way through Aunt Liz's recipes one by one until she found a dish that fit the bill, but apparently she'd struck gold on her first try.

Belle's phone buzzed softly. The redhead glanced at an incoming text. "Diane says she's just pulled into her driveway."

"She made good time," Kim noted. Hoping to be home before Caitlyn finished with soccer practice, Diane had left earlier in the afternoon. Kim's brow knitted. "Is everything all right with her?"

Belle answered with a blank stare. "I didn't notice anything, but then, I've been a little preoccupied." The redhead inclined her head toward her mom.

"She was quieter than usual, and she didn't let that phone of hers out of her sight. But if my daughter was on the other side of the state, I'd want to stay in touch, too," Margaret said.

"I just hope things between her and Tim are all right," Kim mused. The fact that Diane's husband had gone on a cruise without her didn't feel right.

"I don't know. Diane seemed pretty blasé about it. Did you pick up on something?" Belle wanted to know.

"Hmmm, might be nothing." Kim shrugged. "She seemed more content to go along with whatever plans we came up with than the Diane

I remembered as a kid." Despite being the youngest of their generation, Diane had been the one who nagged the others into playing hide-and-seek or dodgeball or exploring the farthest reaches of the inn's property. Kim took a breath and deliberately let go of her concerns. "But then again, it has been a while since we've all gotten together."

"It sounds like we'll see a lot more of each other this next year," Belle commented. "What with the reunion to plan and working on stuff around here." She waved a hand through the air.

"True." Kim turned to her aunt. "I hope you won't get tired of having us underfoot."

"As if that would ever happen," Aunt Margaret scoffed. "I love having you girls around. I just hate that you're having to work so hard."

It had been ages since someone had called her a girl, and having Margaret do it reminded Kim of how much she'd missed spending time with family. "We won't be busy all the time. We'll have some fun, too," she promised.

"Speaking of fun, how long do you think you'll be in Atlanta?" Belle asked.

Kim groaned. Moving was many things. Fun wasn't one of them. The upside was that it wouldn't take her long.

"Not more than a week," she assured her cousin. She was almost embarrassed to admit that it'd take less than two days to pack up the belongings she considered worth keeping and load them into her car. "At least I don't have to worry about the furniture. The super said I could leave anything I didn't want behind and still get my security deposit back."

"You aren't going to rent a trailer and bring all your stuff down here?"

But Kim only shook her head. "My car doesn't have a tow package." Besides, making the six-hundred-mile drive from Atlanta to Emerald Bay in her aging Honda on her own was daunting enough without the added pressure of hauling a trailer behind her. Not that she had enough furniture to fill up a good-sized U-Haul. Her tiny bedroom in the apartment didn't have room for much more than the secondhand futon and rickety chest of drawers she'd picked up at a garage sale. A lumpy couch and a tattered side chair took up all the available space in the minuscule living room. Those pieces certainly weren't worth the trouble of bringing to Florida. She did wish she could hang on to the small kitchen table she'd stripped down and refinished, but it simply wouldn't fit in her car. She shrugged. Someone else would put it to good use.

As for the rest, there wasn't much. Her collection of photo albums and mementos would fill only two boxes. She'd bring her TV and the few potted plants that had somehow survived her many moves. Other than her shoes and boots, most of her clothes would fit into the good-size suitcases she stored in the coat closet. Packing out the kitchen, though, that would take the most time. She wanted to hold onto her pots and pans, including the La Creuset cookware she'd splurged on for her birthday one year. She'd be lost without her set of Hedley & Bennett chef's knives, and she'd give up the TV before she'd part with the top-of-the-line mixer she'd lugged with her from one apartment to another.

"I hate that you're having to leave Atlanta on my account," Margaret murmured.

"If you were the only reason, that'd be good enough," Kim assured her aunt. "But I was going to have to move anyway. My lease is up, and the owners are converting the building to condos." Technically, they couldn't force her to leave, but they could—and had—raised the rent. The new amount was more than she could afford, even if she had steady employment. Which she didn't. "I've already given my notice. The super will probably have demo crews in there the day after I leave."

"I wish we knew someone who could help you. I hate the thought of you cleaning out your apartment all by yourself."

Kim shrugged. It wouldn't be the first time. She'd been so certain she could make it on her own after she and Frank called it quits. She would have, too, if the company she'd worked for hadn't merged with another, bigger firm. The layoffs that followed had caught her off guard, and she'd blown through her savings while she hunted for a new job. A hunt that, thanks to several factors—a recent downturn in the economy, a salary that had risen over the course of her career and, as much as no one wanted to admit it, her age—hadn't been successful. To keep food on the table and a roof over her head, she'd resorted to taking temp jobs. Coming home to Emerald Bay would give her the time she needed to find a new direction for her life and, hopefully, kick it into high gear.

What that new pursuit would be, she had no idea. She just knew that she needed to figure it out and pretty quickly. Otherwise, people around Emerald Bay would start thinking of her as "that poor relative who'd come home to mooch off her better-off relatives."

On her way upstairs a few minutes later, thoughts about the future continued to plague her. In a move that had become old hat over the past two years, she ran down a short list of possibilities. One thing was for certain, she'd never work in corporate America again. She'd had her fill of working for a paycheck in an industry that treated its employees like cogs in a machine. Where one moment you were building a career and the next you were standing on the sidewalk holding a box of personal items and a pitifully small severance check. That said, she'd never get ahead by signing on with headhunters and working temp jobs.

But what else was there?

"Play to your strengths," she'd heard over and over. What were hers? She ticked a few items off on her fingers. She was organized, energetic, and she knew how to get things done. In the corporate world, her ability to break a project down into logical steps and make a plan for meeting a goal had served her well. All of which were good traits, even if they weren't very exciting. Or very specific, she noted. With her skill set she could apply for just about any job. Including waitressing at the Pirate's Gold Diner.

She shook her head. As much as she liked being around food, she didn't really think that was the path she wanted to travel.

A glance at the clock on the nightstand in the Topaz Suite convinced her to shove her concerns for the future aside for now. She'd have plenty of time to figure out what came next during the long drive to Emerald Bay after she closed out the chapter of her life in Atlanta. For now, she needed to throw some clothes into a duffle bag, shower and get some shut eye. She wanted to be ready to hop in the van when Amy arrived in the morning.

Three

Diane

As Diane turned off the quiet street in the exclusive Parkland Estates neighborhood, the garage door at the end of the driveway in front of a two-story brick home ratcheted upward with barely a whisper. She checked the digital display on her car's dashboard and puffed out a breath of air. She'd made good time cutting across the state on Highway 60. Except for a short stretch where the road had narrowed to two lanes and she'd gotten stuck behind a semi hauling a cattle trailer, she'd cruised along at a steady seventy miles an hour. Which, she admitted, was a bit over the posted speed limit, but not so much that she'd attracted lights and sirens. Even with the usual traffic buildup and resulting slowdown as she neared the city on the gulf side of the state, she'd made it home before the end of Caitlyn's soccer practice.

Which was important because they were overdue for a little mother-daughter talk. The last time they'd spoken, the teen had hurled hateful, heated words at her. Words that had crushed her already broken heart.

It had taken every ounce of twenty years of parenting skills to keep her wits about her. She told herself Caitlyn had only been reacting to an unexpected and gut-wrenching discovery. That it was only natural for the teen to strike out after stumbling onto the fact that her dad had left them. Especially when Diane hadn't been able to soften the blow, to explain that she and Tim had hit a rough patch, but they weren't giving up on their marriage. Before Diane had had a chance to wrap her arms around her distraught daughter and offer her comfort and reassurance, Caitlyn had stormed off in a huff.

On the heels of that awful set-to, Diane had received the terrible news about Margaret and had rushed to her aunt's bedside. Had she done the right thing by letting her daughter spend the last few days with Marty's parents? At the time, she hadn't thought she had much choice. Caitlyn had absolutely refused to miss nearly a week's worth of school and soccer practice. Especially not the week before Homecoming. Letting the girl stay with her best friend had been the practical choice. Besides, it had given them a much-needed cooling off period.

Now that the crisis was over, though, it was time to make things right with her daughter. Diane eyed the cooler strapped into the passenger seat. Kim had made a Treasure Coast specialty especially for Caitlyn. The custardy peanut butter pie ought to serve as a dandy icebreaker.

Headlights illuminated the interior of the oversize garage while Diane pulled her car forward until the tennis ball hanging from the ceiling gently bumped the windshield. On the lookout for neighborhood cats—one had gotten trapped in the garage for three whole days last winter—she scanned the corners. The empty corners, she noted with dismay. Tim's prized set of Calloway golf clubs was missing from its usual spot. As was the rest of his golfing equipment.

Her shoulders folded in on themselves as she stared blankly at the space usually occupied by his SUV. As much as she'd known his car wouldn't be here, as often as she'd reminded herself that her husband of twenty-three years had walked out on their marriage—on her—some small part of her had expected to see his car parked in its usual spot.

Anger boiled within her chest. Shutting off the motor, she flung her door wide. The move was one she could never make when both of their cars were in the garage, and her breath hitched. Would she ever complain about the tight space between their vehicles again, she wondered.

Not if Tim never came back.

Her anger dissolved as quickly as it had come. In its place, regret and loss flooded her chest. The sensation was so profound it made her teeth ache.

Tim would come back, wouldn't he? She refused to believe their marriage was over. They'd work things out. They had to. They'd devoted twenty years to building a home and a family. They weren't just going to throw what they'd built together away over one dinner party that hadn't gone exactly as planned.

She sighed. Okay, sure. The blame for that rested squarely on her shoulders. She wouldn't argue the point. She'd promised to spend last Saturday at home, preparing a special dinner for Caitlyn and her friends, and she'd broken that promise.

In her defense, she hadn't planned on going into the office that day. But then again, nothing had gone as planned that whole week. Not the long hours she'd spent away from her family. Not the tête-à-tête with her boss and mentor or his insistence that she take some time off. Certainly not the thinly veiled threats that her services might no longer be required at Ybor City Accountants.

Afraid that the powers-that-be would use even the flimsiest excuse to fire her, she'd done the only thing she could do when the junior accountants had encountered problems with several tax forms. She'd grabbed her briefcase and headed across town.

She'd rushed back home the minute she could. By then, though, she'd fallen hopelessly behind in her dinner preparations. She'd been forced to take shortcuts. To use store-bought salsa and canned refried beans instead of making her own from scratch. To decorate the kitchen table instead of stringing lanterns beneath the big oak in the backyard.

And dinner had been good. Not up to her usual standards, perhaps, but the guests of honor—Caitlyn and two of her friends—had barely noticed.

Tim had, though. For him, it had been the last

straw. They'd fought. He'd packed his bags and walked out.

She ran a hand through her hair. That wasn't exactly the way it happened, though, was it?

This past week she'd been so worried about Aunt Margaret that she'd hardly had time to think about that evening. Now though, her memories rose like floodwaters after a hurricane. With them came the realization that Tim hadn't decided to leave on the spur of the moment. Her husband had arranged for Caitlyn to spend the night with friends, despite the fact that their daughter had signed up to work in the church nursery the next day. He'd emptied his closet and brought his suitcases downstairs before he dropped the first hint about how unhappy he'd been...with dinner...with their marriage...with her. He'd made arrangements to stay at the office, even going so far as to convert the empty space above it into an efficiency apartment. And he'd purchased not two tickets on a cruise liner but one. So no, he'd made up his mind to leave long before that dinner party.

Which meant...

Which meant her marriage was in bigger trouble than she'd thought it was. Sitting alone in the garage, listening to the *tick-tick-tick* of her car's slowly cooling engine, she had to ask if it was over. What if she and Tim couldn't find their way back to each other?

The control she'd kept on her emotions since her departure for Emerald Bay slipped. She'd suppressed her worries, her pain these last couple of days by caring for her aunt. But now, like a genie that refused to stay in its bottle one second longer, her heartbreak broke free. Loss wrapped its arms around her heart. It squeezed so hard she couldn't catch her breath. Fear shook her.

Tim had walked out on her.

Caitlyn hated her.

The career she'd built lay in shambles.

How had things gotten this bad?

Her vision clouded. Sobs wracked her chest until her shoulders shook. Tears spilled from her eyes, cascaded down her cheeks and dampened the front of her T-shirt. Bowing beneath their weight, she leaned forward until the top of her head rested on the steering wheel. Her lips moved. Soundlessly she repeated, "No, no, no."

She desperately wanted, needed someone to turn to, someone who could tell her how to straighten out the mess she'd made of her life. But the sad fact was, she had no one.

Not her mom—a car accident five years ago had seen to that. Since then, Aunt Margaret had been her go-to person. When Tim faced that cancer scare two years ago, her aunt had been her rock. When their son chose a college nine hundred miles away, it had been Aunt Margaret who'd reminded her of how much young people needed to flex their wings. When Caitlyn's soccer team had won a tournament, Aunt Margaret had celebrated right along with her. But her aunt had big enough troubles of her own right now. Diane couldn't, she wouldn't, add to them.

Amy's happy face flickered into her thoughts, and she considered calling her sister or one of her cousins. She gave her head a slight shake. Once upon a time, she wouldn't hesitate. Living and working at the inn when they were younger, the four of them—plus Kim's little sister, Jen— had kept no secrets from each other. Each evening, when they weren't singing along to the radio as they washed and dried the dinner dishes, they'd talked about everything from the cute guy on the baseball team, to their dreams of the future, to which of their friends had gotten called to the principal's office that day. For two solid weeks after Aunt Shirley died, she and Amy and Belle had hauled their mattresses into Kim and Jen's room so their two motherless cousins would know they'd never be alone. Her sister and her cousins had known she'd met a boy she thought might be "the one" before she and Tim had even gone out on their first date. Through the years, the five of them had toasted each other's successes and drowned their sorrows in vats of ice cream. They'd thrown one another wedding and baby showers and promenaded down church aisles in dresses they'd never dream of wearing for someone else.

But sometime in their thirties, the closeness they'd shared had faded. Busy with their own lives, they'd drifted apart. They no longer lived in each other's back pockets, knew each other's thoughts or what mattered most to each other. Unable to confide in them even though the world as she knew it was falling apart around her, she'd bottled up her troubles and set them aside the entire time she'd been in Emerald Bay.

It hadn't been easy. Every mention of Caitlyn or Tim or her job had twisted a knife in one of her heart's many open wounds. Rather than let the others see her pain, though, she'd clamped her lips shut. She'd told herself she didn't want to shift the focus from Aunt Margaret to her own problems. That it was better not to say a word because once she started talking about her daughter or her husband or her career—once she said anything more than the obligatory, "they're fine"—she'd just known the dam would burst and everything would come pouring out. It had seemed like the right decision at the time, but now she wondered if it had been her best move.

The truth was, she'd wanted more than anything to confide in Amy and Belle and Kim. To feel the closeness they'd once shared again. She gulped. Had she missed her chance to renew those bonds by keeping her problems to herself this trip? The question loosed another spate of tears.

She had no idea how long she sat there, her car door ajar, tears dripping from her chin onto her jeans. She only knew that twin wet spots covered her thighs by the time her cell phone chirped with an incoming text.

Her heart leapt. Was Tim coming home? Did Caitlyn want to apologize for the hateful, hurtful things she'd said? She hadn't heard word one from her husband since the night he'd walked out on her. As for Caitlyn, the many texts she'd sent to her daughter had generated one- or two-word replies, the teenage version of the cold shoulder. Diane sniffled and wiped her cheeks. Hurrying, she punched the little green box on her phone. A message from the one person she hadn't expected to hear from appeared in a bubble on the screen.

Hey Sis. I know something was bothering you this week. I respect your privacy, but whatever's going on, I'm here for you. Belle and Kim, too. Anytime you want to talk, we'll listen. We've got your back.

Stunned, Diane sank against the headrest while her sister's words spread a soothing balm across her raw emotions. Her fingers flying, she responded.

You don't know how much that means to me. Things here are such a mess. EVERYthing is wrong. I couldn't talk about it without falling apart but I'll fill you in soon. I promise.

Three tiny dots appeared on the screen followed almost immediately by a whole line of hug emojis.

A lightness she hadn't felt in a while sifted through Diane's chest. Leave it to Amy and her cousins to know exactly what to say. She'd been wrong about that chasm between them. As wrong as she'd been about a lot of things lately. Though she swore she'd run out of tears, a few more leaked onto her cheeks.

When the waterworks had finally slowed to a trickle, she took another slow look around. There were better places to indulge in a crying jag than sitting in a garage, she thought as she grabbed tissues from her purse and mopped her face. A glance in the mirror on the visor told her that smeared eyeliner and mascara had left circles around her eyes, giving her a raccoonish look. She scrubbed at them until the smudges disappeared and blotches that matched her reddened nose took their place. Shuddering a huge breath, she grabbed the ice chest and her overnight bag and headed inside.

As soon as she stepped from the garage into the laundry room that served as a passageway into the rest of the house, Diane sensed trouble. Crossing quickly to the kitchen counter, she lowered the small ice chest onto the granite. Her eyes narrowing, she scanned room. Magnets still held photographs of Caitlyn and Nick in place on the fridge. The canisters that matched the sleek, modern décor Tim favored were lined up against the backsplash, right where they ought to be. Four chairs sat around the kitchen table. Two more stood as sentinels on either side of the picture window.

A quick peek into the living room assured her that nothing there had changed while she was gone. The wide-screen TV still hung on the wall. The half dozen speakers that provided theater-quality sound effects stood or hung in all their usual places. Even the throw pillows on the couch were all present and accounted for.

Hoping she was imagining things, she breathed in air that smelled slightly sweeter than her usual brand of air freshener. She shook her head. Everything looked right, but she couldn't shake the feeling that something was off.

Shoving her concerns aside for the moment, she started to put the pie away. She made it halfway to the refrigerator before her foot hit a slippery spot in the center of the hardwood floor. She skidded forward, one arm windmilling as she regained her balance. When she had, she crouched down. An oily liquid coated her hand when she ran it over the floorboards. She rubbed her fingertips together and sniffed. The faint smell of lemon tickled her nose.

"Furniture polish?" she whispered. Where had that come from? She had some, sure, but she hadn't touched the bottle of lemon oil since last spring when she'd given the baseboards and the staircase a good polishing. Same as she did every year, twice a year like clockwork. Afterward, she'd returned the container of yellow liquid to the laundry room, where it had been sitting on a shelf ever since. So what was furniture polish doing on the floor of her kitchen?

While she cleaned up the spot, she considered possible solutions to the mystery. Had someone broken into the house while she was gone? She discounted that idea almost before she thought of it. The last she'd heard, no self-respecting burglar left a trail of cleaning supplies in their wake.

Clearly Tim had stopped by to pick up his golf clubs while she was in Emerald Bay. Had he inadvertently spilled polish when he cleaned up after himself? She shook her head, answering her own question. Tim was an excellent cook, but she often spent hours washing pots and pans and wiping down counters after he created one of his culinary masterpieces. He'd no more grab a bottle of lemon oil and set to work than he'd take up skydiving. Considering his nearly phobic fear of heights, neither were likely.

Had Caitlyn cleaned house as some sort of an apology? Lord knew the girl owed her one. She paused for a moment to imagine her teenage daughter pushing a vacuum across the carpets or running a dust rag over the coffee table. The image made her laugh. She was fairly certain Caitlyn hated housework more than she hated brussels sprouts. And her daughter absolutely detested the vegetable.

Her gaze sharpening, Diane prowled about

the house looking for signs that visitors—either invited or uninvited—had been in her home. The evidence might be easy to overlook, but it was there. Yes, precisely six throw pillows stood against the arms of the couch, but they were arranged differently from the way she always left them. A load of towels she hadn't washed sat in the dryer. Two years ago, she'd redone the downstairs powder room in a soft green hue that clashed with the pink trash can she removed from under the sink. Flamingos dotted the wallpaper in the upstairs bath where she found a jade green container. After returning the receptacles to their proper places, she stepped onto the back porch to continue her survey.

The lawn service had visited; their mowers had left a fresh checkerboard pattern in the grass. A few leaves lay scattered about the yard, but that was normal this time of year. On the deck itself, someone had shoved three chairs into a group around the chaise lounge. Had Caitlyn, Marty and Sarah rearranged them when they were here for dinner last week? Diane eyed the cushions and arm rests. Was it her imagination, or was there less dust on the outdoor furniture than there should be?

Slowly, she walked the perimeter of the deck. In each corner, brightly colored impatiens cascaded down the sides of large, clay flowerpots. Not sure exactly what she was looking for, she paused at each one and ran her fingers through the dense foliage. She felt foolish when the first three pots contained only the usual mix of flowers and soil. Dusting dirt from her fingers, she skipped the last one. She'd almost reached the French doors that led to the kitchen when she spotted metal glinting from the pot she'd overlooked. Her stomach sinking, she hurried toward it. From among the impatiens, she retrieved a crumpled beer can. The red and blue letters of a popular brand stared up at her.

It wasn't hers. She didn't drink beer. Not ever. Besides, pitching a can in with her flowers wasn't exactly her style. It wasn't Tim's, either. Her husband might knock back an occasional cold one while he manned the grill or watched a football game, but he stuck with locally brewed IPAs. She ruled out their son. Nick hadn't been home since Christmas, and this can was far too shiny to have spent the last six months outdoors in the elements.

That left only one possibility, and her stomach soured at the idea that her daughter had broken their cardinal rule about teenage drinking.

"Crap," she whispered. Clutching the can in a tight grip, she marched down the steps into the yard, where she followed the path to the privacy fence that hid their recycling and garbage receptacles from the neighbors' view. Prying up the top of the recycle bin, she pitched the offensive can inside. It landed with a clang on top of dozens of others.

Diane gasped. "What on earth…?"

The answer was fairly obvious. While she'd been caring for her injured aunt and Tim had been doing whatever men who walked out on their marriage did, Caitlyn and her friends had thrown a party.

How on earth did the child think she could get away with such a thing? And how in heaven's name had she managed to pull it off under the watchful eyes of Marty's parents? There was only one way to find out, and Diane reached for her phone. Realizing she'd left it on the counter in the kitchen along with her purse, she headed back inside.

With each step, the hole in her heart widened. Caitlyn had always been such a good girl. A straight-A student. The only sophomore on the varsity soccer team. Between her grades and her sports, she'd earn a full ride to her pick of colleges. Oh, they'd had moments of the usual mother-daughter bickering. But Diane had always trusted the teenager to do the right thing.

Or she had until now.

But underage drinking? Throwing a party without adult supervision?

Did Caitlyn have a clue? Was she even aware of the repercussions? Lives could have been ruined if someone had had an accident after the party. If the police had shown up, they'd have been well within their rights to arrest her daughter on the spot. Competition to get into the best colleges was so fierce that just one incident like that and Caitlyn wouldn't even get accepted, much less earn a scholarship.

As her head filled with all the possible consequences of Caitlyn's actions, bile rose in Diane's throat. A shaky fear washed over her. She stopped in her headlong rush to her phone long enough to swallow.

Slow down, she told herself. Caitlyn and her friends had been drinking in their house. That was bad enough, and her daughter would be punished for it. But her phone hadn't blown up with news of an accident. No one had been arrested. She'd received no frantic messages to bail her teenage daughter out of jail.

Aware that things could have been worse—so much worse—she steadied herself while she checked her watch. Caitlyn's soccer practice wouldn't let out for another half hour. In the meantime, she had questions that demanded answers. There was only one way to get them, and after scrolling through her most recent phone calls, she hit redial.

Her fingers shook as she pictured the cheerful, airy kitchen in the Madison house. Unlike Diane, Heather was a stay-at-home mom who rarely left home except for the trips to the grocery store or the gym and shopping forays necessary to keep her family fed, healthy and looking presentable.

Not for the first time, Diane wondered how the other woman filled the hours of her day. Did she spend her mornings whipping up scrumptious meals while listening to the news? Or laze on the couch watching soap operas and eating bonbons each afternoon?

Not that last one, she admitted. Heather regularly bragged about still being able to fit into the size fours she'd worn in college. Maintaining such a perfect figure at their age took hard work and dedication. She should know; she'd failed miserably at it. She imagined Heather spent most of her free time hustling from Pilates to yoga classes, stopping at the juice bar only long enough to down a few sips of some bitter-tasting veggie drink between sessions.

A buzzing sound broke the silence as her call finally went through. The phone rang once, twice. After the third ring, Diane listened as Heather's slightly breathless voice blared from her cell phone's speaker.

"Hello, Madison residence."

"Hey Heather. It's Diane," she said, doing her best to keep a potent mix of anger and frustration from spilling into her voice. "I wanted to call and thank you for letting Caitlyn stay with you this week. How did things go?"

"Oh, are you back?" Heather asked, ignoring the question Diane most wanted her to answer. "Caitlyn said you were taking care of your aunt. There was something about a fall, wasn't there? I hope she's all right."

Geez. Diane barely resisted slapping a palm to her forehead. Heather knew full well why she'd had to leave town. The two of them had discussed it in depth before she left on Monday.

"Aunt Margaret is eighty and uses a cane to get around, but that doesn't slow her down much," Diane said, forcing herself to remain calm as she once again went over the details. "She fell trying to fix a gutter. Had to have pins put in her arm, and she'll need to wear a cast for a month or two. But she's out of the hospital now and resting comfortably. Her daughter flew in, and one of my other cousins has moved in temporarily, so I came on home."

She cleared her throat. "I'm sure Caitlyn enjoyed staying with you while I was gone. Especially during Spirit Week." The week leading up to Homecoming was filled with such fun activities as Anything-But-A-Backpack Day and School Colors Day. "I hope she wasn't too much trouble?"

"Honestly, I've hardly seen her or Marty all week," Heather said breezily. "Sarah had them come over to her house for Crazy Hair Day so they could do each other's hair, which saved me a ton of time and frustration."

"I can relate," Diane said, recalling how last year Caitlyn had sworn she'd "die, absolutely die" unless her hair looked exactly like Chrissy's in *Stranger Things*. Diane had scoured the internet for the same big green bow the character had worn on the TV series. She'd spent an hour teasing and taming Caitlyn's hair into a perfect imitation of the star's soft updo...only to have the teenager comb it all out before she left for school. Later that day, Diane had found the green bow in a waste can.

She shoved the memory aside while she pondered the best way to pry the information she needed from Heather. "I can't tell you how badly I hated being away this week," she said, sidestepping into the real purpose for her phone call. "Did the girls have fun?"

"I honestly can't say. Like I said, I've barely seen them. The girls wanted to work on their shirts for Tie Dye Day together, so they've been staying at Sarah's." Heather sighed. "I wish they'd stayed here. I could have used their help getting ready for the big party on Saturday."

Diane doubted a bunch of hung-over teenagers would have been much help, but at least she knew how the girls had managed to throw a party without any of the other parents catching wind of it. She bet Sarah's mom thought all three girls had spent the whole week at Marty's house.

"Marty stopped by this morning just long enough to grab her books for French class," Heather said, as if that excused her lack of oversight.

Diane's breath caught. "Caitlyn wasn't with her?" she asked slowly.

"Marty said she was catching a ride to school with Sarah."

So much for trusting Heather to ever watch her daughter again, Diane thought. The woman had no idea where the teenagers had really been.

"It's too bad you and Tim had to miss out on Spirit Week. At least you'll be here for Homecoming. You are coming to the party, aren't you?"

Diane grimaced. In the past, she and Tim had opened their house for the gathering of teens and their dates before the big dance. Showing up at this year's event without her husband at her side was exactly what she didn't want to do. "With all that's going on here, I don't think I'll make it."

Fake sympathy filled Heather's voice as she whispered, "Is everything, you know, all right with you two?"

"We're fine." Diane couldn't help sounding curt. She'd hoped word about her marital problems hadn't spread, but she realized now how foolish that had been. Caitlyn had almost certainly confided in her friend Marty, who'd no doubt repeated the story to her mom. Attempting to do damage control, she said, "I had to be with my aunt, you know. And Tim went to Miami. One of the speakers at a conference fell ill."

She wasn't exactly lying. Tim had gone to Miami, and she was fairly certain that at one of the thousands of conferences taking place in the US each week, a speaker had fallen ill. What she failed to mention was that from Miami, Tim had boarded a cruise ship and was now sailing around the Caribbean.

"Oh? Well, we'll miss you both."

Realizing she wasn't going to get any more information out of Heather, Diane reached a snap decision. If she wanted to know what had happened while she was on the other coast, she needed to go straight to the source. Instead of waiting for Caitlyn to come home from soccer practice, she'd pick up her daughter from the field.

"I'm headed to the school now to get Caitlyn," she said as she slung her purse over her shoulder. "Do you want me to give Marty a ride home, too?" She couldn't wait to talk to both girls.

"Oh, honey, that's such a sweet offer, but Marty drove to school this morning."

Diane pressed a hand to her forehead. "Huh. I guess that just goes to show how much stress I've been under this week—I completely forgot Marty has her own car now."

"I worry about her being on the road with all those crazy drivers, but it sure is nice to be done with car pools. I don't miss those days at all."

"I bet. Caitlyn's been counting the days until she gets her license." Though, after throwing a beer bash at the house this week, she seriously doubted if her daughter would be getting her license—or going anywhere but to school and soccer practice—anytime soon.

"Do I need to pick up any of Caitlyn's things from your house? Clothes? A backpack?" Silently,

Diane crossed her fingers. As much as she knew she had to make the offer, she really hoped Heather wouldn't take her up on it. The woman was a regular Chatty Cathy. No one ever dropped by the Madison house and walked away in under an hour, but the way she was feeling right now, she didn't think she'd last five minutes there without totally losing her cool.

"No need. Marty can drop off anything she left."

Diane let out the breath she'd been holding. She and Caitlyn had a lot to discuss this evening. It wasn't going to be a pleasant conversation. She bit her lower lip. The sooner they got started, the better.

Diane nosed her car onto the patch of bare dirt that served as a parking lot for the practice field. On the other side of a chain-link fence, the varsity team hustled to the sidelines, where the head coach and her two assistants stood waiting to deliver a few last-minute words. Half the players tugged off the black scrimmage vests they wore over their gold practice uniforms and handed them to the team manager before they grabbed water bottles from wooden benches. Others picked up soccer balls and stuffed them into equipment bags before they, too, joined the growing cluster of players.

People in New England might be admiring the fall foliage and pulling scarves and mittens out of storage, but here in the Sunshine State, temperatures still hovered around the ninety-degree mark. Even from a distance, Diane saw damp hair curled around the girls' faces. From the sweat-streaked jerseys and reddened cheeks, she surmised the practice had been a tough one. She scanned the group of twenty or so who'd formed a rough circle, some dropping tiredly to one knee, others sinking, cross-legged, onto the grass. While the head coach, a woman who'd played soccer at the college level, spoke animatedly, Diane tried to pick her daughter out of the group. When she didn't spot Caitlyn's number on the back of a jersey, she sent a brief message telling her child to meet her at the car.

At last, the coach dismissed the team. The equipment manager loaded bags into a cart and started the long trek to the gym on the far side of the football stadium where fans cheered the Plant High Panthers to victory on Friday nights. Diane fidgeted in her seat while the girls grabbed backpacks and splintered into groups of two or three. Some headed toward the student parking lot near the main buildings. A few trudged across the field toward a gate in the fence that opened onto the makeshift parking area.

Diane's lips thinned when Caitlyn didn't put in an appearance by the time the field had emptied. She checked to see that her text had gone through. Her irritation deepened when a tiny "Delivered" appeared under her message. Her jaw tightened, and she eyed the now-empty field.

Had the teen blatantly ignored her text?

Don't jump to conclusions, she argued. There could be a dozen reasons why Caitlyn hadn't come straight to the car after practice. Maybe she'd turned her phone off. Or maybe it had run out of juice. There was also the fact that her daughter was no longer five but fifteen...and in big trouble. Caitlyn had to know that, didn't she? Even though they hadn't spoken, she had to know a party wouldn't escape her mother's notice and that there'd be consequences. Serious ones. With that in mind, she couldn't blame the teen for dragging her feet. She'd probably do the same thing if their roles were reversed.

Sure enough, she'd barely decided to give Caitlyn five more minutes when she spotted her daughter's long, lean form coming toward her from the other side of the field. Glad she didn't have another item to add to the girl's growing list of transgressions, Diane let her breath escape in a sigh that seemed to go on forever.

Which was half as long as it took Caitlyn to slowly trudge across the grass, her head down, shoulders rounded as if they carried the weight of the world. When she finally did reach the car, she slung her backpack into the foot well. Collapsing, rather than sliding, onto the seat, she mumbled a soft, "Thanks for coming to get me."

Her voice was so tremulous that Diane studied her daughter intently. Caitlyn's cheeks were pale, not ruddy from exercise. No sweat dampened her hair, which hung in lanky strands around her face. Instead of her soccer uniform, she wore jeans and a loose T-shirt. Flip-flops, rather than soccer cleats, graced her feet. Diane drew the only possible conclusion—she hadn't spotted Caitlyn with the team earlier because the girl simply hadn't been there.

"What happened? Why weren't you at practice?" she asked.

"Coach cut me from the team," Caitlyn said, her voice flat and devoid of emotion.

The anger and frustration Diane had felt earlier at their house dissipated. Confusion rushed in to take its place. "For how long?"

"For the whole season, I guess."

Diane's stomach plummeted. This had to be a mistake. "I thought you were doing so well on varsity. Didn't Coach say you'd get a lot of playing time this year?" Caitlyn had phenomenal ball-handling skills, but as a sophomore, she wasn't nearly as experienced as the upperclassmen. Other parents had warned Diane that her daughter would mostly likely ride the bench this year, but Coach had pulled the girl aside after the last scrimmage and promised her a spot on the second string.

Caitlyn's only response was a shrug as she stared out the passenger window.

Despite the circumstances, Diane's heart melted for her daughter. The girl had literally glowed with happiness the day she found out she'd made the varsity squad. Getting cut had to be devastating. On the bright side, the junior varsity coaches would be thrilled to have her on their team.

"You'll get to play a lot more on JV," Diane said, pointing out the silver lining in case Caitlyn hadn't seen it herself.

Caitlyn jerked so hard on her seat belt that the braking mechanism engaged. The safety harness emitted a rough *ratchet-a, ratchet-a* as it clicked in place without allowing so much as a spare inch of breathing room.

"Argh!" Caitlyn yanked on the thick webbing. Unable to loosen it, she threw herself forward, but the seat belt kept her back pinned against the seat. "I can't breathe!" She clawed at the belt. "Why won't this thing let me loose?"

"Here." Diane reached over and pressed the release button on the buckle. Immediately, the belt retracted into the holder. "Start over," she said, using a soft, calming voice. "This time, don't pull so hard."

When Caitlyn was safely buckled in and breathing easier, she tried again.

"So what happened?" she asked as she backed out of her parking spot. "Why is Coach sending you down to JV?"

"You don't get it," Caitlyn said, her voice sullen. "She didn't just kick me off varsity. She cut me from the squad. I can't play JV, either."

The news was so unexpected, so shocking that Diane slammed on the brakes. Off the squad entirely? That wasn't possible. Not after the thousands of drills Caitlyn had run in the back yard. After all the hours she and Tim had spent driving her back and forth to practices. To say nothing of the enormous cost of joining soccer leagues and hiring personal trainers. Or all the travel they'd done to the two-day tournaments in faraway cities, the stays in cheap hotels.

"They can't do that," she sputtered. But even as she said the words, the reality of the situation punched her in the gut. Caitlyn, along with all the other girls on the team, had sworn they wouldn't drink alcohol or use drugs as long as they played for the high school. They'd been warned that breaking the rule would lead to severe consequences. Last year, Coach had proven she didn't make exceptions, not even for her best players, when a starting midfielder had been caught smoking on school grounds. By the end of the school day, the girl had been kicked off the squad entirely. By the end of the week, Coach had called a player up from JV to replace her.

"Did Coach find out you violated the sober pledge?"

"But I didn't," Caitlyn protested. She balled one fist and punched her cupped palm. "Someone told Coach they saw me drinking, but I didn't. Honest."

Diane carefully checked her surroundings before she put the car in drive. At the corner, she turned onto the main road. As much as she wanted to believe her daughter, it was awfully had to overlook the evidence. "So what did happen exactly?" she asked, wanting to hear Caitlyn's side of the story. She glanced into the passenger seat. "And before you say anything, I already know about the party. And the beer."

"Oh, yeah?" A sad smile lifted the corners of Caitlyn's lips. "I told Marty we'd never be able to get away with it. How'd you figure it out?"

Much more gently than she'd planned, Diane ticked off items without lifting her fingers from the steering wheel. "The throw pillows were out of order in the family room. The bathroom waste baskets had been switched. I found a beer can in with the flowers on the back porch." The car in front of her signaled for a turn, and she slowed. "A word to the wise—don't leave beer cans in the recycle bin. Bag them up and send them home with someone else next time." She scowled as she followed the car into Parkland Estates. "On second thought, there better not be a 'next time.'"

"Don't worry. There won't be." Caitlyn sank down in the seat. "I should have double-checked the bathrooms. You're so anal about stuff like that."

"I prefer to think of it as observant," Diane corrected with a half-smile. "The pink trash can goes in the pink bathroom. The green one goes in the green bathroom." She paused. She might have missed all the other signs if it hadn't been for the oily spot in the kitchen. Though she refused to let the conversation veer too far afield, she thought it was worth asking, "What did you guys do, spend all day cleaning the house?" At Caitlyn's surprised look, she added, "Someone spilled furniture polish on the kitchen floor. I slipped in it and nearly fell." She watched as her daughter slowly digested that nugget of information.

"Marty dusted and cleaned the kitchen," Caitlyn said after a minute. "I swept and vacuumed the carpets. Sarah was in charge of the bathrooms." She turned to Diane, her face earnest. "You don't have to worry about the bedrooms. I locked all the doors so no one could...you know."

Thank goodness for that much, at least. That still didn't explain how her normally well-behaved daughter came to have a party in the first place. Or why she'd gotten thrown off the soccer team, though Diane suspected one thing had led to the other. She pulled into their garage and shut off the engine. Turning to face Caitlyn, she didn't try to hide her disappointment. "I have to tell you, I never dreamed you'd have your friends over without me or your dad there to supervise. You know it's against the rules." She and Tim had made those perfectly clear to both children.

"It wasn't supposed to be that big a deal," Caitlyn moaned. "I fu—" She stopped herself before her mom had a chance to intervene. "Everything just got out of control. Me and Sarah and Marty…"

"Sarah and Marty and I," Diane corrected out of habit.

"My grammar? That's what you're concerned about?" Caitlyn gave her an incredulous look, but she continued. "We were all going to Homecoming together. As a group, you know. But last week this guy Marty likes—Brad, Brad Henderson—he invited Marty to go with him. *Sarah and I,"* she said, emphasizing each word, "we were fine with it, but Marty insisted we had to have dates, too. So Brad asked Ricky Carson and Craig O'Neil to take us. They play *Call of Duty* together, and they're really nice."

Many of the kids who attended Plant High had gone through elementary and middle school together. The O'Neils lived just down the street from them in Parkland Estates. Ricky Carson's older brother had been in Nick's class. Diane and Lauren Henderson had worked on the same committee for last year's church bazaar. Though none of the boys Caitlyn had mentioned were athletes, they were all honors students and basically good kids.

"We wanted to get to know the guys a little bit before the dance, you know. So Marty suggested we all go to my house and hang out for a while. It was supposed to be just the six of us. But I don't know… Brad must have said something to some of his friends. Or Ricky did. I don't know how it happened. I just know some older kids showed up, and the next thing I knew, the guys were all hanging out on the back porch drinking beer. But I wasn't, Mom. I swear!"

"You know how dangerous it is to drink and drive? Do you have any idea what could have happened if one of them had gotten stopped on the way home? Or had an accident?"

"We're not stu-pid, Mom. Sheesh!" Caitlyn protested. "Everybody knows better than that. All the guys handed their keys to their dates, and none of the girls drank. Just the boys. The ones who didn't have dates, like Justin Manor, either caught a ride or called an Uber."

A huge wave of relief thundered through Diane's chest. At least Caitlyn and her friends had exercised a small amount of good sense. Still, she couldn't overlook the fact that they shouldn't have been in the house alone in the first place. "Drinking or no drinking, you know you're in trouble, don't you?"

"Duh." Caitlyn's frustration came through

loud and clear. "I, uh, I messed up. I'm probably grounded forever."

"For a start," Diane agreed. After unbuckling her seat belt, she exited the vehicle.

"But Mom," Caitlyn pleaded as she followed Diane into the house. "Mom, you gotta talk to Coach and get me back on the team. She didn't even give me a chance to explain. It's not fair that I'm the one who got punished. I kept my promise. I didn't have anything to drink." Shrugging her backpack to the floor, she solemnly drew a cross over her chest with one finger.

Diane busied herself with setting her purse on the small table by the door while she mulled over her daughter's request. As far as she knew, Caitlyn had never out-and-out lied to her before. She wanted to believe the girl with every fiber of her being.

The coach, though, that was another story altogether. Proving Caitlyn hadn't broken the sober pledge was going to be tough. How did one even go about proving something *hadn't* happened?

"I'm going to have to think about this, Caitlyn. I'll need to talk to some of your friends and their parents. Once I'm sure you're telling the truth—all the truth—I might be able to convince…"

Caitlyn, who'd opened the refrigerator and was peering inside, slammed the door so hard, the bottles on the shelves rattled. "Moo-om! You can't talk to Mrs. Harrison or Sarah's folks. I don't want to get them in trouble."

"I can't help that, Caitlyn. Mrs. Harrison thinks you and Marty spent the night at Sarah's house. I'm betting Mrs. Painter thinks the three of you had a sleepover at Marty's. They deserve to know where their daughters really were this week. I can't keep this secret from them. It'd be the same as lying." She wouldn't compromise on that point, no matter how hard Caitlyn begged her. "If they back up your story, I'll talk to Coach. No promises, though. In the end, it'll be her decision whether or not to let you back on the team."

"Uhhh! You don't believe me!" Caitlyn wedged her back against the fridge, her arms folded across her chest.

A bitter retort sprang to Diane's lips. She swallowed it. Losing her temper with the teen would only make the situation worse. "I'm trying to." She sighed. "You haven't exactly given me a whole lot of reasons to trust you this week."

"Daddy would believe me," Caitlyn taunted. "He'd walk straight into Coach's office right now and get me back on the team."

Diane doubted that very much. She and Tim had both had enough dealings with coaches over the years to know that marching into the athletic office like some entitled Ken or Karen was far more likely to get their daughter kicked off the team permanently than to produce the results they wanted.

"Yes, well," she huffed. "You can ask your father how he'd handle it when he gets back. Until then, I'm all you've got." Inwardly, she groaned as the weight of being a single parent, whether it was temporary or not, pressed down on her.

Caitlyn scoured the kitchen as if she expected to find her father hiding behind the potted plant in the corner. "Where is Daddy? Did you…" Her voice died. When she spoke again, her words came out sounding thin and strangled. "Did you kick him out?"

"No. I'd never do that," she said softly. She pressed a hand to her belly as a fresh barrage of pain and betrayal hit her. She pushed against it, burying her own hurt deep inside while she determined to be strong for Caitlyn's sake, if not for her own. "I wanted to talk to you about your dad and me. That's one of the reasons I came to the school—so we could have some time alone together. But other things—" Her hand cut through the air between them. She had more to say on the subject of her daughter's behavior this past week—lots more—but it would have to wait. For now, she needed to help Caitlyn understand what was going on with her and Tim. "The most important thing for you to know right now is that your dad and I both love you very much."

"So what happened?" Caitlyn demanded. "Where is he? I must have texted him a million times. He never answered. Not once. It's like he fell off the face of the earth or something. He's not... He's not..." Her face crumpled.

"Your dad's fine," Diane soothed as she motioned Caitlyn into a chair in the cozy breakfast nook. "You can't reach him because he's on a cruise." Taking two glasses from the cupboard, she filled them with ice and water while she considered exactly what else she wanted to say. Knowing the truth and nothing but the truth would paint her in a bad light, she admitted her daughter deserved to hear the whole story. Anything less was tantamount to a lie, and as they'd already seen, those never turned out well.

Caitlyn sniffed. "A cruise? Like the one Nick took?" Her brother and several of his friends had taken a Carnival cruise from Port Canaveral to the Bahamas right after graduation.

"Mmmm, sort of. Your brother just went to Nassau and back." She doubted a four-day booze fest was on Tim's agenda, but then again, who knew what men did when they were taking a break from their wives, their marriages? For all she knew, Tim could even now be parading around the promenade deck with some floozy.

Oh, stop. Just stop. Thinking like that was not going to help her or Caitlyn.

Swallowing, she refocused on her daughter and tried to keep her voice upbeat. "Your dad's ship is much nicer. It sails to Colombia and Costa Rica and makes a couple of other stops. He'll be gone for two weeks."

"Sounds like fun," Caitlyn said tentatively. She cast a furtive glance at her mom. "He didn't want you to go with him?"

Diane sipped some of her water. This next part was hard to explain, not that discussing any part of her marriage—the good or the bad—with her teenage daughter was easy. But she was stalling, she realized, and forged ahead.

"He did," she admitted. "He planned the trip as an anniversary present since we didn't get to celebrate it last summer." At the time she'd been so busy dotting every *I* and crossing every *T* in her quest to climb the next rung of the corporate ladder at Ybor City Accountants that she'd nixed the idea of spending a week at an inn near Destin. But rather than forgoing the trip entirely as she'd intended, Tim had booked a stateroom aboard the Celebrity Constellation. "This time, when I explained to your dad that I couldn't take time off work on such short notice, he went by himself."

"Whoa. I would have gone with him."

Diane gave her daughter an indulgent smile. "You have school," she reminded the girl. And soccer, she added silently as she crossed her fingers.

Caitlyn blinked. "So he's just taking a little vacation? He'll be back in another week or so?"

She hated to break her daughter's heart, but the truth was bound to come out sooner or later. Lying to the girl would only prolong the inevitable. Diane shook her head. "I don't think so, honey. Your father... Your dad," she corrected, "has an apartment above his dental office. He's going to stay there for a while."

Tears welled in Caitlyn's eyes. "Don't you want him to come home?"

Though Caitlyn made a half-hearted attempt to avoid her, Diane grasped her daughter's hand and held on tight. "Oh, honey. I want that more than anything else in the world. But your dad and I, well, we have different goals right now.

He's starting to think about retirement and making plans to travel. He wants us to see the world together."

"You don't want to do that?" Caitlyn's eyes widened.

Diane grimaced. How did she explain to her daughter that she still had goals she wanted to achieve? That she'd consider herself a failure for the rest of her life if she gave up now? She took a stab at it. "I like what I do for a living. I'm not ready to hang up my calculator just yet."

"But you're always working, Mom," Caitlyn protested.

Out of the mouth of babes. Diane gulped, but there was no sense in denying the truth. "I've probably focused on my job more than I needed to this past year or so. You're right about that. So's your dad, and I promised him I'd cut back on the overtime and spend more time at home."

Not that striking a balance between home and work would be easy. Not with Jeff Thomlinson's threat hanging over her head. But laying that burden on her daughter's slim shoulders was more than Diane wanted to do at the moment.

"Your dad wasn't satisfied with that. He didn't think I'd keep my promise. So he left." She let that sink in for a long moment before she added, "That doesn't mean that either of us are wrong. It's just that we have different ideas about what we want in the future."

"But you guys are gonna fix things, aren't you? You'll see a marriage counselor or something?"

"We'll do all those things, but…" Sadly, Diane shook her head. Caitlyn wanted reassurance she couldn't give, no matter how much she wanted the same thing. She took a breath. She wouldn't sugarcoat the truth for her daughter. Tim had cut himself out of their lives for the time being. He'd walked away from their marriage, from her, from Caitlyn. None of his recent actions boded well for fixing what was broken in their relationship. "Even when two people love each other like your dad and I do, things sometimes don't work out the way we want them to. Remember when your brother and Lila broke up?"

Caitlyn lowered her head. "I was so upset."

"We all were," Diane agreed.

Nick and the girl down the street had been best friends in grade and middle school. They'd started dating at fifteen and had remained a couple all through high school. Over time, Diane's family had expanded to include the girl as a fixture in their lives. Caitlyn had been thrilled to finally have the big sister she'd always wanted. The parents had gotten along well enough that Diane and Tim had frequently invited the other couple over for cookouts and card games, where the topic often drifted to a future that included the babies Lila and Nick would have once they settled down and started a family of their own.

In the devastation that accompanied the breakup, the friendship between both sets of parents had dissolved, as had Lila's relationship with Caitlyn. As for Nick, he'd been so shattered that he'd switched majors and transferred to an altogether different university from the one he and Lila had chosen to attend together.

"We all thought they'd be together forever. And when it didn't turn out that way, it hurt. But we got through it, didn't we? We came out stronger for it."

Caitlyn's friendship with Marty and Sarah had deepened afterward. Nick, whose grades had been mediocre while he and Lila were together, now regularly made the dean's list in his new course of studies. Diane found it particularly encouraging that, after taking a six-month break to, as he put it, "clear his head," her son had started dating again.

She squeezed Caitlyn's hand. "I'm not giving up on your dad and me. But however things work out with us, you need to know we both love you very much."

"Aw, Mom," Caitlyn said, slipping her fingers from Diane's grasp. "You don't need to worry about that. I know you love me." Scooting her chair away from the table, she glanced at the refrigerator. "What's in that box I saw in the fridge? Can I have some?"

Diane smiled. Teens were a rare breed. They considered a bowl of ice cream or a bag of chips the solution to all the world's problems. "Your Aunt Kim made us a chocolate peanut butter pie. I've been dying to have a slice."

"I'll get the plates," Caitlyn volunteered. She sprang from her chair like a jack-in-the-box.

"I guess I'll cut the pie, then." Diane stood.

A few minutes later, Caitlyn spoke around a mouthful of meringue. "Is it okay if I call Marty and Sarah before you talk to their folks?"

Wanting to savor every bite of the rich dessert, Diane forked up a tiny bit of chocolate custard dotted with sugary peanut butter crystals. "You want to give them a chance to come clean with their parents?"

"Yeah. Otherwise, I'm pretty sure they're gonna hate me." Caitlyn had devoured her slice in seconds. Her fork clattered onto a plate so clean she might as well have licked it.

"I actually think it's a good idea." With all that was going on between her and Tim, to say nothing of Caitlyn's problems with the coach, her daughter would need her friends more than ever in the coming months. "But Caitlyn?"

"Yeah?" Rising, she carried her plate to the sink.

"Make those calls and then leave your phone right there on the counter." Diane pointed to the wooden bowl that served as a catch-all for loose change, pens and hair ties. "As part of your punishment for having people in the house while I was gone, I'm taking away your phone privileges for two weeks."

"Two weeks?" Caitlyn's mouth gaped open in disbelief.

"I can make it longer if you'd like."

"But…"

Diane held up a hand. "It's not up for discussion. You're also grounded for a month. You can go to school and to church and that's all."

"What about Homecoming?" The biggest social event of the season was only days away.

"I'm afraid you'll have to skip it this year."

"Yes, ma'am." Caitlyn's head drooped. She scuffed her foot on the floor. "And soccer?"

Diane sighed. Caitlyn was a good girl who'd

made a mistake and had owned up to it. She'd be punished, yes, but she didn't deserve to have her dreams of playing for Plant High ripped away from her.

"I'll talk to Coach after I speak with Marty and Sarah's parents," Diane promised. "If they back up your story, I'll do everything I can to get you back on the team." She took a breath. "But Caitlyn, I have to warn you, even my best might not be good enough to change the coach's mind."

"I know you'll do it, Mom." Picking up her backpack, Caitlyn slung it over one shoulder. "I'll be in my room."

Ahhh, the certainty of youth, Diane thought as Caitlyn bounded up the stairs a few minutes later. She wished she had half as much faith as her daughter that things would go well with either the coach or her marriage. Unfortunately, she had a feeling the coach was going to make an example of her daughter no matter how many people sprang to Caitlyn's defense. As for Tim, she hoped this time away from them would shake him up and make him see what he was missing, but she wasn't going to hold her breath on that one.

Suddenly feeling nauseous at the thought of what lay ahead, she stared down at the fluffy meringue that topped the remains of her slice of pie. Her stomach tightened when she considered taking even one more bite. Saliva pooled in the back of her mouth, and she swallowed.

What a shame. It really was an excellent pie, she thought, before she crossed to the trash can, scraped nearly the entire serving into the bin and braced herself for the challenges that lay ahead.

Four

Belle

*L*ight slanted through a gap between the curtains. Protesting softly, Belle ran her fingers over her face until she reached the sleeping mask that had slipped down onto her nose. She tugged the padded fabric over her eyes where it belonged. When the sun still seeped in around the edges, she yawned and stretched. Her hands skimmed over sheets worn thin from a thousand wash cycles.

Where were her silky-smooth, bamboo bed linens? For that matter, where was she?

Easing into a sitting position, she pushed the mask onto her forehead, pried her eyes open and gazed about to orient herself. The white wicker rocking chair near the closet was missing an armrest. A stack of books propped up a corner of the dark oak nightstand on one side of the bed. On the other, veneer curled in long strips atop a cherry table. Half the drawer pulls on the painted dresser had been replaced with cheap glass knobs.

Home. She laughed silently.

As a kid, she'd gradually become aware that not everyone lived with a mishmash of furniture. Devouring magazine articles about rock stars who'd made it to the big time, she'd vowed that, once she was discovered, her home would look like theirs. No more living with cast-offs from the various rooms throughout the inn for her. No siree.

She'd stuck to her guns, too. While other people bought cars or fancy clothes with their first paychecks, she'd plunked down cash for a brand-new bedroom set that came complete with matching everything. With the money she'd earned from her first hit single, she'd purchased living room furniture that featured the same trim on the couch as the easy chairs, the coffee and end tables. When she hung her first platinum album on the wall, she'd insisted on outfitting her home office to match the frame.

Now she lived in a New York high rise where absolutely nothing matched, and the irony of it all failed to escape her. But by the time she could afford such expensive digs, the eclectic look had been all the rage. Her designer had absolutely insisted on filling the space with pieces that complemented each other, like her living room's white leather couch, which was flanked by two differently styled chairs, one red and one gold.

But at least her sheets were soft.

She swung her legs over the side of the bed while she quickly reviewed her plans for the day. A good workout was at the top of her list or, failing that, a long walk along the beach. She'd been in Emerald Bay for the better part of a week without once doing the hundred crunches or leg lifts she did every day without fail in New York. To say nothing of the five-hour daily workouts with her personal trainer. She pinched her belly and frowned. Was she getting fat? A lack of exercise and a steady diet of casseroles and fried foods would do that to a person.

Once word had gotten out about her mother's broken arm—and in a town as small as Emerald Bay, the news had spread like wildfire—a veritable casserole brigade had formed at the front door. Since the day she'd brought Margaret home from the hospital, they'd been inundated with a barrage of chicken casseroles with crushed cracker toppings, tuna casseroles brimming with thick egg noodles that swam in a cheesy sauce, and so much crispy fried chicken, people must have thought they were feeding an army instead of two women. Faced with all that food, the no-carb diet Belle usually followed had flown right out the window. Starting today, though, she vowed to do better. If nothing else, she'd call Amy and ask her to bring her a salad. Which would go good with a piece of that tasty fried chicken she'd covered in plastic wrap and stuck in the fridge.

She groaned. Staying in Emerald Bay was going to be the death of her. But where else could she go? Not back to New York. Not after the fiasco in Nashville. The minute she stepped off the plane in LaGuardia, reporters would camp out in front of her condo again. She'd be a prisoner in her own home until someone else caught the media's attention. She supposed she could hide out in the little pied-à-terre she kept in Paris or the much larger villa overlooking Italy's Positano coast. But what would she do about her mom?

Margaret had never traveled overseas, and at eighty, she wasn't about to start. Not that she'd ask that of her mom. Even first-class travel could be taxing. Throw in a broken arm, and it'd be downright miserable. Abandoning the woman who'd given her life wasn't an option, either.

So no, Belle wasn't going anywhere. At least, not until Kim returned from Atlanta. Until then, she'd promised her cousins she'd help renovate the inn.

Speaking of which, she'd better get moving. The carpet salesman had dropped off sample swatches yesterday along with an offer for free installation if she placed an order by the end of the week. As soon as she had the final cost, she'd run the figure by her financial manager.

She hoped Richard wasn't going to be a problem. Lately, he'd been making all sorts of noises about overspending. To appease him, she'd done her best to cut back. Hadn't she stayed at the Best Western in Nashville instead of her usual suite at The Hermitage? She'd flown coach to Florida instead of chartering a private jet, hadn't she? With the money she'd saved on those two trips alone, she ought to be able to make a few improvements around the inn. Nothing outrageous, of course. It wasn't like she intended to gut and redo upwards of twenty bathrooms. Not even she had that kind of money lying around. But she ought to be able to swing new carpet and have the floors refinished. After all, she was Belle Dane, wasn't she?

Refusing to dwell on how little that meant lately, she pulled a thick elastic from her hair.

Her curls sprang free of their topknot and fell onto her shoulders. She finger-combed the loose strands before securing them in a ponytail. Running down her mental checklist, she slipped out of her pajamas and pulled on a loose T-shirt over a pair of leggings. She'd exercise first, then look at the swatches and call about the carpet, and if she could squeeze a little more time out of the day, she'd check into the cost of redoing the floors. Her plans made, she eased open her bedroom door.

"Belle? Is that you?"

Belle froze when her mom's voice whispered down the narrow hall.

"Mom?" She padded softly to her mother's room. Light spilled from the doorway and fell onto the rail-thin figure standing beside the bed. Wearing a cotton nightgown, her hair a messy halo around her lined face, Margaret struggled to slip her cast into the sling draped around her neck.

"How they expect anyone to do that one-handed is beyond me. Here, let me help." Belle crossed the room to her mother's side. It took both hands to position the heavy cast in the canvas holder and adjust the Velcro tabs that ensured a good fit. And that was before she tightened the neck strap that held everything in place. "There," she said when she was finished. "You want to go back to bed now? It's barely six o'clock." She glanced out the window. The day was going to be another scorcher. She'd need to get started soon if she was going to finish her exercise routine before the temperatures climbed above eighty.

"Six?" Margaret started toward the door. "We'd better hurry."

"Hold on now. What's the rush?" Before she'd turned in last night, Belle had spooned coffee into filters, filled reservoirs with water and set the timer on the brew station for this morning. One sniff of the caffeine-laden air told her fresh coffee would be ready and waiting for the inn's few guests when they put in an appearance.

"The Bradys are checking out today. They'll want to get an early start." Margaret tried to lift her arm and failed. "It's going to take me forever to get their receipt ready one-handed."

Belle inhaled deeply while she juggled her priorities. Her workout slipped a notch lower on her list. She tugged gently on her ponytail.

"I assume everything's on the computer?" she asked. She'd spotted a bulky model in the office under the stairs. At her mom's nod, she said, "Tell you what. The little I know about computers wouldn't fill a teacup, but if you sit beside me and tell me which buttons to push, I bet we can knock this out in no time."

"You think so?"

Seeing some of the worry lines slip from her mom's face made postponing her own plans for the day worthwhile. "I'm sure. Now, let's get you into your robe and you can walk me through all this."

Taking the nubby chenille robe from the back of a nearby rocking chair, she looked from the garment to the sling her mom wore and back again. Fortunately, the robe had wide bell sleeves that would slip over the cast. But the sling itself? After all the effort required to get the cast properly situated, she'd have to remove the pouch and start over. There was nothing for it, and moving as gently as possible in order to avoid jostling her mom's broken arm, she set about to do what needed to be done.

A few minutes later, Belle scanned the bare surface of a desk that held only a monitor, keyboard and mouse. "Where's the ledger?" she asked, looking for the thick leather binder where her mom had carefully recorded the check-ins and departures of their guests for as long as she could remember.

"I think Kim still has it, but we don't need it. Everything's computerized now." Reaching across Belle with her good hand, Margaret jiggled the mouse. The screen sprang to life. "As much as I complain about computers, they've made this part of running the inn a whole lot simpler. Nowadays we almost never get walk-ins. People expect to do everything online. Diane installed a system that lets our guests reserve their rooms and place their deposits." She pointed a finger toward a small icon in the corner of the screen. "Click on that and open the program. Then we'll enter the date and print out the Bradys' receipt."

Though Belle had never worked the reception desk, the new system sounded a lot easier than the old method of writing things down in the ledger. From what she recalled, her mom had spent hours updating the information on the thick pages each day, carefully recording each reservation, crossing them out whenever someone had to cancel, scribbling a guest's preferences in the margins. She'd often marveled at how her mom kept track of fifteen suites and six cabins and could tell off the top of her head which ones were available on a particular day. Now, the computer program did all that for them.

Not that getting the job done was as simple as "Mary Had a Little Lamb." Before Belle could work on the receipt, Margaret wanted to check the system for new reservations and handle several other administrative tasks. All of which took more time than necessary, thanks to a computer that was much older—and slower—than the one in Belle's own office. But one hour and only a few choice words later, she held her breath as the ancient printer spat out two copies of the Bradys' final bill.

"There," she said, handing a copy to her mom and carefully placing the other one in a file for Diane.

"This looks perfect, honey," her mom said as she scanned the bill over the tops of the glasses perched on her nose. She held it out. "Could you slip it under their door?"

"Happy to." Belle folded the receipt into thirds and placed it in an envelope.

She stood. Her hands folded together, she stretched her arms over her head. "If that's all you need right now, I thought I might go out on the deck and run through my usual exercise routine."

"Actually, I..."

"Is there something else?" Belle let her arms fall to her sides.

"Never mind. I think I can manage."

Belle lifted one eye. "Manage what?"

"Well, I always sweep the front porch and plump the pillows first thing in the mornings."

Belle closed her eyes for a long second while she let her thoughts drift back over the daily chores she and her cousins had performed so many years ago. "What about the entry hall? Don't you sweep it, too?" When she was younger, her mom had insisted on giving the common areas of the inn a once-over every morning.

Her mother nodded. "Then I walk through the parlors and check for anything out of place. If need be, I'll get the vacuum out and run it over the carpets."

"Mom, I'm half your age, and I'm impressed by all you do," she said. She eyed her mom's arm. "There's no way you can manage those things without bumping that arm, and you know what the doctor said."

"He said it'd heal faster and better if I didn't move it around too much," Margaret said with a long-suffering sigh.

"Right. I tell you what, why don't I help you get settled in the kitchen with a cup of coffee, and then I'll take care of all the stuff you usually do."

Margaret's face brightened. "If you wouldn't mind, honey, I'd love a cup of coffee. And maybe a little bite of something so I can take my medicine?"

Belle felt her face warm. How had she forgotten how much her mom looked forward to her first cup in the morning? Or that she couldn't take her pain medication on an empty stomach?

"Of course," she assured Margaret. She waved the envelope that contained the Bradys' receipt. "Let me drop this off and I'll be right back."

So much for her plans for the day. Belle laughed to herself as she dashed across the first floor to the Diamond Suite, where she left the envelope before hustling back to the office. It was beginning to sound like the only workout she'd get would be the one she got taking care of her mom.

Leaving Margaret to sip some much-appreciated coffee in the kitchen, Belle sped through the first floor, plumping pillows and straightening chairs. She scooped playing cards from a table and returned the deck to its shelf in the game room. Outside, she shuddered as she brushed wispy spider webs from the porch railings before sweeping sand and dust into the flower beds.

Satisfied with her work, she returned to the kitchen, where she expected to find her mom finishing her coffee. Instead, Margaret stood at the counter. As Belle watched, her mom struggled to take a full pot of coffee from the brew station and empty it into an urn she'd placed in the white porcelain sink. Imagining all the ways things could go wrong, Belle rushed to her mother's side.

"Here, let me," she said.

"I can do it," Margaret protested as coffee sloshed over the rim of the pot.

"I know you could, but why should you when I'm here to help?" Gently, Belle took the carafe from her mom and finished filling the insulated dispenser. "Does this go in the dining room?"

Wondering how on earth her mom had planned on getting the heavy urn into the other room, much less lift it onto the buffet, she dried the bottom before positioning it on the long sideboard. At her mother's direction, she filled a second dispenser with decaf coffee, as well. She had just completed that task when Amy rushed into the kitchen carrying a large tray filled with Danish and sweet rolls. Several bulging plastic bags dangled from her fingertips.

"Hey! Need a hand?" Belle hurried to relieve Amy of the heavy tray. As she slid it onto the counter, she eyed the selection of sweet rolls that glistened under a layer of icing and sugar crystals. Her stomach gurgled hungrily while she counted the pastries. "That's over two dozen!" She gasped. She peered into the plastic bags. "And four loaves of bread? How many people do you think we're feeding?" As far as she knew, a couple of twentysomethings on their honeymoon were the only guests other than the Bradys.

"Aunt Margaret asked for twice as much as usual. I thought she must be expecting some guests."

While Amy dashed out the door and on to her next delivery, Belle blinked. From the summers she worked at the inn in her teens, she recalled the flurry of activity that preceded a new check-in. The morning of their arrival, she and her cousins used to clean the suite from top to bottom. They'd double-check the trash cans, dresser drawers and closets for anything a previous guest might have left behind. They'd replenish the bars of soap, bottles of shampoo, conditioner and lotion in each bathroom. As a final touch, they'd place an arrangement of fresh flowers in each suite.

She turned to her mom. "Which rooms are we giving our new guests?" She'd need to inspect each one to make sure they had fresh linens and towels.

Margaret's face pinched. "We checked the reservations this morning. We didn't have any new ones, did we?"

Belle waved a hand over the large order of pastries that would grow stale in a day or two. "Then what are all these for?" she asked, curious.

"I guess everyone wants to be sure you girls are taking good care of me. People have been stopping by every day to drop off food or to make sure I'm doing okay." She gave a one-armed shrug, the best she could manage with her arm in a sling. "I thought we should have some extra goodies on hand to serve them."

Belle nodded. Her mom made a good point. Whoever they were, today's members of the casserole brigade were sure to linger over coffee. It'd be only neighborly to provide light snacks.

"Put half the rolls on the serving trays in the dining room so the Bradys and the Normans can help themselves when they get their coffee." Margaret checked the time on the microwave. "They should be up soon."

"And the rest?" Belle asked.

"I keep some plastic containers under the counter."

Belle held up the loaves. "What about these?"

"We'll need bread for sandwiches and such when Kim gets back."

Belle sucked her tongue. Sandwiches with Aunt Liz's special sauce? No thank you. She hadn't eaten white bread in at least ten years.

She snapped her fingers. "Phooey," she whispered. With all the running around she'd been doing this morning, she'd forgotten to ask Amy to bring her a salad from the bakery. Her tummy rumbled a reminder that she had skipped breakfast. Forget that. She hadn't even stopped long enough for a cup of coffee.

She lifted the still-warm loaf of bread to her face and sniffed. The buttery smell of the yeast made her mouth water. Resolutely, she gave the tie a firm twist. If she couldn't follow her regular fitness routine, she could at least stick to her diet, one that did not include bread. Determined to make room among the frozen casseroles, she headed toward the extra freezer in the laundry room.

The morning passed in a whirlwind of getting her mom bathed and dressed, looking at carpet samples, saying goodbye to the Bradys and making sure Irene and Eunice knew to thoroughly clean the recently vacated suite. By the time Margaret headed in to take a nap after a bowl of soup and a grilled cheese sandwich— which was about the extent of Belle's cooking abilities—she felt like her mom wasn't the only one who needed a rest. Instead, Belle grabbed pen and paper and headed for the one place she was fairly certain she wouldn't be overheard.

Sitting in the shade of an oversize market umbrella a few minutes later, Belle gave thanks for an onshore breeze that made being outside in the heat of Indian summer bearable. The distant sound of mowers provided a steady background while she spoke on the phone with the salesman at the flooring store in nearby Vero Beach. She held her breath while he calculated the cost of recarpeting the upstairs hallway and several common areas. When the figure he quoted was lower than she'd expected, she only relaxed a tiny bit. Carpet was nothing compared to the cost of refinishing the hardwood floors throughout the rest of the inn. She tapped her pen on the cost per square foot and tried not to faint when the salesman gave her the final numbers.

After jotting the figures down on her pad, she scrolled through her contacts list for her finance manager. Realizing she wasn't his sole client—an important one, no doubt, but not his only one— she expected to have to wait for a call back and was mildly surprised when his assistant put her straight through to the man himself.

"Belle. Always a pleasure to hear from my favorite pop star. I hope you're calling to say you've reconsidered my offer and you're ready to run away with me to Bora-Bora."

"Not hardly, Richard." Belle didn't let a single word of the man's harmless flirtations go to her head. Richard had been handling her finances since the very beginning of her career. In all those years, he'd never let the opportunity to propose pass him by. The poor guy would probably keel over in a faint if she ever agreed. He'd been happily married to his childhood sweetheart for more than thirty years.

"Ouch. You wound me, Belle." Richard's dramatic sigh provided the usual prelude to getting down to business. "To what do I owe the honor of this call? Tell me those idiots at Noble have come through with a big advance on your next album."

"I'm afraid not." Belle didn't try to hide her regret. "You know how record companies drag their heels these days." Twenty years ago, when she was just starting out, the big recording studios had enticed new artists to sign with them by offering huge advances and enough air time to guarantee a hit. Sadly, those days had passed.

Richard tut-tutted. "That's a shame, but I expected as much. I'm sure good news like that would be plastered on the front page of *Variety*." The magazine had cornered the market on all the news in the entertainment industry. He paused before venturing a tentative, "They were all over that mess down in Nashville."

"That didn't help matters." Belle's face warmed. The tabloids still featured articles on her disastrous open mic appearance in every edition.

"Don't worry, Belle. You and I, we've both been around this business long enough to know that what happened in Nashville will blow over. It won't be long now before Noble comes around, begging you to come back to them."

Belle winced. Richard had never been one to blow smoke before. Did he really think she was so low she needed that kind of ego boost? She squared her shoulders and, ignoring the man's flattery, got straight to the point.

"Listen, I'm at my mom's place in Florida."

"The inn, right? The, uh—"

Belle heard the click-click-click of someone typing on a keyboard and imagined Richard staring at his monitor.

"The Dane Crown Inn?"

"That's the place." She wasn't at all surprised that Richard had the name of the family business on file. After all, he'd paid all the bills when she'd had the kitchen remodeled several years ago. "My mom fell and ended up in the hospital, so I'm down here helping out until she's on her feet again."

"Oh, I'm sorry to hear that. Please give her my best."

"I will. But that's not why I'm calling. I'm calling because I need some money to help renovate the inn." Waiting for Richard to ask how much she wanted to spend, she paused. When he remained silent, she forged ahead. "The whole place needs a lot of work. One of the cottages has a hole in the roof. The rest need new paint and landscaping. For now, though, I just want to replace the carpet and have the floors refinished."

Unlike all the previous times she'd asked the finance guy to free up some money for this expense or that one, Richard didn't hurry to assure her that he'd handle the bills. Instead, he said, "I'm sorry, Belle. That's just not possible right now. We might be able to do something after your next album releases. For sure after the tour. But right now, you're barely making ends meet. You don't have the money to splurge on a major expense like carpeting an entire inn."

Belle stiffened. She didn't want to lay new

carpet throughout, but that wasn't the point. "What do you mean I don't have enough money?" she asked testily.

Richard oozed reassurance. "Remember, we've talked about this. You haven't had a new hit in a while now. Yet the bills continue to come in. You can't keep that up forever. Eventually, you'll run out of money. I've been telling you we needed to cut expenses wherever possible until the new album releases."

"You said I had to cut back, so I did," she pointed out. "I hardly spent a dime on that trip to Nashville." Okay, she and her agent had chartered a plane for the return trip, but she'd been in such a hurry to shake Tennessee's red clay off her boots, she hadn't stopped to consider the expense. "I sat in coach on the flight here." Richard didn't need to know it had been the only seat available on the first flight to Florida.

"Neither of which were in your budget in the first place. Whether you flew first-class or not, those trips were still deficits."

Belle pressed her fingertips against her eyelids. "I had no idea things were this bad when you said to cut back."

"You're not on the brink of bankruptcy or anything," Richard assured her. "But you've incurred a lot of expense in getting ready for the new album and the tour. We're paying for the dance studio and the choreographer…"

Belle bit her lip. Though she'd had a barre installed in her home gym, she needed a lot more space to practice the routines she'd perform on stage.

"Your band, the sound studio, the song-writers…"

She swallowed. People who weren't familiar with the music business assumed the record label hired the composers, the musicians, and the sound technicians. They didn't realize a lot of those expenses fell on her shoulders. Or, more accurately, on Richard's.

"The numbers mount up. To say nothing of the normal, everyday expenses."

"So, how bad is it?" she asked, dreading the answer.

"I'm not worried. You'll get a huge influx of cash once the new album goes on sale. Even more if it goes platinum. The tour, along with T-shirts and souvenir sales, will generate another source of revenue. As long as you don't run up any unforeseen bills before then—"

"Like remodeling the inn," she suggested.

"Exactly. As long as you don't do that, you have enough to get you through without doing anything drastic."

Belle hesitated. Much as she hated to ask the hard questions, she hadn't gotten where she was by sticking her head in the sand and pretending reality wasn't bearing down on her. "And if it doesn't?"

"What do you mean? If what doesn't?" A note of caution crept into Richard's voice.

"What if there's no album? No tour?"

"Is that even in the realm of possibility?" Richard's voice dropped to a barely audible whisper.

Belle chewed on her lower lip. What would Richard do with the truth? Would he keep her secret? Or would he call the people at *Variety* the minute she hung up the phone? Not that it mattered. The whole story was bound to come out sometime. So far, Jason Dennis had kept his promise not to leak word that her relationship with Noble had ended, but too many people— from the lowly intern at the record label to the money men who sat on Executive Row—already knew she and the record label had parted ways. Sooner or later, someone was sure to feed the news to the gossip rags. It might as well be Richard.

"Yes," she answered.

The quiet tapping of Richard's hands on the keyboard ended. The silence on the other end of the call seemed to go on forever before, without a hint of his usual flirtation, Richard asked, "Do you have any idea what's next for you?"

"I'm considering my options," she said, employing the phrase people throughout the entertainment industry used when they had no prospects whatsoever.

"Well, then." Richard cleared his throat. "This is going to require major surgery instead of a Band-Aid. We need to be thinking of the assets you can afford to unload."

"My jewelry?" Belle suggested. Jewelers lent her the expensive pieces she wore on stage and to events like the Academy Awards, but she owned some nice earrings and a gorgeous five-carat pear-shaped pendant.

"Mmmm. Those would only keep you afloat for a month or so. I'm looking for a long-term solution." He typed for a moment. "You're upside down on the Central Park property."

"Yeah," Belle agreed. A housing crash right after she'd bought the luxurious condo over-looking the Reservoir meant she owed more on the place than it was worth. "What about the villa in Positano? Or the apartment in Paris?"

"I'd have to check with our agents in Italy and France, but I suspect, by the time you paid commissions and taxes, you'd break even if you sold those." Another tapping noise came from Richard's office. "We should sell them anyway if we're cutting costs."

She rarely visited the pied-à-terre, but she'd miss the house in Positano. She closed her eyes and envisioned the home that hugged the rugged hillside. How many mornings had she sipped espresso on the balcony overlooking the clear blue Mediterranean Sea? Or taken a dip in the salt-water pool? Not nearly enough, she acknowledged. Though she wiped a sudden dampness from her cheeks at the thought of never again wandering down the brick-lined streets to the market at the center of town, even she had to admit that owning a house she could only visit once or twice a year was a luxury she couldn't afford.

"Sell them both," she said, resigning herself to the inevitable.

"That's a good start, but you're going to need to come up with something else to tide you through for... What do you think? A year? Two?"

Frankly, she had no idea how long it would take her to figure out the next step in her career. "Let's split the difference and call it eighteen months," she offered.

"Okay, eighteen months. Considering your

current expenses, minus the two properties in France and Italy, that's…"

Belle heard a calculator whirr.

When Richard came back on the line, he cited a number that made her head spin.

"That much?" she gasped softly. "I had no idea." She'd meant it when she'd told Diane that math wasn't her thing.

"Getting to the top of the heap is a lot easier than staying there, Belle. For that, you need a publicity team, makeup artists, housekeepers, personal assistants. The list goes on."

She supposed it did.

"What else can you part with?"

She probably had a hundred pairs of shoes. Designer bags and clothes filled her closet. A couple of cars she almost never drove sat in an underground garage. But if a five-carat diamond wouldn't stopper the dam, none of that would either.

"Things are that bad, Richard?" She willed him to laugh and confess that the whole conversation had been a joke. She'd almost forgive him if he did. Almost.

He didn't.

"We were betting on the album and the tour to generate a new cash flow. Without them, yeah, well, you can't go on living the way you have been. That's for sure. It's not time to panic, but you'll definitely need to tighten your belt."

She pointed her pen to the figure on her pad. "Just so you know, as soon as I figure out a way to pay for them, I'm ordering those carpets."

On the other end of the line, Richard muttered something unintelligible before, with a resigned "You're the boss," he ended the call.

Five

Jen

From her window on the sixth floor of the hotel on the outskirts of Las Vegas, the High Roller Observation Wheel shimmered in the desert heat. As the sun dropped lower in the sky, the temperature in her room rose despite the efforts of an air conditioner that ran constantly. Sacrificing the view of the city's miles of concrete, glass and neon to the gods of cool air, Jen drew the floor-to-ceiling drapes. Then, feeling claustrophobic in a space barely large enough to hold a bed and a built-in chest that served double duty as a TV stand, she resumed pacing from the door to the window and back again. After every circuit, she lifted her phone from the charger and checked for messages.

Other than another message from her sister reassuring her that their Aunt Margaret was on the mend after a short hospital stay, there was nothing. Why hadn't someone from the casino called her yet?

She'd killed it at the interview this morning. And why wouldn't she? She had oodles of experience as a cocktail waitress and, most recently, as a casino hostess. In her last job, she'd even earned a coveted spot behind the velvet ropes where the rich folk played, though she almost wished she hadn't. Things hadn't worked out well for her after that, which was why she'd traded Mississippi's heat and humidity for hotter, drier Las Vegas.

She placed the phone facedown on a minuscule table and resumed pacing. The flat-chested woman who'd handled the interview had said to expect a call from Personnel by four o'clock. It was after that now, and she hadn't heard a word. She paused, propped one hand on her hip and stared at the wall, willing her phone to ring. When it didn't, she had to face facts—she hadn't gotten the job.

Frustration built to a screaming crescendo in her chest. She stifled it by shoving her fisted hand to her mouth and biting down on one knuckle. What was she going to do now? In the week since she'd cruised into town, she'd worn the heels of her best pair of shoes to nubs hustling from the employment office of one casino to another. She'd filled out dozens of applications. Personally handed her resume to another half dozen managers.

In the past, the higher-ups had taken one look at her credentials and hired her on the spot. Not so in Vegas. Here, she'd only gotten three callbacks. Though all the interviews had gone well, she'd hadn't received a single job offer. Not even from the Lucky Diamond, and she'd felt particularly good about that one. Just like her, the interviewer had been in her mid-forties and working hard to make her own way in the world. Jen thought they'd made a real connection. Not that it mattered. Nothing had come of it.

Should she call on the off chance that her number had gotten lost somewhere between the interview room and the Personnel office? With nothing to lose, she dug in her purse for Sally Carter's business card. She listened to canned music for less than a minute before her call went through.

"Sally here. How can I help you?"

Jen took a breath. "Hey Sally. It's Jen Passel." Picturing the tall, thin brunette, she summoned a breezy air. "I wanted to thank you for talking with me about the opening at the Lucky Diamond this morning."

"Oh, hi, Jen. You're so welcome. It was a pleasure getting to know you. Is there something I can help you with?"

She'd been right about that connection, Jen told herself. She could almost see Sally's down-to-earth smile. Relaxing the tiniest bit, she dove right in. "Well, as a matter of fact, you said I should expect a call from Personnel by four today, and I haven't heard anything. I was wondering if maybe there was a problem?"

"You haven't?" Mild surprise edged Sally's voice. "Hold on a second."

More canned music came through the speakers. This time several minutes passed before the other woman came back on the line.

"Okay," Sally said with a distracted sigh. "I'm looking at the list of people we hired. Hmmmm. Your name's not on it. That's odd. You were my first choice. I wonder..." Sally's voice dropped a register. "You know we run background checks on all prospective employees. Do you have something in your past that sent up a red flag? A felony? Prison time? Bankruptcy?"

"No," Jen assured her, although she'd be filing for that last one soon enough if she couldn't find work. "There's nothing like that."

Other than a few speeding tickets, her record was squeaky-clean.

"Huh. Well, that's strange." A tapping noise came through the receiver, as if Sally was bouncing the point of a pen off her desk. "Let me look into this. It might take a while."

"Yeah, sure." Jen hesitated. She'd tried to get on with practically every casino on the Strip without success. Was there a secret handshake she didn't know about? Did the managers in this town expect a kickback? She had to be missing something, but what? She twirled a strand of hair around one finger. She wouldn't get a wink of sleep until she knew why the Lucky Diamond had turned her down. Going all in, she continued. "I hate to be a bother, but I'm having trouble getting my foot in the door around here. Do you maybe have a couple of tips you could share with me?"

"I'm not sure I can be much help," Sally protested. "But I don't mind getting together. You want to meet for a drink later?"

"I'm always up for a margarita," Jen said with a smile. Even if things didn't work out for her at the Lucky Diamond, it'd be nice to make a friend in Vegas. Other than her sister and her cousins, she didn't have many of those.

Sally laughed. "Every bartender in Vegas

claims their margaritas are the best. Personally, I prefer the ones at the Ghost Donkey. Do you know it?"

"No, but I can probably find it." She'd pull it up on her phone as soon as they hung up.

"Don't be so sure," Sally cautioned. "The Ghost Donkey is a speakeasy. It's hidden behind the food court at The Cosmopolitan." She named one of the ritzier places in town. "It's quiet there. We won't have to shout to make ourselves heard over a band. I can meet you at seven."

Knowing the evening would involve alcohol, Jen splurged on an Uber that dropped her off around the corner from the entrance to a towering edifice made up of glass and steel. One thing about living in Vegas, she told herself as she crossed acres of polished marble and carpet in search of the Ghost Donkey, she'd certainly meet her daily quota of steps. With minutes to spare, she wound her way through the crowded tables of the food court until she spotted the donkey someone had painted on what looked like an emergency exit.

A full-fledged grin shaped her lips as she tapped out "shave and a haircut" on the concealed entrance. Her smile widened when someone replied with "two bits" before the door sprang open for a trio of departing patrons.

Scanning the room, Jen stepped into a speakeasy straight out of the Prohibition era. The dark wood panels covering the walls gave the place a charming, intimate feel. Drop lights hung over the wooden bar, where gleaming bottles of top-shelf liquors were on display. A handful of customers nursed drinks poured by a bartender who wore a colorful apron over a crisp white shirt and dark slacks. For the first time since Jen had stepped foot in Vegas, there wasn't a slot machine or keno screen in sight, and she soaked in the quiet atmosphere.

No one occupied the leather banquette that provided seating for a large party in one corner of the room. She chose a smaller four-top tucked into the opposite corner and slid onto a metal chair. While she waited for Sally, she studied the cocktail menu the lone waitress dropped on her table.

"Ooof," Sally said, sinking onto the vacant chair beside Jen a few minutes later. She brushed a damp strand of long, dark hair behind one ear and shrugged out of her suit jacket. "I can't believe it's October already and still a hundred degrees outside."

"Yeah, but it's a dry heat." In her first twenty-four hours in Vegas, Jen had heard the phrase repeated at least a dozen times.

"Which is why I need that margarita. Have to stay hydrated, you know."

Jen laughed, confident Sally knew as well as she did that alcohol and heat could be a deadly combination.

They both opted for frozen margaritas and agreed to split an order of chicken mole nachos that were a house specialty.

"The truffle ones are incredible, but we'll come back and have those after you get your first paycheck," Sally said, pointing to the most expensive item on the menu.

"I like the way you're thinking." Both the part about becoming the kind of friends who would meet for drinks on a regular basis and what they'd be celebrating.

"Have you found a place to live yet?" the brunette asked while they waited for their drinks.

Jen shook her head. "I haven't started looking. For now, I'm at the Rio Villa. Tell me, are hotels in Vegas always this cheap?" She'd lived in places where fifty bucks wouldn't get her a room in a sleazy motel, but the accommodations at the Rio were actually quite nice.

"The casinos figured out early on that people who think they're getting a bargain on their hotel rooms will spend the extra—and more—at the tables each night." Sally smoothed the edges of a gray cocktail napkin. "It's a win-win."

Maybe so, but even at bargain-basement rates, Jen's limited funds would only stretch so far. Unless she found work soon, the nachos and drinks they'd ordered would be the last treat she allowed herself for some time.

It was worth it, she decided after one sip of the frozen concoction made with tequila and elderberry liqueur and topped with a chili-dusted cucumber slice. Savoring her drink, she learned that her new friend had divorced two husbands and was on the hunt for lucky number three. Though Jen suspected they'd reached the decision for very different reasons, neither of them had children, which left them both free to spoil their nieces and nephews. Pleasantly surprised by how much they had in common, Jen reached for a crunchy tortilla chip slathered with a dark peanut sauce and bits of shredded chicken before she brought up the reason she'd asked Sally to meet her.

"So I didn't get the job. Any clue where things went wrong?"

"I told Personnel we'd be lucky to have some-one with your skills and experience working at the Diamond," Sally said without addressing the question directly. "I thought for sure they'd make you an offer."

She had, too, Jen admitted. "It doesn't make any sense. I'm clearly qualified. I've never been arrested. I doubt if I've even been suspected of a crime. People tell me I have lousy taste in men, but I'm working on that." She, too, had two divorces under her belt, but unlike Sally, she wasn't interested in chalking up a third. She scratched her head while Sally sucked the last of her margarita through a straw. Jen signaled their waitress for a refill.

When her new drink sat on the table before her, Sally swiveled in her chair to face Jen. "You didn't hear this from me," she whispered.

Her attention piqued, Jen crossed her heart. "From your lips to my ears and no further."

Sally idly stirred the slushy white beverage with her straw. "Vegas looks like a big city, but it's a tight community. The managers of all the big casinos work together. If a shark hits the Sahara, word spreads all the way to the Tropicana in less than an hour." The two casinos stood at opposite ends of the Strip.

"Got it," Jen breathed. Movies and television romanticized the card counter who made a big score and saved the family farm from bankruptcy. In real life, though, most card sharks were professional thieves who did their best to fly under the radar. They employed an ever-evolving bag of tricks, from lasers that tricked the slot machines into making big payouts to devices that literally hid an ace up a player's sleeve. When they hit town, they raked in a certain amount at one casino and moved on to the next before they attracted too much attention. In that way, they could easily rake in hundreds of thousands in a single day. With so much money on the line, the casinos in Biloxi had worked together to catch the cheaters.

"What you might not know is that if, say, your old casino the River Delta gets hit, the casino manager at the Lucky Diamond will know about it before the end of the day."

It made sense, Jen acknowledged. When things got too hot for a crew in Biloxi, the swindlers would most likely move on to Vegas, Tahoe or Atlantic City.

"The thing is, the managers, they share other information, too. Not just about the cheats and the scam artists, but employees."

"Like a blacklist." Jen lost interest in the taco chip she'd taken from the tray. She lowered it to her napkin.

"Not in so many words. But yeah. If someone runs into trouble in Biloxi, they can't just show up in Vegas without the boys upstairs knowing about it."

Despite her best efforts to keep them straight, Jen's shoulders slumped. If word of her problems in Mississippi had spread to Nevada, her chances of landing a good-paying job here were practically zero. She might as well pack her bags and leave town first thing tomorrow. Tears gathered in her eyes. She blinked them away and fought to keep her composure.

She should be grateful, she told herself. Her new friend had just saved her from uselessly spinning her wheels in Vegas until her money ran out. She needed to return the favor.

"I know you hear this a thousand times a week, but what happened in Biloxi wasn't my fault." When Sally simply smiled into her drink, Jen continued. "You know the founders of Preservation?"

"The video game?" One of Sally's eyebrows lifted. Everyone knew the rags-to-riches story of the two nerds who'd developed the hottest video game of the decade by working at their parents' dining room table. Earlier this year, they'd sold their baby to a major distributor and walked away with millions in their pockets.

"Yeah. Those two. Ralph and Garrison." Jen held up a hand. "I'm only telling you this so you can warn your floor managers about them. They're a piece of work. They breezed into the high roller section one night like they owned the place…and the girls who worked the floor. Garrison was particularly obnoxious. He thought I was part of his personal entertainment package. When I refused to sit on his lap, he lost it. Upended a tray of drinks. Made all kinds of accusations. None of it was true, but it didn't matter. His partner demanded satisfaction. The casino manager comped their entire stay—which ended up costing the Delta a pretty penny. I, of course, was fired on the spot."

Sally cupped her chin in her hand. "It's a lot easier to replace a cocktail waitress than two well-heeled whales."

"The thing is, one of the other hostesses told me they'd pulled the same stunt in Atlantic City."

"Infuriating," Sally said simply. "Those two made enough money to buy a small country when they sold Preservation. You'd think they'd be above such shenanigans."

Jen's head bobbed. It felt good to finally tell someone her side of the story. "After that, I couldn't find another job in Biloxi, so I ended up here. But I guess I'll be moving on."

"Don't be in such a hurry," Sally cautioned.

Jen didn't see much point in sticking around.

"Before you pack your bags and hit the road, check out some of the smaller casinos. The big places like the Sahara, the MGM, the Bellagio—"

"Places on the Strip or right downtown," Jen contributed.

"Yeah. You're going to want to steer clear of those. The smaller places are going to be more willing to take a chance on you. If that fails, every hotel in the state has a casino of some sort. One thing they all have in common—they provide free drinks to their players. So they all need waitresses."

Jen mulled the information over while Sally polished off the last of the nachos. By conserving her pennies, she could give Vegas another day or two. But that was all. Any longer and she wouldn't have enough gas money to make it back to Emerald Bay, the one place she could always take refuge.

"Hold on a sec," Sally urged. Reaching into her purse, she pulled out her phone and sped through several screens. "Got it," she said a few seconds later. A sly smile wreathed her face when she turned toward Jen. "Card-A-Val has openings for three cocktail waitresses. They must be desperate. They're offering a $500 signing bonus."

"What's the catch?" She'd applied for a job at more than thirty casinos. Not one of them had offered a bonus.

"The big casinos are all owned by huge corporations. Card-A-Val is Vegas's version of a mom-and-pop diner. You should give it a try." Sally scribbled an address on a cocktail napkin.

When she slid the napkin across to her, Jen carefully pocketed it.

Sally pushed her empty glass to the center of the table. "That's it for me," she announced. "Two's my limit. Spunky's going to want his dinner."

Jen signaled their waitress, who hurried over with their check discreetly tucked into a leather book.

"Dog or cat?" Jen asked as they added a tip and divvied up the bill. She was a dog person herself.

"Cat. He's my baby." Sally grinned. "I found him beside a dumpster on my way to work one morning. He was so tiny, still had his eyes closed. The others in the litter didn't make it, but he had spunk so I named him Spunky." Sally's dark eyes took on a faraway quality. "I bottle-fed him for six weeks."

"Whew!" Jen breathed. "That's a commitment." She pushed the book to the edge of the table where the waitress could easily retrieve it. "How'd you manage that and your job?"

"Oh, I brought him to work with me." Sally laughed. "I kept him in my desk drawer whenever no one else wanted to hold him, which wasn't often. Everybody fell in love with him. I still bring him in once in a while so everyone can fawn over him. He loves the attention." She stood and brushed a few crumbs from her skirt. "This was fun. We'll have to do it again sometime."

"Yeah, let's." Jen slipped her purse strap over one shoulder. "As soon as I get my first paycheck." She patted her pocket. Tomorrow morning, bright and early, she'd try her luck at the Card-A-Val employment office.

The wind coming off the desert cooled the sweat that trickled down the back of Jen's neck as she walked the short distance from her car to the rear entrance of the casino. For once, the heat hadn't caused the sudden rise in her temperature. No, the blame for that belonged to the stack of carefully altered resumes she carried in her purse. Resumes that omitted any mention of the time she'd spent at the River Delta. Would leaving off that information improve her chances of getting a job? She shrugged. It certainly couldn't hurt.

She swigged water from the bottle she'd refilled before leaving the hotel this morning and took her place at the end of a short line. She didn't bother asking if she was in the right place. A sign stuck in the ever-present brown gravel read "Job Fair" above a bright red arrow that pointed the way toward a set of tinted double doors.

She sized up her competition as she brushed a spec of dust from the suit jacket she'd worn over a silky white shirt and tight skirt. Surely, she was a better choice than the twentysomething with last night's mascara still smeared under her puffy eyes. Or the lanky blonde who hadn't bothered to fix her hair before squeezing into a pair of jeans and pulling on a sweatshirt. Or the young mother who'd showed up with a toddler on one hip and a diaper bag slung over her shoulder. Feeling more confident by the moment, Jen tightened the top of her water bottle while she gave herself a stern reminder not to count her chickens before the eggs hatched. After all, this was Vegas, and so far, the town hadn't exactly welcomed her with open arms.

But maybe her luck was changing. As if offering up an example, the line moved much quicker than she'd expected. In almost no time at all, she stepped across the threshold and into a casino that had seen better days.

"What position are you applying for?" asked a young man who held a clipboard. At Jen's answer, he handed her a sheaf of papers to fill out before directing her down the hall to a row of empty chairs. Taking one on the end, Jen began filling out forms that requested all the usual information. She'd made it halfway through the second page when the door opened. The girl with the disheveled hair stepped out.

"I didn't want to work here anyway," she grumbled, letting the door swing shut behind her. "This place is the pits." She huffed and retraced her steps to the exit.

Watching the young woman eat her sour grapes, Jen had to admit the Card-A-Val was no Taj Mahal. On her way to the job fair, she'd driven past the casino's main entrance. The red exterior walls had faded beneath the rays of the harsh sun and should have been repainted long ago. The entrance itself hailed from a different era, but what did she care? A foot in the door and a paycheck, that's all she wanted. Once she had a job history in Vegas, she could use it to get a better position in one of the posh casinos on the strip.

A door swung open, and a woman who wore her gray-streaked hair in a severe bun beckoned her into a cramped office.

"I'm Marge Friedly. Have a seat, Ms., uh…" Marge extended her hand for Jen's paperwork.

"Passel, Jennifer Passel. Everyone calls me Jen." She greeted the woman of indeterminate age whose bright red lipstick had bled into the fine wrinkles around her mouth. Fighting the urge to hand Marge a tissue, Jen sank onto a hard, plastic chair, crossed her legs and pulled her shoulders erect. A rush of nerves made it hard not to fidget while the woman quickly flipped through the pages.

"You've been out of work for the past sixteen months?" Marge stared down at Jen's altered resume.

"Yes." She summoned the sad smile she'd practiced in the mirror of her hotel room. "An illness in the family. We were very close."

"I'm sorry for your loss," Marge said, making an assumption that Jen didn't bother to correct. The rest of her questions were simple and straightforward, and Jen did her best to answer them honestly.

"This all looks in order," Marge said, holding the pages in her hand and tapping the edges against the desk to straighten them. "We'll run the standard background check, of course. You can yourself some embarrassment and me some money if you tell me right now whether something will show up or not."

"No, ma'am. You won't find any red flags." Jen refused to squirm beneath Marge's penetrating stare.

"Good," Marge declared as she apparently reached a decision. "Because you don't have any recent job experience, you'd have to begin at the bottom," she warned. "We're open twenty-four seven. You'd be working the graveyard shift, midnight to 8 a.m. We'd start you off on the main floor with the slot machines. After six months, we'd move you up to the gaming tables. Does that interest you?"

It was an entry-level job, but she couldn't very well demand a better position without admitting that she'd been employed for the last year and a half at the River Delta. A move that would get her fired before she even started. Jen swallowed her complaints. "And the salary?"

"Minimum wage, plus tips, which you may choose to split with the bartenders. Most of our wait staff do."

Jen faked a cough to hide her laughter. She'd been around long enough to know that sharing her tips with the bartenders was not optional.

Not if she expected her orders to get filled quickly and accurately.

Marge stamped the top of Jen's application and scribbled her name across it. "Stop in at Personnel and fill out the paperwork so Uncle Sam gets his cut. Then, see Gus in Uniforms. He'll get you outfitted. You'll have to provide your own hose—skin tone only—and black shoes. You can wear flats, pumps or heels, your choice."

"I, um, I got the job?" Jen asked, just to be sure. The whole interview had taken less time than it took to do her hair this morning.

"Yes," Marge confirmed. "Your first shift starts tonight at midnight. Get here early enough to change into your uniform—the dressing rooms are behind the main floor. Gus will show you around."

As she was preparing to leave, Marge stopped her. "One more thing." She handed across a blue binder. "We tell all our employees to commit this to memory, but you'll get along fine as long as you obey three rules: Leave your phone in your locker—they're not allowed on the floor. Never drink on the job—it's grounds for immediate dismissal. Never cheat. You can't get away with it. We have cameras everywhere."

For the first time since she'd opened the door

fifteen minutes earlier, Marge smiled, a move that stretched her red-tinted lips into a grimace. "Welcome to the Card-A-Val."

Jen gave the woman a heartfelt "Thank you" before she tucked the rule book under one arm. With the papers Marge handed her in her other, she headed down the hall in search of the Personnel Office.

As she walked, she let out a relieved sigh. She'd gotten off on the wrong foot in Vegas, but she'd made a new friend, and thanks to that connection, she'd landed a new job. Things were finally looking up. Maybe now that she had some good news to share, she'd give Kim a call and catch up on all the happenings back in Emerald Bay.

Six

Kim

Kim glanced away from the stove as the door to the deck opened. Air scented with orange blossoms rushed into the kitchen along with Belle. Her dark red hair in tight, damp ringlets, she mopped sweat from her cheeks and forehead using the ends of the towel around her neck. As she took another step into the room, her head lifted. She sniffed the air.

"What is that incredible smell?" Belle asked.

"Celery, onions, green peppers." Kim stirred the finely chopped vegetables in the pan. "Otherwise known as the holy trinity."

"That can't be everything. What else are you cooking?" Belle took a long swig from her water bottle.

Kim eyed the counter, which was littered with plates of browned sausages and chicken thighs along with various bottles and cans of spices. She caught the faintest whiff of the mussels that soaked in a brine mixture. Diced, smoked ham sat on a nearby cutting board. In the fridge, another bowl held shrimp marinating in a mix of lemon juice and oregano. She recited the ingredients.

"Are you… Tell me you're not making paella." Belle licked her lips.

"I am. It'll be ready around six."

"Gosh. I haven't had a good paella in…" Belle paused to think. "To tell the truth, I think the last time I had it was right here. Aunt Liz cooked up a batch the night before I left for Juilliard."

"That was quite the celebration," Kim said, thinking of the night they'd gathered to give Belle a good send-off. "Your mom was so proud. She told everyone who'd listen that her daughter had earned a full ride to the most prestigious music school in the country."

Belle sank onto a kitchen chair. "Sometimes I wonder what my life would be like if I'd stuck it out there." After two years, she and three of her fellow students had formed The Julies. Soon, they traded practice sessions and tutors for a life on the road.

"I think you've done quite well for yourself." Kim grabbed bottles and packets of seasoning and sprinkled the spices over the sautéed veggies.

"I was lucky. After The Julies broke up, I literally ended up singing for my supper. On a New York street corner, no less. I was so sure I'd blown my chance." She shrugged. "But that's where I met Lisa, and from there I was on my way. I still ask myself what might have happened if I'd stayed at Juilliard, if I'd finished my studies. Who knows where I would have ended up. Carnegie Hall, maybe?"

Kim stirred wine and chicken broth into the vegetable mix. She gave the mixture a slow stir while she considered what to say to her cousin. Though Belle hadn't mentioned the fiasco in Nashville, she'd seen the tabloids with their glaring headlines about her cousin's ill-fated venture into country music. She'd even picked up one of the so-called newspapers at the little sundries store in the Melbourne Airport. She read through it on the plane to Atlanta. Though she'd never been in Belle's shoes—and honestly, whoever forced her cousin to wear those ludicrous pink cowboy boots should lose their fashionista license—she thought she could relate to what Belle was going through. Lowering the heat to a bare simmer, she turned away from the stove.

"How much do you know about my marriage to Frank?" She leaned against the counter for support.

Belle's perfect features scrunched. "Just what you've told us—that he considered himself an entrepreneur but was notoriously bad with investments. You warned everyone against putting money into any of his business ventures. Why?"

"Frank is a con man," she said bluntly. "His schemes have ruined a lot of lives, including mine." When Belle began to protest, she waved her off. "This isn't a pity party. I have a lot of regrets about our marriage, but the one thing I don't regret—I don't regret falling in love with Frank. If I hadn't loved him—warts and all—I wouldn't have Natalie or Josh."

"Hmmm." Belle's green eyes narrowed. After a long pause, she gave her head a shake. "I don't get the connection."

"I'm saying you left Juilliard to pursue your dreams, and you succeeded in making them come true. Would things have turned out differently if you'd stayed in school longer? No doubt about it. Oh, you'd have found another path to the top of the mountain. But you'd never have known *this* success, never have recorded *these* platinum records."

"Whoa," Belle breathed. "That's heavy."

"Sorry. I didn't mean for it to be." She'd only wanted to help Belle see that second-guessing the choices she'd made in life wouldn't bring her happiness. She took the wooden spoon from the spoon rest. Lighting one of the burners, she slid the pan with the butter over the flames. "I really should stick to cooking and leave the psychology stuff to the shrinks."

"No. I think you hit the nail right on the head. In fact, if I weren't so sweaty, I'd hug you." Belle's features brightened.

"You had a good workout, then?" The butter had melted nicely. Kim poured the rice she'd premeasured into the pan.

"If by 'good' you mean, do I have jelly legs? Yes. I'll be sore tomorrow. That's what happens at our age when we don't exercise for a week." Standing, she stretched. "I wage a constant battle against getting old."

Stirring the rice with a wooden spoon, Kim sautéed it to a golden brown. "Tell me about it. My knees creak and pop so much when I go up and down the stairs, I keep waiting for someone to ask, 'Where's the fireworks?'"

Belle's laughter trailed off as Kim prepared to

scoop the browned rice into the broth. "Hold up," she said. When Kim turned to look at her, she asked, "Is it absolutely necessary to add the rice? I can do without all those carbs and calories. Can you make paella without it?"

Lowering the pan, Kim tapped the recipe she'd taken from the cookbook she'd found in a cabinet. "According to Aunt Liz's recipe, rice is a key ingredient. But I can set some aside without it for you. It won't be as hearty—it'll be more like a soup, but it'll still taste good. Or I can take something out of the freezer and heat it up. There are loads of casseroles and such in there."

"And pass up Aunt Liz's paella? No, that's okay. I just won't eat until dinner, and I'll work out extra hard tomorrow."

"Now that I'm going to be here for a while, I plan to go for a run along the beach in the mornings. You're welcome to join me. We can start tomorrow." She would have gone today, but she'd wanted to unload her car as soon as she got up. The drive down from Atlanta yesterday had been a long one.

"Sure." Belle took the towel from around her neck. "What time?"

"Five. I'll need to be back in time to help Aunt Margaret. She gets up at six."

"Tell me about it." Belle groaned. "I don't

know where I got the idea that I'd have time to work on my music while I was here. Between taking care of her and keeping things going smoothly with the inn, I haven't had a moment to myself all week."

"Well, now that I'm back, we can share the load. What was it Aunt Liz used to say? Many hands make light work?"

It had been after eleven by the time she'd pulled into a parking space, her car loaded to the brim with everything worth keeping from her apartment. Rather than wake the household when she hauled her belongings inside, Kim had locked the car, then slipped quietly up the stairs to her room, where she slept like the dead until morning. Scrounging for something to eat for breakfast, she'd been amazed when she checked the freezer and found what had to be a half-dozen casseroles on the shelves. "Where did all those dishes in the freezer come from anyway?"

Belle laughed softly. "I guess the preacher must have mentioned Mom's broken arm at church last Sunday. Ever since, one of the ladies shows up around four each day armed with a casserole or fried chicken and all the fixings. They usually sit and visit with Mom for a while." Belle sniffed her armpits. "It's a good thing they do. It's about the only time when I can sneak off and get a shower."

"I'm sure Aunt Margaret loves the company, but I'll put the word out that we don't need any more food. We already have enough to feed an army of teenage boys for a month." Kim made a mental note to contact the church office.

"Speaking of Mom, where is she?"

Kim followed Belle's glance down the hallway to the family quarters. "She was dozing off in her chair after breakfast. I think the pain pills make her sleepy. I tucked her in for a nap." She checked the time displayed on the microwave. "She should be up any minute."

"You don't mind if I take a shower when she wakes up, do you?"

"Of course not." She'd no sooner spoken when Kim heard muffled noises coming from the small apartment off the kitchen. "In fact, there she is now." Kim turned the heat off on all the burners. The rest of the preparation for tonight's dinner would have to wait a bit. "Actually, I'll help Aunt Margaret today. It's the least I can do since you've been responsible for her the whole time I was gone."

"You're sure?" Belle asked, her expression a mix of disbelief and hope.

"Go on." Kim flapped the hem of her apron at

her cousin. "I can manage. Besides, I'm sure your mom and I have plenty of catching up to do."

"You don't have to tell me twice."

Watching Belle disappear down the hall to the family suite, Kim smiled to herself. Belle had put up a brave front, but being responsible for her mother and the inn, as well as seeing to the needs of their albeit few guests, was probably a tough gig for someone like her cousin. Someone who employed a staff whose sole purpose was to cater to the star's every need.

Must be nice, she thought. Even during those flush times when Frank's enterprise of the moment was going well and the money was flowing in, she'd never known that kind of luxurious lifestyle.

Minutes later, Kim lugged one of the boxes she'd unloaded from her car into the kitchen, where she'd left her aunt nursing a cup of coffee. The box was heavy, and she slid it onto the table with a soft grunt.

"What's all this?" Margaret asked, moving her coffee cup out of harm's way.

"When I was packing last week, I ended up with a bunch of things I didn't need anymore but were too good to throw out," Kim explained. "I thought we could look through them in case there's something you want for the inn. Do you see anything you like?"

She began lifting the items, one by one, from the box and arranging them on the table. Margaret chose a blue table lamp for the Lapis Suite and a pair of bookends for the library.

"I'm afraid that's all," the older woman said after she'd scanned the assorted serving utensils, table linens and knickknacks. She ran one finger over a fragile porcelain doll dressed in a yellow porcelain gown. "This one's pretty, though. Where'd you get her?"

"It was Natalie's. She had several of them, but she broke most of them over the years. This one's the only one left." When she was ten, Natalie had developed a fascination for china dolls dressed in ball gowns. But like so many of her daughter's other hobbies, Natalie had lost interest in her "fancy dolls" after only a short time. "I've been hanging onto it in case she ever wanted it, but she said I should get rid of it." Kim carefully wound bubble wrap around the figurine before returning it to the box.

"She's far too pretty to end up in the landfill. What will you do with her and the rest of all this?" Margaret nodded to the odds and ends still on the table.

"I'm going to donate it all to the church thrift store. That way someone will get some use out of it."

"Excellent idea," Margaret agreed. "I'm sure someone will buy her." She sipped her coffee before asking, "Did you stumble across anything else interesting during the move?"

"As a matter of fact, I did." Kim grinned as she loaded the rest of the stuff into the box.

"Oh?" Margaret's blue eyes sparkled.

"You'll have to wait until dinner tonight to find out what it is. I've asked Amy to join us. I think she'll find it interesting, too."

"Now you've really stirred my curiosity. Don't you want to give me a hint?"

"I'm afraid you'll have to wait like everyone else," Kim chided. She checked the time. "And now, I need to put the finishing touches on dinner if we're going to have anything worth eating tonight."

Kim removed her apron and hung it on a hook next to the refrigerator. Turning, she surveyed the table.

The paella was the star of the show, so she'd deliberately kept the décor simple. In the center of the table, greenery sprang from three tin cans wrapped in raffia and arranged in a rustic wooden box. Around it, she'd placed tall green glasses, sage stoneware plates, and shiny silverware on four woven placemats. The rolls Amy had brought from the bakery sat in a lined wicker basket. Pitchers of water and iced tea stood at the ready, along with a bowl of freshly tossed salad. The usual accompaniments—salt and pepper, butter and assorted dressing choices—were scattered about.

"Perfect, if I do say so myself," she whispered.

A twinge of regret struck her, and she blinked it away. Her Aunt Liz had taught her to take pride in her cooking, and she'd often dreamed of following in her aunt's footsteps and opening a small restaurant of her own one day. But then she'd met Frank. Fast-forward a couple of years and she'd put her own dreams aside to become a wife and a mother. Not long after that, she'd found herself working a dead-end job to make ends meet, all the while believing her husband's promises that one day his business schemes would pay off. Something that had never happened.

Argh! Why was she thinking about Frank?

She'd meant it earlier when she told Belle that it didn't do any good to play the coulda-shoulda-woulda game, but ever since she and her cousin had spoken this morning, her thoughts kept straying to her ex-husband. Which only brought up bad memories, memories she'd sworn she was over and done with. She gazed around the kitchen. The dinner she'd worked so hard on would be ruined if she stood here too much longer. Determined not to dwell on a past she couldn't change, she gave herself a rueful shake and got moving.

She summoned Amy and Aunt Margaret in from the deck, where the pair had been watching a flock of monk parrots settle in for the night. The birds had arrived several weeks earlier and had apparently decided to make a home in the inn's stately palm trees. "Does anyone know where Belle got off to?" she asked as she helped her aunt to her seat.

"I'm here. I'm here." Belle bustled into the room. "Sorry I'm late. I was on the phone with the carpet people. I hope I didn't hold everyone up." She paused, her huge eyes growing even wider. "Kim, this looks amazing."

"Yes, it does," chimed Amy. "And it smells divine. Things were so busy at the bakery today, I skipped lunch. I'm looking forward to making up for it now."

Kim felt her cheeks flush as a burst of pride rushed through her. "I hope everything tastes as good as it smells. If not, blame the cook, not Aunt Liz's recipe."

She crossed to the oven, where she removed the platter of paella from the warming tray and carried it to the table. As she lowered it onto the table, Amy let out a long, low moan.

"Oh, that looks better than any picture in a cookbook or magazine," she declared.

Kim had to admit her cousin was right. Succulent shrimp, meaty chicken thighs and spicy sausages peaked out from their bed of flavorful yellow rice. Green peas and chopped tomatoes added little spots of color. Around the edges of the dish, bright orange mussels in their shiny black shells lay atop thin lemon slices and strips of red pimiento. Steam wafted upwards, flavoring the air with a mixture of spice and seafood.

"Oh, my gosh." Not standing on ceremony, Amy forked a mouthful of the rice. She smacked her lips. "It's every bit as good as it smells and then some."

"Hold on a sec." Kim made another trip to the oven, this time returning with a soup bowl brimming with all but one of the paella's ingredients. "I made yours without the rice, Belle."

Belle sucked in a breath. "Kim, you are too much. Honestly." She clapped her hands. "Okay. Let's say grace so we can dig in."

Kim's mouth watered in anticipation as Aunt

Margaret gave thanks for the food and other blessings. The older woman's quavering "Amen" had barely faded before Amy grabbed the serving spoon and piled a generous helping of the rice dish on her own plate. Belle, meanwhile, carefully separated the meat from a chicken thigh and cut shrimp and sausage into bite-size pieces for her mom who, due to her broken arm, couldn't wield a knife.

"I'll never eat that much," Margaret protested when Belle slid the plate in front of her.

"Give it a try. You might surprise yourself," Kim encouraged. Only ten days had passed since Margaret's accident, but already their aunt's lean frame looked narrower.

Margaret speared a piece of shrimp. "Oh, that is good, Kim," she said, chewing thoughtfully. She scooped up a bit of rice.

Sitting beside her mom, Belle dipped a spoon into her bowl and came up with a chunk of sausage. She chewed, her eyes rolling back in her head with pleasure. Amy practically moaned with every bite as she scarfed down a substantial helping of paella and salad. What followed was a string of compliments that made Kim's chest warm. The initial burst of praise gradually faded into the sounds of everyone enjoying a good meal. Other than asking each other to pass the rolls or salad, they barely spoke until, one by one, they cleaned their plates.

"Who wants seconds?" Amy asked, reaching for the serving spoon.

Belle chased her spoon around her empty bowl before she lifted it. "I'll have some. A little rice couldn't hurt, could it?" She waited until Amy gave her two full scoops before she withdrew her hand.

"Aunt Margaret?"

"Maybe just a tiny bit." Though she'd sworn she couldn't possibly eat everything on her plate, she had done that and wanted more.

"This takes me back, Kim," Amy gushed after she'd taken another bite. "Paella has always been my favorite, but I think yours is even better than my mom's."

"I wouldn't go quite that far." The warm feeling in Kim's chest spread. Even she had to admit the dish was one of her better efforts.

"No, truly. It's that good." Amy chewed and swallowed. "You should come to work for me at the bakery."

Kim hesitated. "Thanks, but…"

Amy paused, another forkful suspended in midair. "But what?"

"Much as I love to cook, I'm not much of a baker," Kim confessed. "You can ask Natalie or

Josh. Every time they were supposed to bring brownies or cupcakes to school, they'd beg me *not* to volunteer."

Amy laughed. "Okay. I get your point. But this—" She speared a fat chunk of sausage— "This is amazing."

"What about the diner?" asked Belle. "You can certainly out-cook whoever they have there now."

"Don't let Vivi Borders hear you say that." Amy's dark curls shook. "She fancies herself a chef. Her sister Denise runs the front of the house. They only hire people to wait and bus tables. Kim would be better off looking somewhere else."

Belle tapped her spoon against the side of her bowl. "Okay, if not the diner, then what about opening a small catering business?"

Kim blinked. She'd followed the bouncing ball of conversation while Belle and Amy batted her fate around like she wasn't in the room. Now that she thought about it, though, she didn't hate the idea of going into business for herself. But was Emerald Bay large enough to support a catering business? "How many people around here hire someone to handle their birthday or wedding celebrations? Not that many," she said, playing devil's advocate.

"True." Belle cupped her chin in one hand while she gave the matter some thought. "But everyone loves a home-cooked meal. You could open a small subscription service and deliver meals straight to your customers' homes. Start out slow, maybe two, three times a week until you see how it goes."

"A home delivery service? Like Hello Blue or Fresh Apron?" Kim named two companies that provided all the makings for easy-to-prepare meals.

"Yeah, like that, only yours would be fully cooked, fully prepared. Just heat and serve," Amy corrected.

A kernel of excitement unfurled in Kim's midsection. "I'd need to try out some recipes. If I came up with a dozen sure-fire entrees and the side dishes to go with them, I could offer them on a rotating basis throughout the month."

"A business like that wouldn't require a huge amount of capital. You'd need small ice chests to pack the frozen meals in. Aluminum tins. Labels," Amy suggested. "Except for the chests, we have plenty of supplies at the bakery. I could lend you whatever you needed to get started."

"No need," Kim protested. After watching Frank take advantage of all their friends, she'd vowed never to follow his example. That included not taking supplies and such from Amy's bakery. "I have a little bit of savings, enough to get something like this off the ground. Plus, I'm getting my entire security deposit back from the apartment in Atlanta. Mr. Phipps, the building manager, tried to argue, but I refused to back down. The check should arrive next week."

"Good for you," Aunt Margaret said.

"There's just one problem." Amy stared down at her empty plate.

"What's that?" Belle asked.

"You'll need access to a commercial kitchen. The bakery has one, but it isn't equipped for this kind of cooking. Plus, my bakers work round the clock. I don't think we could share kitchen space."

Kim deflated like a balloon that had sprung a leak. The state and local governments had strict guidelines for businesses that provided food to the public. And with good reason. No one wanted to be responsible for an outbreak of food poisoning or salmonella. But the equipment needed to outfit a commercial kitchen was expensive and, while she had enough money to cover the start-up costs for a new business, she certainly didn't have the funds needed to meet all those regulations.

They all fell silent for a long moment.

"Maybe this isn't the right time to go into business for myself," Kim said at last.

"Don't be so sure," Margaret argued. She cleared her throat while the others looked at her expectantly. "You do know we had this kitchen certified as a commercial kitchen, don't you? We had to bring it up to code when we refurbished it."

"That's right!" Belle snapped her fingers. "I'd nearly forgotten that." She pointed to a series of jets discreetly installed around the big gas stove. "The fire marshal insisted on an automated fire suppression system. The refrigerator and freezer are commercial-grade. There were some other upgrades, too."

"I thought one requirement was a triple sink," Kim said, eyeing the oversize farm sink.

"We use plastic tubs to divide the sink at the bakery. Works like a charm." Amy grinned.

"And you wouldn't mind if I cooked here?" Kim studied her aunt's face.

"Not as long as I get my meals for free," Aunt Margaret said without hesitation.

"Always. And thanks." Leaning across the table, Kim squeezed her aunt's good hand. She stanched tears of gratitude with her napkin. "Still, I don't want to get too far ahead of myself." One question still remained, and it was a doozy. "Do you really think there'd be a market for a service like this in a place the size of Emerald Bay?"

"I can't answer that, but I know someone who could," Margaret said immediately.

Kim stared into the lined blue eyes that crinkled with humor. "Who?"

"Your friend Craig," her aunt answered firmly.

By an act of sheer will, Kim refused to blush. If anyone in Emerald Bay had a finger on the pulse of business enterprises in the area, it'd be the mayor, she supposed. "I've been meaning to call him to bring him up to date on the National Registry. I guess it wouldn't hurt to run something like this by him."

"That's right, dear," Aunt Margaret said as she gently prodded Kim's arm. "You should call him first thing tomorrow."

"I'll do that," Kim promised. A sudden warmth flooded her as she scanned the faces of her aunt and cousins. Whether she ever got this new business venture off the ground or not, she'd always be grateful for her family's support. *How did I get so lucky?*

Once everyone had eaten their fill of the spicy paella, Kim still had a couple of surprises in store for her aunt and cousins. She walked to the refrigerator after they'd cleared the dinner dishes. Taking a plate that held an inverted Bundt cake pan from the top shelf, she carried it to the table.

"Everyone cross your fingers now," she ordered. This was her first attempt at the recipe Diane had given her. She held her breath while she rapped the plate sharply on the table. Grasping the pan by the edges, she lifted it to reveal dark, sugary syrup dripping down the sides of a perfectly formed flan. The oohs and aahs that followed sent another burst of happiness through her. "I thought we might want something cool and creamy after that spicy meal."

"It's perfect," Amy gushed. Hurrying to her feet, she rushed to the cabinets, where she grabbed four dessert plates and spoons.

"Just a taste for me," Belle said. "I already cheated on my diet enough with the rice." She patted her flat stomach.

Kim honored her cousin's request before serving everyone else generous slices of the custard. Another round of compliments rose as they all sampled the dessert bathed in a decadent coating of melted sugar. Not used to being the center of attention, Kim felt a sudden urge to change the subject. She turned to Belle. "Didn't you say something about the new carpets earlier?"

"Yes. Just before we all sat down to this feast." Belle broke off a tiny bit of flan. "Now that we've chosen the sample we like the best..." She shot a deferential look at her mother, who nodded.

"I think that rust color will look splendid against the dark wood floors," the older woman said.

"I do, too, Mom," Belle agreed. "Based on our choice, I have a final estimate on refinishing all the wood floors and laying the new carpet. It's not cheap." She paused only briefly before announcing, "The whole job will run twenty grand."

"Yikes," Kim exclaimed. "That's a lot more than I expected."

"Me, too," Belle confessed. "It's also more money than I'm able to free up right now, but I'm working on it." When her mother expressed concern, she added, "Don't worry. We'll get it figured out. But there's something else we all need to think about in the meantime."

Amy pushed her empty plate aside. "What's that?"

171

"The flooring guy—his name is Darren, by the way—he wants to refinish all the floors upstairs before he tackles the downstairs. He says he'll need two weeks to do the whole job. And another couple of days to lay the carpet."

"Two weeks." Trying not to gasp, Kim watched as, across the table, Amy bit her lower lip.

"Why can't they do one room at a time?" Margaret asked.

"They could, but Darren says it'll save us thousands and we'll get a much more uniform finish if we have them do the entire job in one fell swoop instead of piecemeal," Belle explained.

"From his perspective, moving the equipment from one job site to another would be time-consuming." Kim rubbed her upper lip. "Which would make it more expensive for us."

"Plus, you're bound to run into delays when you spread a big job out like that," Amy added. "I ran into a few of those when we remodeled the bakery. And don't forget the smell," she cautioned.

"Oh, right." Margaret's white curls bobbed up and down. "That stuff they seal the floors with is potent. What's it called?"

"Polyurethane," Kim provided. "It stinks to high heaven."

"Yes, that's it. Polyurethane. How could I forget? Eric used it whenever he repaired furniture. We always had to let the pieces sit in the shed for several days before we could bring them inside."

"Remember when we replaced the furniture in the Opal Suite?" Belle asked. "Daddy said he'd fix up that old dressing table and let me use it. I was dying to have it, and I convinced him to put it in my room before it finished curing." She waved a hand under her nose. "Boy, was that a big mistake. My clothes smelled like lacquer for weeks."

"That pretty much settles it. If we had Darren and his crew do one room at a time, you'd be dealing with that smell for months on end. I'm sure your guests would complain, Aunt Margaret," Amy said sympathetically.

"Wait, though." Kim ran her fork through a smear of caramel and licked the tines. "Doesn't that mean Aunt Margaret will have to close the inn for two weeks?"

Margaret's expression turned positively glum. "I don't know how I could do that. I've already booked several reservations through spring."

"Hmmm. Waiting that long might be a problem." Belle clucked her tongue. "I'll have to check back with Darren. I don't know how long he'll honor this bid."

"What if…" Margaret's voice faltered. "Never mind. That probably won't work."

"What, Mom?" Belle prodded.

"Well, you said you were going to refurbish the cottages anyway. What if you started with those before we work on the main house? Do you think that's possible?"

At her aunt's tentative suggestion, Kim felt certain they'd hit on a plan. "That's a great idea," she declared. "It would let us put all the guests in the cabins so we'd be free to do the floors and whatever else needs working on without inconveniencing anyone."

"We'd need to take a good look at the bookings for the next couple of months," Belle said.

"I can help you find a time when you don't have too many reservations," Amy offered. "I do that all the time whenever someone at the bakery needs to take a vacation."

"No need." Margaret tapped the side of her head with one finger. "I've got everything I need to know right up here. The holidays are our best bet. The Jamisons have the only confirmed reservation for the week before Christmas. They're checking out Christmas Eve. The Edisons,

Clarks and McGraws check in the day after Christmas and plan to stay until New Year's. The first couple of weeks in January are slow, too."

Two very different emotions swirled in Kim's head. She was, of course, relieved that Aunt Margaret had so quickly chosen a time to work on the floors. But she had to admit, she'd always loved Christmas at the inn—the tinsel and the lights, the scent of pine that filled the entire house, the good smells of gingerbread and Aunt Liz's fruit cakes baking in the kitchen. She'd hate to miss all that this year.

Apparently an altogether different worry had struck Amy. She gazed around the table at her cousins. "That only gives us two months to get the cabins ready. Can we do it by then?"

"What do you think, Kim? You're the one with the list."

Lost in memories of Christmases past, Kim didn't hear the question until Belle nudged her arm. "What?" she asked. She replayed the conversation in her mind. "I think it's doable," she said slowly. "Regala doesn't need much work. Once Helen leaves, we can give it a fresh coat of paint inside and out. We should be able to knock that out in a few days."

"She came over for coffee yesterday," Margaret offered. "Her book is going better than she expected. She said she plans to finish it and check out by the end of the week."

"I spoke to Max on the phone last week." The handyman had been polite and reassuring when Amy had reached him. "He says it'll only take a day to repair the gutters and fix Carmen's broken window. He'll also pressure-wash the rest of the cabins to get them ready for painting. He's not a roofer, but he has a friend who can handle the repairs to San Roman and Trinidad. Max is bringing him out here this week to look things over and give us a bid."

"Any idea what that's going to run?" Belle asked.

"The bungalows are small, so I don't expect it to be too expensive, but if you smile just right at him, he might give us the friends-and-family discount," Amy teased.

"I'll do my best."

Laughter rippled through the room when Belle struck a pose.

"Okay, so we'll see how much it'll cost to put a new roof on San Roman," Kim said when the laughter died. "Someone put a tarp over the leak, and there's surprisingly little damage inside. It needs paint inside and out. Rosario needs the least amount of work. We'll start by painting it."

She continued down her mental checklist. "In

the meantime, La Popa has been used for storage. It'll need fresh paint, too, but we'll need to empty it out before we can tell what else needs to be done in there."

"How about a painting party this weekend?" Belle suggested. "Diane said she'd be here. That'll give us an extra set of hands."

"Sounds good. By then, we should know how much it'll cost to reroof Trinidad and if there's enough money in the bank to cover it." Kim looked at Amy. "What about you? Are you available this weekend?"

"Saturday is our busiest day at the bakery, but we're closed on Sundays. What if I provide lunch on Saturday and plan on being here all day Sunday? Will that work?"

Kim gave a thumbs up sign.

"If we can pull this off, it'll give me a couple of months to come up with the money for the carpet and flooring," Belle mused.

"As long as we don't run into any surprises," Amy cautioned.

"Speaking of surprises, I have one I think you'll like." Kim stood. "Don't anybody move until I get back." Seconds later, she raced up the stairs. From the floor of the closet in the Topaz Suite, she took a laundry bag that held a bulky object. Walking into the kitchen, she held the bag aloft. "Guess what I found when I was cleaning out the apartment."

"A teddy bear?"

"A throw pillow?"

"A pair of shoes?"

"No, no and no." Kim laughed. She tugged open the drawstring. Reaching inside, she pulled out the old, leather tricorne hat they'd used as kids when they hunted for buried treasure. "Remember this? Josh must have brought it home. It was mixed in with a box of his stuff."

"Oh, my gosh. I haven't seen that in ages," Belle declared. They'd drawn straws, and whoever had the shortest one got to be captain of the pirates for the entire day.

"The captain always wore the hat *and* carried the treasure map. I never thought it was fair that they got to do both." Amy's hand darted toward the hat. Grabbing it, she jammed it on over her curls. "Avast, ye maties!" she cried.

Fine grains of a whitish powder dribbled out from under the brim and onto Amy's nose.

"What is this stuff?" she demanded as she swept the leather tricorne from her head. It plopped onto the table, where more of the powder sifted onto the dark wood. Looking for all the world like someone who'd run into a spider's web, Amy vigorously ran her hands through her hair.

"Here, let me see that." Belle turned the hat over. The stained linen liner crumbled when she ran a manicured finger over it. "Hmmm, maybe we shouldn't wear this anymore."

"Before Amy so rudely snatched it away from me"—Kim gave her cousin a teasing look—"I was thinking we should put the hat in a shadow box and display it. What do you think?" She turned to her aunt.

"That's a fine idea," Margaret said. "If we ever find the map that went with it, we could put them in the same display."

"We'll be on the lookout for it when we fix up the rooms and the cabins," Kim promised. "Who knows? Maybe it'll turn up, too."

The strains of "The Old Rugged Cross" faded. Over the clatter of dishes and the sounds of running water that came from the kitchen, Belle sang the opening bars of "Amazing Grace." When she reached the first chorus, Amy provided the harmony.

"I could listen to them sing together all night." Margaret swung her legs up and into the bed while Kim plumped the pillows.

"They do make a sweet sound, don't they?" After Margaret leaned back against the pillows, Kim pulled the covers over her aunt's lean form. "Do you want to read for a little bit?" Margaret usually kept at least one book on her nightstand. Tonight was no exception. Kim hummed along with the music.

"I'll pretend to," Margaret said, reaching for the book Kim handed her. She yawned widely.

"Do you want me to send Belle in to say good night?" She brushed a kiss onto Margaret's forehead. Her aunt had tired visibly not long after they'd finished dinner.

"No. I'm just going to listen for a while." Margaret's eyes drifted closed. "Ask them to keep singing, will you?"

Kim agreed. Leaving the door to the family suite ajar, she joined the others in the kitchen. At the sink, she picked up a fresh dish towel and began drying the pots and pans that Amy had washed and Belle had rinsed and left to drain on the counter, just like they'd done when they were younger.

"Okay, do you remember this one?" Belle asked after the last notes of "Grace" faded. She hummed the opening bars of "I'll Fly Away."

Kim grinned. Leaning her back against the counter, she eyed Amy. As if forty years hadn't passed since the last time they'd sung with Belle, they both came in on the downbeat with Amy taking the high tenor and Kim singing the lower baritone in the three-part harmony.

Water dripping from her fingers, Belle high-fived each of them at the song's conclusion. "I've performed with some amazing singers over the years, but no one—and I mean no one—does it better than you guys. You're the best."

Kim felt her face flush at the compliment. She glanced at Amy. Twin spots of bright red color stained her cousin's cheeks while she studiously watched the last of the sudsy water swirl down the drain. "You make us sound good," she whispered.

"Nah," Belle protested. "It's more than that."

"We should sound good together. We've been singing as long as we've been doing the dinner dishes. Which was..." Kim paused.

"Gosh, since we were old enough to reach the counters," Belle suggested.

"On those little plastic step stools," Amy added. "Remember, Mom would line five of them up in a row. One each for the three of us and two more for Diane and Jen."

"Heaven help us if we missed a spot on one of the dishes. Aunt Liz would make us start over and rewash every dish."

"I never understood why she didn't have a dishwasher back then," Belle said.

"I asked her about that once." Kim smiled. "She said she already had five of them."

"It didn't take her long to buy one after we moved out, did it?" Amy pointed to the under-the-counter unit.

"Don't you dare tell Mom, but I actually miss the days when we used to clean the kitchen together each night." Belle paused. "Speaking of Mom, has she gone to bed already?"

Kim nodded. "I think she was sound asleep by the time I reached the hallway, but she said to tell you how much she enjoyed listening to you sing."

"She's always been my Number 1 fan," Belle said on her way to the wine rack. Bending low, she examined several labels before she chose a bottle of red. "It's such a pretty night. I feel like sitting out on the deck for a while before I turn in." Deftly, she opened the bottle using the corkscrew she found in the drawer above the wine rack. "Anyone want to join me?"

"Count me out." Amy clasped her hands and stretched them over her head. "I need to get home. Some of us still have to work for a living, you know."

"I'm in," Kim said. A little one-on-one time with Belle sounded like the perfect ending to a busy day. Even better, spending time with her cousin would banish the thoughts about Frank which, like the proverbial boomerang, kept coming back.

Seven

Kim

"Hello?" Kim eyed the empty reception desk at the front of the squat, one-story building that served as Emerald Bay's Town Hall. When no one answered, she let her voice rise. "Hello? Is anyone here?"

Not so much as a piece of paper stirred. Had everyone gone out to lunch? She pulled her cell phone from her pocket and checked the time. Sure enough, the morning had completely gotten away from her.

She took three deep breaths, expelling them slowly to combat the frustration that buzzed around her head like a cloud of bees. When she'd made her list of errands to run today, she hadn't factored in Aunt Margaret's insistence on double-checking every booking around the holidays.

Not that she blamed her aunt. If she were an innkeeper, she'd want to make sure to inconvenience the fewest possible number of guests while the main house underwent major repairs. But Kim couldn't very well force her aunt to use the hunt-and-peck method when accessing the computer, and the older woman's cast prevented her from doing anything else. So Kim had dutifully manned the keyboard in the tiny office while she and Margaret spent an hour examining every booking from now through the spring. Only when Margaret was satisfied that the information in her head matched that on the computer had Kim set off on a lengthy list of errands. From the looks of things, the delay had cost her the chance to talk with Craig.

Disappointment sank deep roots into her core. She hadn't realized how much she'd been looking forward to seeing the man. She'd been hoping to hear the deep timbre of his voice, to gaze into his gray-blue eyes. She shook her head. If she didn't know better, she'd say she had a little bit of a crush on the mayor of Emerald Bay. Which was ridiculous, of course. Women her age didn't have crushes. Even if they did, she certainly wasn't looking to start a new relationship, not with her life in its current state of flux.

She swept another look over the Town Hall's reception area, which had been designed with function, if not beauty, in mind. Behind her, chairs built more for sturdiness than comfort lined the wall. In front of her, a service counter stretched out on either side of a short swinging gate. The space between the counter and the back wall housed several desks, all vacant at the moment. An open door led to a long hallway lined with offices.

Could someone in one of the offices tell her where she could find Craig?

Her gaze returned to the gate. It was locked, right? She shrugged. It wouldn't do any harm to check. If she couldn't pass through, she'd leave a short note on the receptionist's desk and go on about her business. She gave the gate a tentative shove and was surprised when it swung open on well-oiled hinges. Before she could think better of the plan, she strode past the desks and headed down the hall.

Modest signs mounted on industrial green walls identified the offices of the city clerk, council members and various administrative staff. She moved on without encountering a single soul until she reached the end of the corridor. There, another sign simply read, "Mayor's Office." The door stood ajar. Curiosity got the best of her, and she pushed on the wooden surface.

She caught Craig in the middle of shrugging into a lightweight jacket. "Oh, hi!" she said, her cheeks burning. "I called out, but no one answered. I wasn't sure anyone was here."

"Kim." The smile lines bracketing Craig's lips widened. "What brings you to Town Hall?"

"You, actually. I wanted to let you know what I found out about the National Registry and to ask for your advice." She glanced at his windbreaker. "I've obviously caught you at a bad time. Maybe we can chat later?"

Craig's smile deepened. "As a matter of fact, I was just heading to the park for lunch." He lifted a bulging paper bag from his desk. "If you don't mind peanut butter and jelly, you're welcome to join me."

After gorging herself on paella and flan last night, Kim had sworn she wouldn't eat again for a week. At Craig's tempting offer, however, she was suddenly ravenous. Forcing herself to play it cool, she teased, "Depends. What kind of jelly?"

"Orange marmalade, actually. My wife used to make her own jams and jellies. Orange marmalade was her favorite."

A burst of sympathy shot through Kim. Aunt Margaret had told her Craig's wife had died in a tragic accident. "I was sorry to hear about Vivian," she said softly. "I knew her in school, of course. Everyone did." Though Vivian had been part of the "in crowd" while Kim definitely had not, she and the captain of the cheerleading squad had been in the same senior English class. "She was good people."

"She was." Craig nodded.

"How long's it been?" Kim asked.

"Two years ago last month. I didn't think I'd ever get over losing her, but I finally accepted that she wouldn't want me to spend the rest of my life grieving for her. Life has a way of making you move on, you know." He dusted his hands lightly. "So here I am. Mayor of Emerald Bay. Doing my part to make the world a better place. Right now, that means having lunch." Paper rustled as Craig held the door for her.

"I hear you on that," Kim said. She glanced sideways at the bag he held. "Do you always brown-bag it?"

"Whenever the weather is nice enough. I like the peace and quiet." He held the door for her as they stepped out onto the sidewalk a minute later. "I deal with people and their problems day in and day out. It's nice to take a break from all that once in a while."

Kim stopped in her tracks. "Hey. I don't want

to be a bother. I can make an appointment for later on this week."

"Don't be silly. You could never intrude. Seeing you is the best thing that's happened all day." He turned toward the park that lay just beyond the Town Hall.

Was that a compliment, she wondered, or was Craig just being a good politician? Before she could figure out the answer, Betty Lauder, the woman who'd worked as a receptionist in Town Hall for as far back as Kim could remember, bustled toward them.

"Taking a late lunch again, Craig?" she asked.

"Yes, ma'am." Craig ducked his head like a kid who'd been caught sneaking out onto the playground in the middle of math class. He aimed a palm toward Kim. "You know Kimberly Dane, don't you? Margaret Clayton's niece?"

"Why yes. Kimberly, how are you?" Instead of waiting for an answer, Betty leaned in for a hug that enveloped Kim in a cloud of Jean Nate. "I haven't had a chance to see you since you've been back in town," Betty exclaimed, smashing pillow-soft breasts against Kim's chest and wrapping plump arms around her shoulders. "How long are you staying?"

"I'm not sure, exactly," Kim said. Trying not to gag on the smell of Betty's perfume, she extricated herself from the hug. "I'll be here at least until Aunt Margaret's cast comes off." After that, well, that's part of the reason she'd wanted to talk with Craig.

"I hope you stay for a nice, long visit, dear. Did you get the flowers we sent?" Betty asked. She glanced up at Craig. "The city sends a get-well bouquet whenever one of our business owners is ill." Now that she had the mayor's attention, she continued, "Don't forget, you have that two o'clock with the police chief. The shuttle will be here to pick you up at four."

Kim had expected the woman to pass along a few reminders and move on, but Betty evidently had a particular grievance she needed to discuss with the mayor. When she began to do exactly that, Kim stepped away. Not wanting to intrude on town business, she pointed to a picnic table in the shade of a sprawling oak tree. "I'll wait over there, if you don't mind."

Turning in to the park, she picked her way down a sidewalk lined on either side with knee-high hedges. A breeze gently rocked the empty seats on a nearby swing set. A small fountain burbled in the middle of an open area. Beyond it stood an aging amphitheater where the county symphony performed concerts on summer nights.

She hadn't been waiting long when footsteps sounded on the path behind her. Seconds later, Craig slid onto the bench opposite hers, offering a wry, "Sorry about that."

"I can see why you need to get away from it all at lunch," she said with a soft laugh.

Craig chuckled. "Betty knows more about this town than I ever will, but when she gets a bee in her bonnet, there's no stopping her."

"Tough day in the Town Hall?"

"Tom Medford took over the Spring Fling planning committee last year after Josiah Jenkins retired. Tom's called five times this morning. He's already spent more on the Fling than we allowed for it, and he wants me to approve the extra expenses. Betty explained to him that all budget matters have to be approved by the Town Council, not just me. But he won't take 'no' for an answer. I think she's at her wits' end with him."

Kim lifted one eyebrow. "What's the Spring Fling?"

"An arts and crafts fair," Craig explained. "One weekend a year—this one's in March—vendors from all over the state line the streets of Emerald Bay. The event draws thousands of visitors into the area. It's great for local businesses, and since the city gets a cut of all the sales, it helps us keep the lights on. Or it will as long as Tom Medford doesn't blow through all the profits."

"You've been doing this for a while, I take it." The festival hadn't existed when she'd lived in Emerald Bay.

"This will be our twentieth year."

"Hmm. Seems like by now things ought to be routine."

"You'd think. But Tom has some new ideas. They're not bad. They just cost money. For instance, he wants to hire a band and block off the streets for dancing in the evening." Craig shook his head in disgust. "Of course, that means bringing in beer and food trucks. Which means we need a bigger police presence. Which costs even more money. Frankly, we don't make enough off the craft fair to justify the expense."

"You could charge an entry fee," Kim suggested.

"No one pays to get into a craft fair," Craig protested.

"Not for the fair itself, no." She hadn't worded that right and hurried to explain. "Just for the dance. And instead of letting the beer and food trucks handle the money, you could sell food-and-beverage tickets. So many tickets needed for a beer. So many for a taco. That way, the city would get a little bit of profit on each item—enough to pay for the extra security."

Craig tilted his head toward one side. "Has anyone told you lately that you're brilliant? I'm going to suggest that idea to Tom and have him work up a proposal."

"What's the going rate for solving problems down at Town Hall?" Glad she could be of help, Kim smiled.

"How about half a sandwich?" Paper crackled as Craig ripped open his lunch bag to reveal a peanut butter and marmalade sandwich, a handful of grapes and a bag of multigrain chips.

"Throw in a couple of those grapes and you've got yourself a deal."

"A bargain," Craig declared with a smile that warmed her heart. His eyes narrowed slightly. "You mentioned the National Registry? Did you have any luck?"

"I wish it had worked out, but it doesn't look like the Dane Crown Inn qualifies." Kim plucked a grape from the cluster Craig had set on the bench between them. "The requirements are pretty stringent. As far as I can tell, no world leaders have ever stayed at the inn. No famous poets took up residence in the attic. Our house wasn't designed by I.M. Pei, and Ponce de Leon did not make landfall on our beach."

"That's too bad. I was really hoping it would work out." He chewed thoughtfully on a bite of sandwich.

"No more than I was. We could have used some grant money to fix the place up."

At Craig's frown, she hurried to ease his concerns. "We're not throwing in the towel. Aunt Margaret wants to host a family reunion next Memorial Day weekend, and we've all decided it's the perfect excuse to get the place in tip-top shape."

"Seems like a lot of work to do with just…"

Kim interrupted him. "Craig Morgan, if the next words out of your mouth are 'a bunch of women,' we're going to have a problem." She summoned her most serious glower.

"No, not that. I'd never say that." Craig threw his hands into the air in mock surrender. He shot her a look that was pure jest. "What I was going to say before I was so rudely interrupted, is that it'd be a lot to do for a small crew. Men or women."

"Don't worry. We're calling in the experts when we need to," she assured him. "We have a quote for new flooring. Amy asked Max to inspect all the railings and make whatever repairs he can handle. He was at the house this morning, pressure-washing all the cottages so we can have a painting party this weekend. Diane's driving over for it."

"Sounds like you're headed in the right direction." Apparently mollified, Craig broke a grape in half and tossed the pieces to a couple of robins who picked through fallen leaves at the base of a nearby tree. "I may have heard something about that family reunion." Craig grinned as he took one of the chips from the bag and popped it in his mouth.

"You did?" Kim didn't try to hide her surprise. As far as she knew, only immediate family knew about the gathering.

"Word spreads fast in Emerald Bay. You've had quite the parade of visitors out at the inn this week, haven't you?"

"I was in Atlanta most of the week, but yes. Several of Aunt Margaret's friends and some of the women from her church dropped off meals. Which we all appreciate more than I can say," she hurried to add.

"If your aunt even hinted at the possibility of holding a reunion, that's all it took. The news of a Dane Family Reunion was all but included in the bulletin at church on Sunday."

Shaking her head, Kim laughed. She'd forgotten how fast word spread in a small town like Emerald Bay. She eyed Craig thoughtfully. She wouldn't want news of her new business venture to get around before she was ready.

Could she trust him to keep her own plans under wraps? She rolled the grape between the tips of her fingers while she gathered enough courage to broach the topic.

"Why'd you go to Atlanta?" he asked.

The question caught her off guard. She recovered quickly and shrugged. Without intending to, Craig had provided the perfect segue into the very subject she wanted to discuss. "The lease was up on my apartment. You're looking at Emerald Bay's newest resident." She smiled, hoping he'd be pleased by her announcement.

"Welcome to town. If I'd known ahead of time, we could have celebrated with something better than peanut butter and jelly. Rain check?"

"Sure," Kim said as an image of a table for two, flickering candlelight and glasses of wine flashed through her head. She felt a sudden urge to go shopping for a new dress but applied the brakes to that idea. For one thing, she was watching her pennies. For another, she doubted whether Craig's thoughts had veered in the same direction as hers. His *rain check* was probably nothing more than coffee at the Pirate's Cove Diner. Which was fine with her. After all, hadn't she just reminded herself that she wasn't looking for a relationship?

She blinked, vaguely aware that Craig had asked a question. "What was that?" she asked.

"I wondered what you plan to do now that you're moving to Emerald Bay."

Firmly pushing all thoughts of candlelight and a nice bottle of wine to the back of her mind, she straightened. "Well, I'll be helping Aunt Margaret until her arm heals. And working on the inn, of course."

"Of course."

She took a breath. "I'm also thinking—and this is just the beginning of an idea, mind you— but I might open a catering business."

Craig's eyebrows lifted the slightest bit. "Here? In Emerald Bay?" Swiveling toward her, he eyed her carefully. Interest flickered in his bluish gray eyes.

Was that good or bad? Suddenly nervous, she gave him a quick rundown of her plans. "My goal would be to deliver heat-and-serve meals to people who sign up on a monthly basis. I'd use the kitchen at the inn as my base—it meets all the food service guidelines. At first I'd make deliveries two, maybe three, times a week. I'd start with a very limited customer base—no more than ten subscribers. I'd gradually expand as the business proves itself viable." Her heart hammered in her throat as she asked the one question that would determine the fate of her fledgling idea. "Do you think there'd be a need for something like that in Emerald Bay?"

Instead of answering directly, Craig pointed to the remnants of his half of the sandwich. "I can barely boil water, much less cook for myself. How soon can I sign up?"

Tension bled from her shoulders at his lighthearted response.

"You haven't even tried my cooking yet," she said.

"I'm going out on a limb here and trusting that your Aunt Margaret wouldn't support such an idea unless you were a very good cook." He tapped his chin thoughtfully. "I assume your target market is busy working moms and retirees. We sure have plenty of those in town. Throw in a few singles like me, and I think you have all the ingredients for success."

"You really think so?" She could hardly believe it. She was finally going to make her dream of going into business herself come true.

"I do." Craig nodded firmly. "Plus, building trust is one of the biggest difficulties in getting any new business off the ground. Somebody new moves into the area, hangs out their shingle and claims to be the best roofer in the state. Who's going to believe them?" In quick succession, his shoulders lifted and fell. "Not anyone in Emerald Bay. It'll take years of doing consistently excellent work before people around here will recommend them. You have an advantage over most out-siders. People here know and trust you because you spent a large part of your childhood here in Emerald Bay."

Trust.

As they had off and on this past week, thoughts of Frank filled Kim's head. Her ex-husband had been one of the least trustworthy people she knew. Yet she'd stayed married to him for more than twenty years. What would people say about her if they learned the truth about Frank? Would they consider her guilty by association?

Would Craig?

Considering the idea that her marriage, no matter how long ago it had ended, could ruin her chances to see her dreams come true, she suppressed a groan. If her connection to Frank could come back to hurt her, she wanted to find out now, before she invested what little money she had in starting a business. The same went for her friendship with Craig.

She folded her hands tightly together and held them in her lap. Afraid she'd see doubt and mistrust creep into Craig's expression, she refused to look up. Instead, with a deep, shuddering breath, she confessed.

"I don't know how many people in Emerald Bay know this, but my first husband, the father of my children, was…" She stopped herself. The only way she was going to get through this was to be completely honest. "Is," she corrected. "Is a con man."

Her blood thundered so loudly in her ears that she barely heard Craig's dry, "Oh, really."

Feeling more miserable by the moment, she hit the highlights. "For as long as I've known him, Frank has come up with one fantastic get-rich-quick scheme after another. One time, it was a newly discovered oil reserve in the Amazon. Once, it was the inside track on a promising but underfunded cancer drug. The thing is, he's really good at getting people to trust him. So the next thing I'd know, we'd be at a backyard cookout and all our friends and neighbors would be clustered around Frank, practically begging him to let them invest in his latest idea. Of course, he never said no."

"Everybody wants to get rich, but not many are willing to work for it. They're always looking for an easy buck," Craig said on a long breath.

"Exactly." Kim's jaw tightened. "For a while, things would be great. The first 'gusher' would come in, or the drug would pass the first set of clinical trials with flying colors, and everybody would make money. Not as much as they originally invested, but enough to make them want to buy more shares. They'd tell all their friends, who'd also want in on the deal. The thing is, though, none of it was real. There were no uncharted oil fields in South America. No cancer drugs, no clinical trials."

"How'd he keep people from finding out the truth?" Disbelief colored Craig's tone.

"I—I don't really know." She wasn't particularly proud of that fact and let it show. "Between taking care of the kids and the house and my own job, I was always busy. Too busy to ask a lot of questions. The few times I did ask about his investments, he launched into some highly technical explanation of how crude oil is refined or the odds of developing cardiac toxicity following a regimen of chemotherapy. I'd get so lost in the gobbledygook that I'd lose sight of the fact that he hadn't really told me anything. And life was good, you know? We drove new cars and had country club memberships and there were trips to theme parks."

She took a deep breath and forced herself to tell him the rest of it. "Sooner or later, though, one of Frank's investors would need to cash out, and things would fall apart. Of course, I didn't know that. I only knew that one day, Frank would come home from work and announce that he'd been transferred, and we had to leave the next day. We'd throw what we could in the car and move to a new city, make new friends, and the cycle would start all over again."

"You didn't know what was really going on?"

A tear slipped down her cheek. "Not for much longer than it should have taken me to figure things out. The first couple of times his schemes fell apart, I convinced myself he just didn't know how to run a business. I couldn't accept that the father of my children would actually steal from our friends, our relatives. But when the same thing kept happening over and over again, I had to admit the truth. That's when I left him."

"That had to be a difficult decision."

"It's one I've never regretted." Straightening, she looked up at Craig. To her immense relief, the same caring concern she'd noted on his face earlier hadn't wavered. Still, she had to be sure. Aware there might be more at stake than her business proposal, she asked, "Do you think my marriage to Frank will be a problem?"

"I don't see why it should. It's not like you were involved in his schemes or privy to his plans." Though Craig's expression didn't change, he shot the cuff of his jacket and glanced at his watch. "I'm afraid I have to run," he announced. "I have that two o'clock with the police chief." He began gathering up the remnants of their lunch. Tucking the plastic bags inside the paper one to save for another day, he stood.

"That's okay. It's so pretty here, I think I'll just sit for a while." It had felt good to come clean about her relationship with Frank, but thinking about her divorce had stirred up the usual anger and resentment. She wanted to take a minute to deal with those before finishing her errands. Besides, though she tried to brush the feeling aside, Kim couldn't help but question whether Craig was more in a hurry to get to his meeting or to put some distance between them.

"Don't forget—you owe me a rain check," she said, hoping she was wrong about the sudden coolness in Craig's manner.

"Right," he said slowly. "Let me check my schedule and I'll…call you." With that, he began retracing his steps to the Town Hall.

Watching him go, Kim shook her head. His parting words had been the classic brush-off. "Don't call me, I'll call you," she whispered to his retreating back.

Eight

Diane

*I*n tense whispers, the twenty junior accountants and admin staff who crowded around the long, mahogany table questioned whether or not they'd still have jobs at the end of the meeting. The consensus was that they had every right to worry. Not one of the people in the room could say with any certainty that they'd make the deadline. Worse, with less than twenty-four hours left in the IRS's filing window, they'd run out of work to do. Someone wondered aloud whether their lack of new assignments was a sign that the axe was about to fall.

Lingering just out of their sight in the hallway, Diane tapped her foot impatiently. She wanted to reassure her staff. They deserved that much. But here she was, cooling her jets while she waited for her boss and mentor to put in an appearance.

It wasn't right for Jeff to keep the people in the conference room on pins and needles. She'd caught enough snatches of the conversations drifting through the open door to know how upsetting they'd found the situation. To be honest, she didn't blame them a bit for being concerned. Not when she'd disappeared without a moment's warning just days before a deadline so etched in concrete that missing it was grounds for immediate termination.

Deciding she'd give Jeff one more minute to show up before she put an end to the suspense, she checked her watch. She'd braced herself, prepared to accept the fallout for addressing the group without him, when she spied the founder's long, lean form rounding the corner at the end of the corridor. Relief sighed through her as he closed the distance between them. She squared her shoulders, ready to deliver the news that would put an end to all the speculation.

"You remember your lines?" Jeff asked when he reached her.

Diane nodded. She wasn't entirely convinced

her staff was in the mood for a joke, but she'd voiced her concerns earlier. Jeff had overridden her objections.

"Let's get going, then." Jeff rubbed his hands together.

An expectant hush fell over the room as they entered. Eager to put everyone at ease, Diane let a warm smile break across her face.

"I want to thank you for all your hard work these past months. I'm especially pleased with how well you've handled things while I dealt with a family emergency these last few days." Each of the people under her supervision had risen to the occasion, not only completing their assignments but doing them flawlessly. She should know. She'd spent the morning reviewing their work. There hadn't been a single mistake on any of the returns.

She scanned their faces, happy to note that some of the tension in the room had dissipated. She swallowed a knowing grin. The rest of her staff's stress would soon evaporate quicker than dew on grass.

"That would be reason enough to celebrate," she continued, "but you went above and beyond by emptying our queue." She upended the wooden box that had once held a towering stack of tax filings. Not even the tiniest scrap of paper fell to the floor. "Congratulations on being the first group to make the deadline!" Three other teams, including her rival Blake Larson's, were still burning the midnight oil in their efforts to file their tax returns on time.

A collective gasp rippled through the room, followed by a burst of applause. When it died down, Jeff stepped forward.

"Great work!" the founder said, grinning broadly. "In appreciation for a job well done, each person on Diane's team will receive a five-hundred-dollar bonus."

When a handful of people clapped politely, the founder reeled back as if he expected a more positive response. His eyes widening, he turned to Diane. "How much did you promise them?"

Diane winked at her team and folded her arms across her chest. "More than that." She played her part just like Jeff had asked her to do.

Holding out his hands as if he were shushing a crowd, Jeff said, "All right, then, we'll make it seven fifty."

"More!" Diane coaxed.

"More?" Relishing his role, Jeff shot her a horrified look. At her nod, he shook his head. "You drive a hard bargain," he declared. His shoulders rounding in apparent defeat, he sighed audibly. "All right. One thousand dollars," he conceded as if that hadn't been the amount promised to members of the winning team all along.

The announcement met with nervous laughter and a smattering of applause. Diane sympathized with her staff's lackluster response. Each of the people gathered around the conference table, from the lowliest admin to the most senior accountant, had spent the last month working eighty-hour weeks. A mere thousand dollars would hardly make up for the time they'd missed with their families, friends and loved ones.

Signaling for quiet, she stepped forward. "Spend the rest of the morning wrapping up any loose ends. There'll be pizza in the break room for lunch on me." She'd already ordered an assortment of pies from Bella's, her favorite pizza joint. "Then take the afternoon off. You deserve it."

"You don't think giving them the rest of the day off was a bit much?" Jeff asked after the last of her team had filed out of the room.

"No, sir," she answered firmly. "Some down time will do them all good. They'll come back tomorrow ready to tackle the next project." Now that her staff had filed their allotted share of the October tax returns, they'd return to the normal

accounting tasks that were Ybor City Accountants'
bread and butter.

"Well, some time off seems to have worked
for you," Jeff acknowledged. "You're looking
well-rested and more like your usual self."

"The circumstances weren't ideal, but it was
good to get away for a bit." Knowing the importance her mentor placed on appearance, she'd
taken pains with hers before returning to work.
In between the difficult calls she'd placed to
Marty and Sarah's parents last night, she'd given
herself a fresh manicure and pedicure. This
morning, she'd paired her favorite silk blouse
with a navy power suit and put some extra effort
into her hair and makeup.

"I want you to sit in on a meeting with Joe
Smalley and me this afternoon. Now that your
team has proven it's not afraid of a little hard
work, I'd like them to take over the WEXX
accounts."

"I'll be there." Diane lifted one eyebrow.
"I take it things have gone well with the
negotiations?" Landing the WEXX account was a
huge feather in Ybor City's cap, but she didn't
fool herself. It also meant more work for her and
her beleaguered staff.

"They'll be coming on board the first of the
year. The next three months, I'll want you and

your team to liaise with their current accounting firm to ensure a smooth transition."

"What time is the meeting?" she asked while she considered how she'd break the news to her staff that their reward for all the hard work they put into making the most recent deadline was…more work.

"Two."

She was on the verge of assuring the man in charge that she'd be in his office at the appointed time when her phone vibrated. Knowing she'd silenced the device at the start of her workday, she frowned. Only a short list of callers could get through when her phone was in Do Not Disturb mode. She considered the most likely suspects, ruling out her husband and daughter. Caitlyn's phone was sitting on the kitchen counter, while Tim couldn't very well reach her from the middle of the ocean. Had something else happened to Aunt Margaret? Imagining the worst, she flinched when her phone buzzed again. She held up a finger.

"Excuse me a minute, Jeff. I need to take this."

Ignoring her boss's scowl, she pulled the device from her jacket pocket. Her pulse jumped the instant she glanced down and saw several missed calls from Plant High. Images of armed intruders and frightened children filled her head.

She brought up the school's chat loop and drew a shaky breath when there was no mention of a school lockdown.

"Problem?" Jeff asked in a tone that implied there better not be.

Diane shook her head. "A message from Caitlyn's school. It's probably an announcement about Homecoming." Idly, she wished the school wouldn't clutter up her inbox with trivial matters. Deciding to deal with the messages later, she didn't bother reading them before she returned the phone to her pocket. "I'll see you at two," she assured her boss.

But as she headed toward her office, her phone buzzed again. Annoyed by the insistent interruptions, she once more retrieved the device. She tapped the latest message and stumbled to a stop when she saw the principal's name displayed in all caps. The woman didn't waste a moment in getting to the point.

Ms. Keenan, your daughter Caitlyn Keenan has violated the school's zero tolerance policy on violence. She has been suspended for ten days, starting immediately. Please come to the office as soon as possible.

Diane blinked and read the message again. The words didn't make any more sense the second time than they had the first time she read them. Caitlyn had been suspended? How was that possible? Her daughter had problems—what teen didn't?—but she didn't have anger issues. This had to be some kind of mistake.

She executed an abrupt about-face. "Jeff. About that meeting—I'm not going to make it after all. There's been a problem at the high school. I have to pick up my daughter."

"I'm sorry?" Jeff asked, not sounding the least bit sympathetic. He closed the gap between them. "I thought you were going to use the last couple of days to get your priorities straight."

Diane swallowed a harsh retort as her respect for the man in front of her plummeted. Jeff didn't have a clue about what was important in life. He'd readily admitted that he valued Ybor City Accountants above everything else. Above his wife—or, in his case, his ex-wives. Above his children. He obviously expected that same level of dedication to the job from her.

Well, she was sorry—not sorry—to disappoint him. She might be the best accountant in the firm, might be next in line for a corner office on Executive Row. But that's just how she earned a living. Her family came first and foremost in her life. She might have lost sight of that for a minute, and her marriage had suffered because of it. But her son and daughter would not.

They'd always be more important than her work.

She squared her shoulders. Her priorities were straight, and right now, Caitlyn was at the top of her list.

Hoping for a word with Caitlyn before she spoke with the principal, Diane scanned the row of hard plastic chairs in the school office. Although students occupied several of the seats, her daughter was not among them. Diane's pulse shifted into overdrive. Had Caitlyn been injured? Was she, at this very minute, being treated by the school nurse or on her way to a local hospital?

She rapped loudly on the counter that separated the administrative staff from students and visitors. "Where is my daughter?" she asked in a voice she reserved for the most dire of circumstances. With no Caitlyn in sight, this certainly qualified.

Mrs. Barnett, the school secretary, looked up from her computer keyboard. The younger woman's features hardened. "Mrs. Keenan. Principal Goshen has been waiting for you. I'll let her know you're here."

Diane dredged the secretary's first name out

of her memory banks. "Bonnie, where's Caitlyn? Has she been hurt?"

"She's fine." Bonnie Barnett's rushed assurance knocked Diane's panic down a peg or two.

"But where is she?" She'd expected to find the teenager waiting for her outside the principal's office. That's where she found Nick when she was summoned to the school after her son had aced the SATs. She supposed the staff had a different system for handling unruly students, but where was she?

"She's in the clinic, but she's all right," Bonnie repeated. "Jeremy Cook is with her." As the school resource officer, Jeremy Cook was Plant High's first line of defense against outside threats. When he wasn't busy guarding the entrance, he regularly patrolled the grounds looking for kids who were smoking and cutting class.

"A police officer?" Diane's voice climbed an octave as she pictured her fifteen-year-old daughter being interrogated by a man in a uniform.

"Well, he's not really a police officer," Bonnie huffed. "He works for the school board. All the kids love him."

"I want to see my daughter," Diane insisted. To make her point clear, she growled, "Now."

"But Principal Goshen…" The woman who routinely stared down belligerent teens took one look at Diane's no-nonsense expression and gave in. "Come with me." She beckoned.

They walked down a hall, past the gym and through a door that led to a portable trailer that housed the school's clinic. Diane's breath seeped unsteadily over her lips when she spotted Caitlyn sitting on a sturdy cot, an ice pack pressed against her face. Her daughter's red-rimmed eyes and blotchy cheeks left no doubt—Caitlyn had been crying. Diane hurried across the room and wrapped her arms around the child.

"What happened?" she whispered into Caitlyn's hair.

If she expected the teen to melt into her arms, she was wrong. Refusing to lift her head, Caitlyn stared at her lap and shook her head.

"Caitlyn." Diane cupped her daughter's chin in her hand. "Look at me. I need to know what happened before I speak with Principal Goshen."

"Marty and I had a fight." A fresh round of tears welled in Caitlyn's blue eyes.

"You and…Marty?" That didn't make any sense. The girls were best friends.

"Yeah. Surprised the he—" Caitlyn hiccupped. "Surprised me, too."

Diane glanced over her shoulder at the young

man who stood, his back against the wall, on the other side of the room. "Could I have a moment with my daughter...alone?" she said, making sure the officer knew it wasn't a request.

Once the door had closed behind Jeremy's retreating form, Diane murmured, "Let me see." Gently, she pushed the ice pack away from Caitlyn's face. Her breath hissed between her teeth at the clear imprint of a hand on her daughter's cheek. "Keep that ice on it," she said, gently replacing the cold pack. "Did she hit you anywhere else? Any other injuries?"

When Caitlyn assured her the bruised cheek was the worst of it, Diane squatted before the girl. "Okay, tell me what happened so I'm not going in blind when I speak to Principal Goshen."

"I've never seen Marty so angry. She hates me." Tears laid fresh tracks down Caitlyn's cheeks. She sniffed. In an unsteady voice, she continued. "Her parents grounded her and won't let her go to Homecoming. They called off the party at their house, too. Everybody's mad at me about it, but Marty's the worst. She—she blames me, says it's all my fault, that I ratted her out. I—I tried to tell her I was grounded, too, but she wouldn't back off. She got in my face about it. She hauled off and slapped me and I—I pushed her away. She fell on her a—butt." She eyed the door. "That's when Officer Cook showed up."

"Was Marty hurt?"

"Nah. She was mad as…" Caitlyn grimaced. "She's fine."

"Where is she now?" Marty hadn't been in the office, or Diane would have seen her there.

"Soccer practice, I guess."

Diane's eyebrows rose. "She didn't get suspended?"

Caitlyn looked up, confusion written across her features. "Suspended?"

"No one told you?" A thready sigh eased between Diane's lips. "I received a text from Principal Goshen. You've been suspended for violating the school's no-violence policy."

"For an argument?" Disbelief dripped from Caitlyn's voice. She dropped the ice pack.

"Marty hit you. You pushed her. That's violence. It draws an automatic suspension." The punishment had been spelled out in the student handbook Caitlyn brought home at the start of the school year.

"But she started it," Caitlyn whined.

"As far as the school's concerned, you're both at fault. I'll talk to Principal Goshen, explain that you were merely defending yourself. Once she learns the facts, she might let you off with a warning."

Mentally, Diane crossed her fingers. Her daughter had no idea how much today's little set-to could affect her future. Suspended students weren't allowed to make up class work or tests, so a ten-day suspension meant Caitlyn would most likely fail all her classes this semester. Her GPA would plummet. Which meant she could forget about getting any kind of academic scholarship when she went to college. Assuming she'd even get accepted, that is. One blemish on her permanent record could ruin her chances.

Diane swallowed her panic. She was getting ahead of herself. She hadn't even spoken to the principal yet. Perhaps the woman would understand that the incident was nothing more than an argument between best friends. She stood. "Let me see what Principal Goshen has to say. Maybe we can get this straightened out and no one will be suspended."

But fifteen minutes later, Diane walked out of the principal's office defeated. The woman had been adamant. Though she promised to look into Marty's role in the matter, Officer Cook had personally witnessed Caitlyn push her friend to the ground. That left the administration with no choice—they had to suspend Caitlyn for ten days. But that wasn't the worst of it, Principal Goshen had warned. As a matter of policy, the school board reviewed all disciplinary actions. Caitlyn would only be allowed to return to Plant High with their recommendation. Without it, the girl faced a transfer to an alternative school for troubled teens or worse, expulsion.

Nine

Kim

Trying to give Belle some privacy while she finished up a phone call on the deck, Kim arranged glasses and a bottle of wine on a tray. From the slump of her cousin's shoulders, Kim could tell the person on the other end of the line had given Belle bad news. She wondered if the mess in Nashville had anything to do with it and tsked. So far, the pop star hadn't said one word about her short-lived foray into country music, but Kim had read about it on her trip to Atlanta. If things had gone only half as badly as the tabloids reported, Belle had good reason to be upset. Knowing it wasn't good for anyone to keep their feelings bottled up, Kim hefted the tray as soon as Belle lowered her phone from her ear.

It was time for a little cousin-to-cousin talk.

"I brought wine," she said as she stepped out onto the wide back deck. On the western horizon, the final rays of a golden sunset had faded from the sky, bathing the back porch in darkness. After lowering the tray, Kim pulled a pack of matches from her pocket and lit the lemon eucalyptus candles that sat in the middle of the table. Almost immediately, a light, citrusy scent drifted on the breeze. She glanced at Belle, who still stood, her phone clutched in her hand. Not wanting to intrude, Kim asked, "Do you want company?"

"I guess."

The low-pitched reply confirmed Kim's suspicions that her cousin was down in the dumps. While she splashed generous pours into the glasses, she considered the best way to get Belle to open up. Deciding to do away with subterfuge, she tackled the subject straight on.

"You want to tell me what's going on? Or do I have to keep guessing?"

Belle's head snapped up. "What are you talking about?"

"C'mon, Belle. You've barely left the house since you got here. That's not like you. You always make a point of seeing everyone in town when you're here."

"I've been a little preoccupied taking care of Mama," came the defensive reply.

In the flickering light from the candles, Kim glimpsed Belle's pursed lips. "It's more than that, and you know it," she said, not willing to let her cousin stew about whatever was bothering her. Even on a day as dark as Uncle Eric's funeral, Belle had managed to look like she'd just walked off the set of a magazine shoot. The night of Aunt Margaret's accident, she'd flown incognito from New York, showing up looking like an adorable waif in an oversize touristy T-shirt. It wasn't like her to let her appearance go to pot. "This is the second day you've worn those clothes." Kim pointed to the loose tunic Belle wore over a pair of leggings. "Your hair's a rat's nest, and you're not wearing a lick of makeup."

"Thanks, I think." Collapsing like a soufflé fresh out of the oven, Belle sank onto one of the chairs.

"For what?"

"For noticing. No one else has."

"Not true," Kim corrected. "We all love you enough to know when you're hurting. Everyone's just been giving you space."

"Why are you talking to me about it, then? Did you draw the short straw?"

"Nope." Kim grabbed her glass of wine and

sank onto the chair closest to Belle's. "I'm the only one brave enough to confront you."

"It's a good trait—bravery."

Belle leaned back in her chair and sipped her wine for so long, Kim thought that might be all her cousin had to say on the topic. After a bit, though, she took a breath and blurted, "I'm in big trouble."

"What happened in Nashville was not your fault," she insisted. Kim had suspected Belle's less than stellar appearance in the birthplace of country music might be weighing on her cousin.

"Thank you for saying so." Belle bowed briefly over hands clasped as if in prayer. "But I'm not talking about Nashville. I made a fool of myself there, but that's not the worst of it. All of that hubbub will blow over in a news cycle or two. My other problems, though, they aren't so easy to deal with."

Kim fought an urge to scratch her head. With all her fame and fortune, what on earth could Belle have to worry about? Unless...was she sick?

"I've got major financial woes."

"Wow! Didn't see that coming." Kim blinked as a heady mix of relief and renewed concern filled her chest. "I thought you were loaded."

"I was, but..." Belle sighed. "I blew it."

"You didn't get taken in by some shady investment scheme, did you?" Even as she said the words, Kim prayed her ex-husband hadn't somehow gotten his clutches into her cousin. It'd be just the kind of trick Frank would pull.

"No." Belle's laughter was filled with pain. "This is a disaster of my own making, I'm afraid. Do you know how long it's been since I had a hit song?"

When Kim started to protest that everyone loved Belle's music, the star held up a hand to stop her. "Don't blow smoke. I get enough of that from people in the business—my agent, my publicity people, even the intern at Noble Records. They're all trying to 'yes, ma'am' their way onto my good side. But I'm fully aware that my last couple of albums have, shall we say, tanked."

This was not the time to agree with her cousin, Kim told herself. To avoid speaking, she took a deep pull from her wineglass.

"I was resigned to joining the ranks of aging rock stars. You know who I mean. The ones who only show up at Grammys to get a lifetime achievement award. If they're mentioned in magazines at all, it's in one of those 'Where Is She Now' columns."

Kim shook her head, unable to picture her

vibrant cousin fading quietly into the background.

"Then the producers of what was supposed to be a summer fill-in on cable TV chose 'Jimmy, Jimmy, Oh' as their theme song. And dang, if that little rom-com didn't hit it big. Just like that, my star was on the rise again." Belle snapped her fingers for emphasis.

Kim grinned. She'd had the TV on for background noise while she made her lunch for work one night last fall when she caught the familiar strains of Belle's big hit. She'd immediately called their cousin Amy, and they'd watched the show together.

"Ron Dees—we've worked together forever—Ron said Noble would get behind a comeback album. They'd send me out on tour with all the bells and whistles. The only thing was, I had to come up with the songs. I poured everything I had into that album. Hired some of the best songwriters in the country to help me with the lyrics. Paid exorbitant amounts of money to get the words set to music. Got the old band together for weekly and then daily practices. Anticipating appearances at Madison Square Garden and the Hollywood Bowl, I hired choreographers and dance instructors and a whole team of personal trainers to get me in tip-top shape."

"That certainly worked." Kim ran several miles most days of the week, but she didn't have nearly as much stamina as Belle. She didn't know many fifty-two-year-olds who did.

"Yeah. It all worked. I was crawling out on a very thin limb, but I knew if just one song on the album climbed the charts, I'd earn back every penny I'd spent. The tour would generate another boatload of cash. But first, we had to get that album finished. We were supposed to go into the recording studio and start laying down tracks two weeks ago. That's when Noble pulled the plug. Ron Dees retired. His replacement wanted me to take my music in a different direction."

"Country," Kim said, finally understanding why Belle had gone to Nashville, of all places.

"Yeah. That." Belle's nose wrinkled. "By then, though, I'd already invested every penny I had in the new album. I have nothing to show for it except a handful of songs, and I'm so broke I can't even afford to take them into the recording studio." Pointing to her phone, she cleared her throat. "That was my finance guy, Richard. He wants me to let the members of my band go. 'The sooner, the better' is how he put it. Some of them have been with me for twenty years."

"That's gotta be tough," Kim murmured.

She'd experienced a layoff firsthand during the Collins merger and knew the process wasn't easy on anyone involved. Her boss had actually had tears in his eyes when he'd delivered the bad news.

"I keep hoping something will change, that the folks at Noble will realize their mistake and get back behind this album," Belle moaned.

"That's unlikely after Nashville," Kim said, not pulling any punches.

Belle's head snapped up. She clapped a hand over her chest. "Ouch!"

"I call them as I see them." Kim shrugged. "Look." She let her breath out in a long, slow whisper. "Things are only going to get worse if you don't deal with this head-on. If you pull the wool down over your eyes, hoping the sky will suddenly open up and rain money into your lap, you're giving your creditors the upper hand. That never turns out well." If things were as bad as Belle said they were, it was important for her cousin to do something about it. That was another little lesson she'd learned from personal experience.

"You're right. I know you're right. It just hurts, you know?"

"Believe me. I do. And I sympathize. Honest. But you can't sit around and mope about it. You have to take action if you have any hope of turning things around."

"Okay. No more sitting around. I need to take action." Belle stood and paced to the end of the deck. On her return trip, she paused near Kim and asked, "Have you got any suggestions?"

Kim smiled despite the seriousness of the situation. "You're teetering on the verge of losing everything, right?"

When Belle nodded, Kim straightened. "What do you have that you can sell for immediate cash? Jewelry? Fancy cars? Swiss chalets?"

Belle's melodic laughter filled the air. "I wish!"

"C'mon, Belle. Be serious."

"I am," she insisted, sinking onto her chair and retrieving her wineglass. "My cars are leased. I owe more on the co-op in New York than it's worth. I've already told Richard to sell the properties in Paris and Italy, but he sees that more as a cost-cutting measure, not one that'll generate the kind of positive cash flow I need to dig myself out of this hole."

"What about that gorgeous green pendant you wore on the *Oh, Baby* album cover? That has to be worth a small fortune." According to *Variety Magazine*, the emerald that hung from a diamond-and gem-encrusted choker weighed more than ninety carats.

Belle shook her head. "That piece was on loan from Bulgari," she said, naming one of the world's top jewelers. "As were the armed guards who never let it out of their sight. Most of the jewelry I wear is either borrowed or fake. I do have a really nice diamond, but selling it would hardly put a dent in the amount I owe, much less keep me afloat until I figure out what to do next."

"Isn't there anything you could get rid of?" There had to be something.

Belle tapped her fingernails against her wineglass. "Well, I do have the Twombly."

"The what?" A thrill of anticipation rushed through Kim. Anytime people stuck a "the" in front of something, it had to be expensive.

"The Twombly. It's a painting. The artist is very popular," Belle said, shaking her head. "Frankly, he's not my style, but when I bought the condo in New York, my decorator insisted on hanging a focal piece in the main salon."

"Oh, yeah?" Kim didn't know much about art, but *the* Twombly sounded pricey. "What's that worth?"

"A lot," Belle confessed. "Enough to pay off all my debts with a little bit left over."

Kim whistled. "Girl, what are you holding on to that for?"

"Good question." Belle poured them each more wine. "Prestige? Ego?"

A Scripture she'd learned as a child popped into Kim's head. "God opposes the proud but gives grace to the humble," she quoted. "Maybe it's time for your life to be filled with grace."

"That…" In the flickering light, Belle visibly paled. "That old hymn, 'Amazing Grace'—I haven't been able to get it out of my head lately. I guess now I know why. I'll do it. I'll sell the Twombly." Her fingers trembling, she held her glass aloft. "I'm glad we had this talk. To Kim."

A peculiar sense of peace settled in Kim's chest as she lifted her glass to meet Belle's. But a few seconds after the toast, she heard a car door slam. She frowned. "Are we expecting guests?" The newlyweds had checked out of the Garnet this morning, leaving the downstairs suites empty for the time being.

"Maybe Helen ran into town for something?" Belle suggested.

If she had, the author would walk right past them on her way to her bungalow. Kim studied the darkened path that wound from the parking lot to the cottages. "We really need to install solar lights for nights like this." A thick layer of clouds overhead obscured the moon and stars, leaving only the light that spilled from the inn's windows to illuminate the pavers.

When another car door slammed, followed by muffled voices, she and Belle stilled. They listened for the sound of footfalls on the path and watched for the wavering glow of a flashlight. Seconds later, a commotion at the back door drew them to their feet.

"That's not Helen." Kim's pulse thudded. "She wouldn't use the employee entrance."

With Belle right behind her, she hurried to see who'd shown up this late at night. As she moved, she ruled out possibilities. Not guests—they entered and exited through the front door. Not Amy—her cousin had left a message saying she was working late at the bakery tonight. Not Scott—he'd called from the courthouse this afternoon to make sure Aunt Margaret was behaving herself. That left... Kim's footsteps slowed as she considered the possibility that the unexpected new arrivals were intruders. Wondering if she should grab a rolling pin or a frying pan, she held her breath.

Air seeped from between her lips when, clutching a pillow to her chest, a young girl emerged from the hallway that led past the pantry to the kitchen.

"Caitlyn?" Kim glanced over the girl's shoulder when Diane trailed her daughter into the room, carrying an overnight bag. "Diane? We didn't know you were coming, did we?"

Belle didn't wait for an answer but surged forward with open arms. "Caitlyn!" she exclaimed.

Kim didn't know if her famous cousin couldn't read the "hands off" expression on the girl's face or chose to ignore it. Regardless, Belle wrapped her arms around the teen and squeezed tightly while a stream of greetings poured out of her. "I'm so glad to see you! You look all grown up! How long has it been?"

"Hi, Aunt Belle." Caitlyn issued a grudging reply while keeping her pillow firmly tucked between them.

Not to be deterred, Belle tugged on the girl's ponytail. "Look at you, all grown up. You were supposed to stay a baby. Didn't anyone tell you that?"

While Belle continued to ooh and aah over the child who was more niece than second cousin to them all, Kim concentrated on not letting her mouth hang open. In the two years since she'd last seen Caitlyn, the girl had changed—a lot. Not only had she grown at least a foot taller, she'd lost all her baby fat, replacing it with the kind of lean muscle that came from daily workouts and playing team sports. Gone were the round, chubby cheeks the women in church had loved to pinch. All of which made it easy to see that Caitlyn had inherited her mother's deep-set brown eyes along with her father's chiseled jaw. The blond hair, though, that was all her own. She wore it long and secured in a ponytail, though a few wisps had worked loose, probably during the ride from Tampa. With hair softly framing her face in lanky strands, Kim had to admit, the girl possessed the kind of striking good looks envied by women everywhere. Caitlyn might even be beautiful if she smiled the tiniest bit. As it was, she wore the pinched expression of someone who'd just eaten a lemon.

She looked to Diane for some explanation for the teen's sour mood, but her cousin had dumped the bags she'd carried into the house and disappeared. Kim shrugged. Her own children had been known to get moody from time to time. To tell the truth, they still did.

"Let me have a turn," she said, playfully nudging Belle aside. She held Caitlyn at arm's length and tried to ignore the girl's stiff posture. "You've grown so tall, Caitlyn," she exclaimed. "And so pretty. I think she could be a model." She looked over her shoulder at Belle. "Don't you?"

Belle grabbed her niece's hand and splayed the girl's fingers across her own forearm. "Look at those fingers. So long and elegant. She's still growing." She eyed Caitlyn up and down. "Yep. Definitely model material," she pronounced.

Interest flared in Caitlyn's dark eyes. "You mean like on commercials and stuff?" she asked quietly.

"Exactly," Kim confirmed. "You've already mastered the pouty look it takes those runway models years to perfect." She grinned, not at all surprised to see the first glimmer of a smile break across the teen's lips.

Caitlyn's smile disappeared, though, when Diane reappeared in the hall with a large gym bag slung over one shoulder. She pulled a sturdy, wheeled suitcase behind her.

"Hey!" Kim called to her cousin. "Need some help? We weren't expecting you before the weekend."

"Long story," Diane said as she traded glances with Caitlyn. She dropped the gym bag to the floor. "You sure you don't need anything else tonight?"

"I'm sure," Caitlyn answered dully.

Diane patted the handle of the lavender roller bag. "We'll bring the rest in from the car tomorrow." She expelled a thready breath. "Let me get us settled upstairs. Is it okay if we take Beryl and Quartz?"

Kim rubbed her chin. "Irene and Eunice just finished working on those yesterday. They're yours if you want them, but are you sure you don't want something bigger?" Tucked into a corner of the second floor, the inn's smallest suites shared a sitting room and a bath.

"Those'll be fine. It'll be like having adjoining rooms."

"Great," said Caitlyn in a tone that let everyone know she didn't think the idea was at all great.

Diane toed the gym bag toward her daughter. "You want to get that?" When Caitlyn appeared on the verge of refusing, Diane prodded. "It's your stuff. You can carry it."

"Do you need help taking things upstairs?" Belle asked.

"Nah, we'll get it," Diane said firmly.

"Are you hungry? There's meatloaf left over from dinner. I'd be glad to heat some up for you." Kim had fixed another of Liz's favorites for supper that night.

Diane glanced at Caitlyn, who answered with the merest shake of her head. "We're fine. We grabbed supper at a drive-through in Vero," she said, directing Caitlyn toward the staircase. Following her daughter, Diane paused just before she reached the hall. With an imploring look, she asked, "You'll still be up for a little while?"

Kim stifled a yawn. She'd gotten up before Aunt Margaret, who rose at six each morning, and she'd been on the go from then until her aunt retired for the night. If she didn't get a full eight hours of sleep, she'd be mainlining coffee all day tomorrow. But one look at Diane's face and all thoughts of getting to bed at a reasonable hour faded. "We'll be outside on the porch."

"I'll open another bottle of wine," Belle offered.

"What do you think of Diane and Caitlyn just showing up like that?" Belle asked when they were once more seated at the table.

"I guess we'll find out soon enough, but I don't think it's a good sign." Kim traced circles on the glass tabletop. Temperatures earlier today had been in the eighties, but the air had cooled considerably once the sun went down. She pulled the edges of her sweater closer.

"She said things were strained at home. You don't think she and Tim have called it quits, do you?"

"I don't see how. Didn't she say he was out of town for a couple of weeks?"

Belle nodded. "That's right. He went on a cruise."

"Here she comes," Kim said when she spied Diane walking into the kitchen.

The French doors squeaked open on rusty hinges. "Whoof!" Diane plopped into a chair, exhaustion showing in every line on her face. "What a day."

"We gathered as much," Kim said as she handed Diane a glass of wine. "It's not every day you show up unannounced. And with Caitlyn, no less. Doesn't she have school?" Though her own mom couldn't have cared less whether she played hooky, Aunt Margaret and Aunt Liz had been sticklers about attendance, not just at school but at church, too.

"She got suspended today." While Kim and Belle listened in deepening shock, Diane filled them in on the party Caitlyn and her friends had thrown and how that led to the fight. "I don't understand. Caitlyn's always been such a good girl. Nick's the one with the temper. I would understand this kind of behavior from him. But Caitlyn? Never. I can't help but think it's all my fa—"

Stopping Diane in mid-sentence, Belle held

up a hand. "Wait a second. Tim packed his bags and left without saying a word to his daughter, and you think it's your fault she's acting out? There's plenty of blame to go around here. I think Tim needs to shoulder his own share."

"But if I hadn't spent so much time at work…" Diane started to protest.

"Or if Amy's husband hadn't been a surf bum. Or Frank hadn't been a con artist or cheated on me." Kim folded her arms across her chest. "Finding out your parents' marriage is in trouble is devastating to any child, no matter what the cause. Or how old they are." Her own kids had been quite a bit older than Caitlyn when she and Frank went their separate ways, and they'd still struggled with the breakup. "Getting kicked off the soccer team on the heels of having her dad leave must have destroyed Caitlyn. And if that wasn't bad enough, her best friend picked a fight with her at school." Kim whistled. "She's really been expelled?"

"Not exactly, but she might as well have been. Principal Goshen suspended her. For ten days."

Kim sucked in a breath. "Hard to come back from that."

"My thoughts exactly." Sadness clouded Diane's features. "She's a straight-A student, but she'll fail all her classes this term. Rather than wait for that ax to fall, I pulled her out of Plant High and enrolled her in home school. She'll take all the same courses she was taking, but everything's done by computer. She'll start bright and early Monday morning."

"I don't know how you moved so quickly on all this—I'd still be curled up in a ball in a corner somewhere," Belle said.

"No, you wouldn't," Kim argued. "You say that, but you're stronger than you give yourself credit for. Look at all you've endured over the past couple of weeks. You've had the rug pulled out from under you, career-wise. Your mom had an accident and needed surgery. But I don't see you crying 'Oh, woe is me.'"

Diane took a healthy sip of wine. "That's why I brought Caitlyn here. I want her to be surrounded by strong women who don't surrender at the first sign of a Jolly Roger on the horizon. They fight the pirates and succeed."

"We've all got a few battle scars," Kim admitted.

"But we refuse to give in." Belle raised her glass. "To Caitlyn and helping her see how much she's loved."

"And to her success," Kim chimed as her glass clinked against Belle's.

"Here, here," Diane agreed.

When they'd all taken a sip, Kim turned to Diane. "What about your job? Isn't this a busy time of year for you?"

Diane folded her arms across her chest. "Yeah, about that. Officially, I'm on vacation."

"And unofficially?"

"The owner of the company is not very happy with me at the moment. He, uh, he didn't understand when I skipped a meeting with a new client after the school called about Caitlyn. And when I told him I was bringing her here..." Diane's breath stuttered. "I might be looking for a new job."

"That stinks. You've poured your life and your soul into that company," Kim said, as if her cousin wasn't already well aware.

"Yeah, well, that's part of the problem, isn't it? I've put my job first for too long. But no more." Diane swirled the rest of her wine and downed it in one gulp. Setting her glass on the table, she held up a hand. "There's so much going on right now that I don't even want to think about work. That's a bridge I'll cross when I get to it. For now, Caitlyn and Tim are my only concerns."

"I'll drink to that," Belle said. Dividing what was left of the wine between them, she emptied the bottle.

They sat talking quietly for another half hour before Belle joined her fingers together and stretched her arms over her head. "I'm going to turn in," she announced. "I'll have to get up before the chickens if I'm going to catch a flight in the morning."

"You're going somewhere?" Diane asked, her surprise evident in the flickering light from the candles.

"To New York." Belle picked up her wineglass and started toward the door.

"What about this weekend? Aren't we supposed to paint the cottages?"

"Don't worry. I'll be back in plenty of time. This is just a quick trip. One night, two at the most."

"You're going to sell the Twombly?" Kim asked.

"As quick as I can. I'll break the news to the band and take care of a couple of other things. It's time I did more than run and hide when there's a Jolly Roger on the horizon." Belle spun on one heel. "Diane, Kim can fill you in, but you both should know you've inspired me tonight."

Ten

Belle

*D*rawing herself to her full height, Belle propped one hand on a hip that had a bit more padding than it had two weeks earlier. With the air of an entitled superstar firmly in place, she turned her haughtiest expression on the man who bent close to the Twombly. As if the matter had ever been in doubt, she repeated herself. "So you'll take it."

"Hmmm. I suppose." The folds of Harold Carstair's black smock swished when the appraiser turned to face her.

Belle smothered a smug smile. She refused to be fooled by Harold's cool attitude. She'd glimpsed the art expert's eagerness in the split second it had taken him to carefully mask his features after seeing the Twombly for the first time. In that instant, she'd known she could practically name her own terms and he'd accommodate them if it meant landing the impressive piece of art—along with a very handsome commission—for his auction house.

"It's late notice." Harold continued sounding put-upon. "But we should be able to add it to our March auction catalogue."

"March?" Belle let her disapproval show. She gestured toward the living room. "I want to turn my decorator loose in here before the holidays. We've decided on earth tones. The blacks and reds in the Twombly clash with the new color scheme."

She plucked an imaginary piece of lint from the jacket of her black suit and straightened the signature lapels of a well-known designer. "I suppose I could ask Christie's. Didn't you say they have a sale in December, Gretchen?" She hiked one eyebrow at her personal assistant.

The demure young woman referred to a digital tablet. "Yes, ma'am," she said, playing along.

"I suppose I at least owe it to myself to contact a few other houses," Belle hedged while she strove to convey the image of a woman who was eager to get on with a remodeling project, not one who wobbled on the tipping edge of bankruptcy. "But I want to get this taken care of while I'm in New York this week."

Not about to lose the artwork to his competition, Harold offered a rare concession. "I assure you, Ms. Dane, interest in this piece will be extraordinary. No doubt we'll entertain several offers well above your reserve price before March if we take possession of the Twombly right away."

"Really?" Belle feigned a bored disinterest. She'd chosen Harold's auction house specifically because it was one of only a handful that accepted preemptive bids and would sell an item outright if a buyer was willing to pay substantially more than the piece was expected to fetch at auction. To do that, though, the gallery had to have the artwork on its premises so they could immediately deliver it to the new owner.

"Oh, yes." Harold's eagerness to land the Twombly seeped out from behind his mask. "I can practically guarantee it."

"That certainly would simplify matters." She hesitated, as if thinking the matter over. Finally, she shrugged and said, "I believe we have a deal. If you'll have the paperwork sent over by close of business today, I'd like to wrap this up before I leave."

She turned once more to Gretchen. In their

preliminary talks, Belle had insisted on having a trusted employee witness the exchange when the auction house took possession of the artwork. "You'll oversee the transfer?"

"I'd be happy to," Gretchen assured her.

Belle jotted a mental reminder to herself to give her assistant a well-earned bonus once the Twombly actually sold. The young woman had definitely gone above and beyond these last few weeks. Not only had she fended off the never-ending demands from reporters for interviews and made sure everything ran smoothly while Belle was in Florida, she'd researched all the major auction houses in New York and lined up appointments with Belle's top three choices. Harold had been the third appraiser they'd seen this morning. The first two had been just as eager but couldn't fit the piece into their upcoming auctions.

"Gretchen, see Harold out, would you?" Belle swept from the room.

Minutes later, she discarded the air of entitlement along with the designer suit in the dressing area of a sumptuously appointed walk-in closet, where a crystal chandelier hung over a tufted bench. Stepping into her favorite pair of black skinny jeans, she asked whether she'd made a mistake by cramming so much into the short trip to New York. She shrugged the question aside as she buttoned a tailored white shirt. Selling the Twombly was her first priority, but she couldn't put off the meeting with her band. Much as she dreaded breaking the news to them, they deserved to hear it from her own lips. After that, she absolutely had to see Lisa. The agent would never forgive her if she left town without at least meeting for drinks. The final item on her agenda had been tacked on at the last minute, but she wouldn't dream of canceling the late-night dinner Jason had requested.

Did he want to talk about her return to Noble Records?

Buttoning the cuffs of the long-sleeved shirt, she eyed the stacks of sweaters neatly arranged on open shelves. With a nod to the crisp autumn temperatures, she chose a cropped one that went well with her coloring. She slipped her feet into a pair of four-inch heels taken from dozens in a lighted display case and checked her image in the three-way mirror. She nodded. Paired with the black leather car coat waiting by the door, the outfit she'd chosen showed off her best features while letting her blend in on New York's crowded sidewalks. Which, with reporters on the lookout for her everywhere she went, was an absolute necessity.

Tucked into a corner booth of a Midtown bar an hour later, Belle clutched her glass of club soda and lime for support. Nausea churned her stomach. "And that's it, guys. I'm as sorry as I can be that it's come to this." She brushed heartfelt tears from her eyes.

"Hey now." Vic Haskel, one of the best bass guitarists in the country, leaned across the table to take her hand. "None of that. We've had a good run."

Belle returned Vic's squeeze while she concentrated on not letting tears drip onto the man's calloused fingers. "I know we were all counting on this album and tour. I hate to let you down."

Vic gave her hand a final press before he leaned back against the red leather. "Not one of us is gonna be hurtin' for work." He surveyed the faces of the other men who, along with their wives and girlfriends, crowded the booth or sat on chairs they'd dragged away from nearby tables. Vic singled out Daniel, the newest member of the group. "How 'bout you, Dan? You got something else lined up?"

The young man nodded. "I've been getting feelers from Sizzler and BTK," he said naming two bands that were immensely popular with the younger set. "I'll land on my feet." Beside him, his wife linked her arm with his in a show of support.

"Bill? Hank?"

Belle battled more tears. Except for Dan, who'd joined them after her longtime lead guitarist had a mild heart attack, she'd worked with these men for years. They'd traveled the world together, performed before sellout crowds on every continent, logged countless hours in practice studios and knew one another better than most relatives. Saying goodbye hurt worse than she'd anticipated. She had to admit, though, it helped to know she wasn't ruining their lives, their careers.

"I, for one, am glad we aren't going on tour. I'm getting too old to be crawling into my berth on the bus at 2 a.m. and never knowing what city I'll wake up in." Bill rubbed a grizzled beard that was more salt than pepper these days. The rhythm guitarist stretched. "I got a good thing going with my online classes. I set up a sweet little music room at home, and no one cares if I show up in sweats and a T-shirt." His sideline gig had turned into a veritable gold mine.

"I don't mind telling you, I wasn't looking forward to spending three months on the road. I'd have to give up my studio work." Hank rubbed his thumb against two fingers. He possessed an uncanny ability to play a flawless rendition of a piece of music the first time he saw it, which made him a highly sought-after studio musician. "Plus"—he lifted his chin, pointing toward a woman who stood at the bar—"me and Sherry got a good thing going. It's new, you know. Not sure it'll last. I can almost guarantee it won't if I have to be out of town for months on end." Five years into their marriage, Hank's first wife had tired of the musician's late nights and weekend gigs. Word had it her new husband kept banker's hours.

Belle's stomach settled. It certainly sounded as if breaking up the group wasn't the worst thing that could happen to the men at the table. It might even turn out to be a good thing all around.

Now that she didn't feel quite so ill at ease, hunger gnawed at her. Belle eyed the remains of the appetizers that dotted plates and baskets on the table. Gretchen had ordered every starter on the restaurant's extensive menu, and the group had done a good job of polishing them off. Though she hadn't felt well enough to eat a single bite earlier, her mouth watered as she cast a glance at the leftovers. They were cold, she told herself, battling back the urge to grab one of the Parmesan-dusted fries and dunk it in the accompanying sauce.

Resisting the temptation, she signaled their waitress to clear away the plates and bring another round of drinks. As for herself, she sipped the last of her club soda. Though long shadows darkened the streets, she still had a long night ahead of her.

"What about you, Belle?" Bill asked.

"Yeah, what's next?" Vic peered at her through a pair of wire-rimmed glasses.

"Not exactly sure," Belle admitted. "It's probably not going to be country, though," she said, managing a smile.

"You're more of an uptown girl," Bill acknowledged with a mock bow.

"I'm sorry you had to go through that mess on your own. Why didn't you call us?" Vic gestured to the rest of the group. "Any one of us would have done a better job of accompanying you down in Nashville."

"Ain't that the truth," Dan said as the rest nodded in unison.

"Thanks. I appreciate the thought," Belle said, meaning every word. "But the owner insisted I use an in-house musician. Something about leveling the playing field for all the participants." Not that it had been level. Not by a long shot.

"I heard Teddy Baynard's been bragging about how he single-handedly took you down." Vic fisted one hand and punched it into his other palm.

Belle grimaced. Vic's words confirmed her own impression. She'd sworn all along that the young guitarist had recognized her and deliberately set out to trip her up. It was just the kind of trick a teenager might pull. Not that she'd play the victim to the members of her band, who were weighing in with their own thoughts.

"We got your back on this one, Belle."

"Yeah. He's dead to us."

"None of us will ever work with him."

"No, guys. Stop." Belle held up her hands, horrified. "Starting a war with Teddy wouldn't be good for anyone. You gotta play nice." Teddy Baynard was so young, acne still pocked his cheeks, but the kid was immensely talented. Once he had a few more hits under his belt, there was no telling how bright his star would shine. Or how much power he'd wield.

"This community is too small for you to refuse to work with anybody, particularly with someone like Teddy. Besides, he had a point. I didn't give him a break on that last song." The music critics had belittled Belle for not sharing the spotlight with the guitarist. "I've apologized. And to make up for it, I sent him a very nice gift basket." She smiled her sweetest smile. She wasn't lying. The basket had set her back a few hundred bucks. The pacifier she'd had attached to the ribbon, though, that was just her own not-so-subtle way of telling the boy wonder to grow up.

As their waitress appeared with the next round of drinks, Belle caught Gretchen's discreet signal. She slipped quickly out of the booth.

Her palms flat on the tabletop, she leaned toward the group. "Listen, guys. I have to go, but before I leave, I just want to say it's been a pleasure working with each and every one of you."

When Vic began to slide across the bench seat, she motioned him to remain seated. "This is not goodbye," she insisted. "Stay where you are. Have dinner. It's my treat." The ever-organized Gretchen had handled all the arrangements. "We'll see each other again soon," she insisted and spun away from the table before anyone could see her tears.

"Valerie's is only a few doors down, but we can take the car if you'd like." Gretchen made the suggestion as they headed for the exit.

Belle silently weighed the pros and cons. While New York wasn't a hotbed of country music like Nashville, plenty of the genre's fans lived and worked in the Big Apple. Getting accosted by one of them wasn't on her list of things to do today. On the other hand, she couldn't hide forever, and a short walk would go a long way towards giving her the time and space she needed to get her emotions under control. To say nothing of loosening joints that had grown stiff during the two hours she'd spent commiserating with her band.

"It'd feel good to stretch my legs a bit," she admitted. Belle fell into step beside her assistant. "You did a great job of setting things up in there. The appetizers were a nice touch." She hadn't expected those, but they'd been a welcome surprise.

"Thanks. There's nothing like a little comfort food to soften bad news." Gretchen stepped aside for a jogger.

Careful not to catch one of her heels in a crack in the sidewalk, Belle ignored her rumbling tummy as she inhaled the smells that drifted through the open doorway of a deli. Dinner at the restaurant Jason had chosen was still two hours away, and she'd vowed not to ruin her appetite.

Her footsteps slowed when she spied the decorative green tiles and dark gray trim that framed the picture window of her agent's favorite Midtown bar.

"Someone got a jump on the holidays," Gretchen noted. Clusters of festive garland dipped down from a wide ledge over the entrance to Valerie's. A row of miniature evergreen trees lined the doorway.

Anticipating the clean, fresh scent of pine, Belle sniffed the air. She shrugged aside her disappointment when the vinegary smell of olives and oregano from the Greek restaurant next door overpowered all the other scents on the busy, crowded street. She started for Valerie's door but turned back when she realized Gretchen was no longer beside her. "Aren't you coming in?"

"I'll wait in the car, if it's all right. I want to make sure your flight is on time." Her brow furrowed. "Are you sure you won't let me get a charter for you? You'd be more comfortable."

Belle shook her head. Her days of being the only passenger on the plane were over. "I'll be fine," she assured the younger woman. "You got me a first-class ticket, and it's a direct flight."

"Yes, but I'd still feel better if someone else were flying with you," Gretchen said doubtfully.

Touched by the girl's concern, Belle offered reassurances. "The airline has arranged for the usual concierge service." Someone would meet her at the curb, take her to the VIP lounge and escort her to the plane. "Once I'm on board, I have a window seat. I'll wear a big, floppy hat and keep my head down." She lowered her chin to her chest to demonstrate. "After the day we've had, I'll probably be so exhausted I'll sleep the whole way home."

Horns honked on the busy street. Brakes screeched, and somewhere nearby a driver loosed a string of curses. Belle shook her head. "Only in New York," she murmured. "I'd better go in. Lisa doesn't like to be kept waiting. Pick me up in an hour?" She aimed a glance toward the car and driver that had tailed them from the other bar.

"Sure," Lisa agreed. "Text me if anything changes."

After assuring the assistant that she would, Belle grasped the brass door handle and slipped inside. She paused in the threshold just long enough to scan the restaurant, automatically noting the bouncer seated at the far end of the bar, the bartenders and wait staff she recognized from previous visits, the usual crowd of regulars sprinkled throughout the long room. Light poured through a towering wall of yellow glass behind the bar and bathed the polished wood in a golden glow. On the right, brass rails lined a wide staircase that led to a second floor. Tucked into the space behind the stairs, the table where Lisa normally held court sat empty. As gracefully as possible—and considering her short legs and the chair's long ones, that was no mean feat—Belle slipped onto one of the stools at the high-top. Settled, she studied the enormous wreath suspended in front of shelves that held enough sparkling bottles of alcohol to satisfy half of New York. In no time at all, a waitress appeared at her elbow. The young woman lifted a House Gibson from the silver tray she carried and placed the drink in front of Belle with a flourish.

"You always remember, Cici. Thank you," she murmured without needing to glance at the girl's name tag. The golden spear perched atop the martini glass held a single pickled onion. She nibbled on the spicy treat while she waited for Lisa, who breezed through the double doors a fashionable ten minutes late.

"Darling, I was so surprised to hear from you," Lisa exclaimed. The agent clutched both of Belle's hands in hers while they exchanged air kisses. "I thought you were staying in Florida until the whole Nashville thing blew over."

"Oh, you know how it is," Belle said with a sigh. "I needed to take care of a few things here in town. I won't be here long. I flew in yesterday, and I'm headed back tonight."

"And you wanted to see me while you're here?" Lisa pressed one hand flat against her chest. "I'm honored." She barely acknowledged their waitress as Cici slid Lisa's usual Spiced Gin and Tonic in front of her. She sipped from the glass before asking, "How's your mother?"

"Better than I expected," Belle admitted. She'd be forever grateful to Kim and Amy for taking such good care of her mom the night of the accident. "I think she's finally accepted the sad truth that she can't run the inn on her own anymore. My cousins and I have agreed to help her sell it." Knowing Lisa wouldn't understand, she didn't bother mentioning the family reunion. Unlike Belle, who considered her cousins to be the sisters she never had, the agent had only the most tenuous of relationships with her own family. A profound sense of loss swept over her as she imagined handing the keys to the Dane

Crown Inn to a new owner in the very near future. She swished the spear through the murky depths of her gin while she fought for composure.

"Sorry," she whispered, wiping a traitorous tear from her cheek a moment later. "It's been an emotional day."

"And no wonder. You've had a rough couple of weeks." Lisa fished one of the apple slices from her drink and bit into it. Chewing, she asked, "Will you move your mother into the Eldorado with you?"

Belle started. "Mama, here?" She shook her head. "I suggested it, but she thinks New York is too cold and too crowded. She's not wrong." She nodded toward the front of the bar. On the other side of the windows, rush-hour traffic clogged the street. "I haven't given up, though. In fact…"

She'd thought long and hard about the best way to explain her decision to sell the Twombly. Admitting she was flat broke wasn't an option. Despite what had happened in Nashville, she did have an image to protect. At the same time, she couldn't tell an outright lie. Tensing, she drew in a cautious breath and tried her story out on Lisa.

"Just in case Mama changes her mind, I'm making a few changes at the condo. If she does come up, I want her to feel at home, so I'm softening the look of the place a bit. Of course, that means the Twombly has to go." The decision had been a difficult one to reach, and she had no trouble looking as if she regretted it.

"Oh, no! Not the Twombly," Lisa protested. "You know it's my favorite." Eddies formed in her drink as she spun the glass stem between her fingers. "Do you need a good broker? I can recommend several."

"Thanks, but I've already made arrangements with Harold Carstair. You know him, don't you?" She lifted a questioning brow, though she was quite certain Lisa knew everyone who was anyone in the art community.

"Hmmm." Lisa tapped her fingernails against the bowl of her glass. "The 27th Street Gallery?" In the heart of the Chelsea Art District, the gallery specialized in modern art.

"That's the one." Bella flashed the thumbs-up sign. "We signed the paperwork this morning. His people are coming to pick it up next week. Not that there's any rush," she hurried to add, lest Lisa uncover her true motivation for selling the piece. "Mama's not going anywhere for quite a while. She needs to recover completely first. After that, well, we'll see."

Sensing Lisa's attention had drifted, she turned the conversation to the agent's favorite topic—herself. "So what's new in your life? How've you been? How's Greg?"

"Oh, Greg and I are fine. Things around the office have slowed down a bit until you and Noble sort things out." She gave a nonchalant shrug. "Did I tell you I've taken on a new client? A young Taylor Swift type."

"Replacing me already?" Though Bella laughed, she was only half joking. Lisa hadn't said a word about bringing on new talent.

"Never!" Lisa clasped Belle's hand in hers. In the dimly lit bar, sincerity shone in her dark eyes. "We go all the way back to the beginning, you and me. No matter what you do next, I'll always be here for you."

"Thanks," Belle whispered. "That means a lot. I thought you might give up on me after Noble Records cut me loose."

Lisa blew a soft raspberry. "You won't get rid of me that easily. Every star has their ups and downs. You've hit a dip in the road, that's all. You'll be back on top in no time."

But how, Belle wondered. Noble Records had taken a firm stance against renewing her climb up the pop charts. Country was out—she'd never willingly show her face in one of those bars again. That left what, exactly?

A faint hope stirred in her chest. There was

something new on her horizon, but for now, she had no idea what it was. Resigned to wait and see what came next, she propped her chin in the palm of one hand. "Tell me more about this new singer of yours," she ordered. The meeting had taken an unexpected turn. It was time to get things back on track.

"You'd love her. She's singing at Paddy Reilly's tonight. Why don't you stay over and come listen to her with me? You can fly home tomorrow, can't you?"

Though Belle had been known to frequent the Irish music pub in Manhattan, she shook her head. "Sorry. No can do. I promised the gang I'd be back in time for a painting party this weekend." She also had dinner plans later this evening. Not that she'd share those with Lisa.

"One of those things where you sit around and drink wine while an art instructor shows you how to paint a landscape?" The mock horror that dawned across Lisa's face told Belle the agent wouldn't be caught dead at such an event. "Stay here instead. We'll hit some galleries this weekend, find something to hang in your living room."

"It's not that kind of painting party." Belle laughed. "Mama swears she'll put the inn on the market but only if we find someone who promises to keep the place open. In order to attract that kind of buyer, we're giving the inn a much-needed facelift. We're starting with the cottages this weekend."

"You holding one of those big old brushes and a bucket of paint? That's priceless! We'll dress you in overalls and tie a red bandanna around your neck. Your fans will eat it up."

Belle considered the idea. Closing her eyes, she pictured herself posing for a few candid shots. Yeah, right. It would never be that simple. If she knew her agent—and after working with the woman for the better part of thirty years, she knew her better than most of her husbands—Lisa wouldn't be satisfied with hiring a local photographer to take a few snapshots. The minute Belle showed the tiniest bit of interest in Lisa's plan, an entire team would be camped out on the inn's front lawn. There'd be hair and makeup artists to tame her curls and slather her in pancake, a wardrobe supervisor who wouldn't be satisfied until she tried on at least ten different pairs of overalls and six red bandannas, a caterer to keep the crew hydrated and fed while the photographer waited for "the perfect light." In the meantime, Diane, Kim and Amy would be barred from so much as touching a paintbrush. How, exactly, would that help get the job done?

"Maybe another time," Belle hedged.

"I'm just saying, it'd be good PR, and quite frankly, you could use some."

"I know, but this weekend is all about family," she insisted and tried not to react when the agent gave the expected eye roll.

Lisa polished off her drink and signaled to the waitress for another. "How about you?" she asked, eyeing the Gibson Belle hadn't touched.

"No, thanks. One's my limit."

When Cici hovered near the edge of the table, Lisa announced, "I'm starving. How about splitting one of those scrumptious Caesar salads with me? There's more than enough for the two of us."

When in New York, do as the New Yorkers do, Belle told herself with a sigh. Personally, she'd much rather have one of Amy's gooey cinnamon buns than a few pieces of crisp Romaine lightly coated in a lemony dressing, but the salad wouldn't ruin her dinner. That was one thing she could be thankful for.

"We're almost there," the driver announced. He cruised past a corner bodega, a Colombian restaurant and a law office specializing in immigration before he pulled to the curb in the middle of the block. The white façade of Uncle Georgio's stood out in the center of the two-story red brick buildings. Far in the distance, the New York skyline stretched across the horizon.

Gretchen's brow furrowed. "Are you sure this is the right place?"

Belle pulled her phone from her bag and checked the address Jason had given her. "According to this, it is." Not that she blamed Gretchen for asking. With its beige awnings and nondescript signage, the restaurant certainly didn't look like the kind of place that would earn hundreds of five-star reviews on Yelp. "Let's hope appearances are deceiving." After starving herself all day, she was in the mood for a good meal. And, much as she hated to admit it, she was eager to learn what Jason had in mind.

The assistant cast another doubtful glance at the restaurant's smallish window and the single glass door with its metal push plate. She tapped a stylus against the electronic notebook she never seemed to be without. "Maybe I should come in with you."

Belle smiled at the assistant. It was nice of her to care, but she was a grown woman; she could take care of herself. "I'm sure you have better things to do. You've worked hard this week.

Take the evening off. Have dinner. Enjoy yourself. I'll text you when I'm done, and you can send the car back for me." She could take a cab to the airport, but she'd hired the car and driver for the entire day. She might as well get her use out of them.

Gretchen peered out the window while Belle unbuckled her seatbelt. "Is that him?" she asked.

Belle pushed down the surge of warmth that flooded her chest when she spotted the tall man who emerged from the restaurant. "That's him, all right."

Gretchen whistled softly. "He's not hard on the eyes."

Belle's face crinkled. She'd thought Jason cut a fine figure in a business suit, but the jeans and cream-colored pullover he wore now made a definite improvement. She felt flush and could pretty much guarantee it wasn't due to another one of those pesky hot flashes. She issued a stern reminder to her hormones that the head of Noble Records was no more interested in her than she was in him. He'd asked her to dinner tonight merely to check up on her, the same way any business associate might. At least, that was her story and she was sticking to it until she found out something different. Still, she couldn't let Jason's handsome features go without at least one comment. "It should be illegal for him to look that good," she said, agreeing with Gretchen's assessment.

Sliding across the leather seat, she slipped the strap of a large tote over her shoulder. Up ahead, a light stayed green. Traffic zipped past, making it impossible for the driver to exit the vehicle and come around to help her from the car. She was growing just the tiniest bit impatient when Jason solved the problem by opening the door himself.

"Belle," he said, taking her hand in a warm grasp that sent tingles up her arm. "You look amazing, as always."

She retrieved her fingers and brushed her hair over one shoulder. "I probably look a fright," she protested. "I've been on the go all day." She kept the fact that she'd reapplied her makeup after leaving Valerie's to herself. A girl had to have some secrets, after all.

His gaze shifted to the dark interior of the car. "Is someone joining us?"

"No. My assistant, Gretchen, will send the car back for me later." She waved goodbye.

Jason scanned the street for another town car. "Lisa isn't coming?"

"Nope. It's just me." She couldn't fault him for asking. Her agent accompanied her practically everywhere. But for reasons she couldn't explain, she hadn't mentioned her dinner plans to Lisa. She shivered, though the sudden chill had nothing to do with the temperature, which had dropped once the sun sank below the taller buildings across the street.

Jason's hand slipped past her wrist to her elbow. "In that case, let's get you inside where it's nice and warm."

They stepped into a cozy restaurant where the air was redolent with garlic and basil. Candles in glass sconces with bronze fittings cast a romantic glow over the room. Belle barely had a second to glimpse several rows of tables dressed in white linens and set with gleaming silverware before a dark-haired man in a suit stepped from behind a short bar that held stacks of leather-bound menus.

"Jason. It's good to see you again."

Belle stepped aside when the maître d' pumped Jason's hand with more enthusiasm than she'd seen on display in most restaurants. "It's been too long. How've you been?"

"Good, Donny. Good. I moved back to the city a few months ago." Carrying a tray laden with heaping plates of food, a waiter emerged through a swinging door. Jason's gaze traced the man's footsteps. "When did you move up to the front of the house?" he asked.

Donny shrugged. "After Dad retired. What's it been, two years now?"

Jason's expression softened. "I was afraid they'd carry him out of here on a stretcher. How is Georgio?"

"Mama keeps him busy. He doesn't come into the restaurant much anymore, but he still keeps his finger on the pulse, if you know what I mean."

"I wouldn't expect anything less." Affection shone in Jason's eyes. "And Little D—he must be, what, sixteen now?

"Eighteen and not so little anymore." His palm cupped, Donny held it several inches higher than his own head. "He works in the kitchen, alongside his Uncle Joey. D'll make a fine chef one day." Pride shone in the man's face.

Jason turned to Belle. "I'm afraid we're neglecting my guest." The smile he beamed down at her earned her instant forgiveness. "I hope you don't mind the walk down Memory Lane. Donny and I both went to PS 148," he said, naming a local public school. "I think I spent more time at Georgio's as a kid than I did at my own house. Let me introduce you—"

But Donny's lips had formed a round *O* while his gaze shifted from his old friend's face to Belle's. "You're here with this guy?" he asked as if he couldn't believe it.

Belle grinned. It had been a long time since she'd walked into a room and not instantly become the center of attention. It surprised her how much she liked the feeling.

She extended her hand. "A pleasure to meet you, Donny."

Donny responded with an awestruck glance that was all too familiar. The restaurateur tipped his head to his taller friend. "I was going to put you at that little table where we used to do our homework."

"The one the kitchen door bumps every time someone goes in and out?" Jason inclined his head toward the swinging doors.

"But now..." Donny smiled broadly. "Now, you get the best table in the house." With an expansive gesture, he indicated a nearby four-top.

Belle coughed lightly. So much for a quiet dinner for two, she thought. People would be stopping by their table to ask for pictures and autographs all night.

Jason chuckled. "I've known you all my life, but I have to bring her with me to get a good seat?" His voice dropping, he pointed to a table tucked into a small recess. "Would you mind putting us over there? Belle and I have things to talk about tonight, and we'd rather not be on display for everyone to see."

"Of course. Right this way." Donny didn't hesitate. Grabbing two menus, he led them to the out-of-the-way spot where gleaming glassware sat on white linens and a bud vase in the center of the table held a single white rose. Tiny spotlights recessed into black ceiling tiles added to the ambience.

"Thank you so much. This is perfect," Belle whispered as Donny held her chair. She took the thick leather binder he handed her.

A server hurried over to fill their water glasses. Their waiter appeared shortly after with bread wrapped in a cloth napkin. He made a show of adding oil to a mix of various herbs while he recited the specials for the night.

"Can I start you off with an appetizer? Calamari, perhaps? Ours is amazing."

"Oh, no," Belle blurted before she could stop herself. A childhood run-in with an octopus had left her with a lifelong aversion to anything with tentacles.

"I guess that's a no," Jason said with a laugh. "Want to order then?"

Belle nodded. Tossing aside her usual no-carb rule for the night, she opted for one of the specials—grilled shrimp with a creamy risotto that sounded divine. Seated across from her, Jason chose the chicken piccata which, he admitted, had been one of his childhood favorites.

"Thanks for agreeing to see me," he said as they sipped a very nice Beaujolais a few minutes later. "I wasn't sure you would after our last meeting."

Belle shook out her napkin and draped it across her lap. "Tempers were high that day. Yours. Mine. Things in Nashville hadn't exactly gone the way either of us had hoped."

Jason's gray eyes sought hers. "I should never have doubted you when you said you did your best down there. I've, uh... I've seen the video. The whole thing—not just the snippet they've been showing on the internet."

"And?" She stilled. He'd accused her of deliberately throwing her initial foray into the country music scene, something she'd never do. If they were going to have any kind of relationship going forward—business or otherwise—he'd have to admit how wrong he'd been.

Jason expelled a heavy breath. "I owe you a huge apology. You did an amazing job on those songs. Considering the mix-up with your music, no one could have done better."

She was ninety-nine percent sure the snafu had been a deliberate attempt to sabotage her performance, but she'd meant every word when

271

she'd spoken with the members of her band earlier. What Teddy Baynard had or hadn't done was between the boy and his Maker. She wouldn't judge, and she absolutely wouldn't condemn the young man.

"It's good to hear you say that," she admitted, letting the final bit of resentment she'd harbored toward her former boss slip from her shoulders. Satisfied that she and Jason could start fresh, she broke off a chunk of bread and dipped it into the oil. The morsel filled her senses with a heady blend of spice and herbs. While she chewed, she questioned again why Jason had asked her to meet him tonight. And why here, in particular. Did he have a business proposition he wanted to discuss with her? If so, surely something in Midtown would have been far more convenient.

Or was there something else on his mind? At that last thought, she quieted an odd flutter in her chest by studying the rest of the dining area from the safety of their nearly hidden alcove. The restaurant was slowly filling. Chairs scraped against the hardwood floors. Silverware clinked against plates. Occasional bursts of laughter punctuated a low buzz of conversation. Through it all, the attentive wait staff circulated. When she considered the flickering candlelight and the white linens, she had to admit, the restaurant conjured up images of romance and heart emojis more than contract negotiations and spreadsheets.

Was that what this was? Were she and Jason on a date? Tugging on the hem of her jacket, she wondered if she should have dressed up for the occasion.

She cleared her throat. When she'd met with him at Noble Records, Jason had mentioned the pressure he faced to cut her loose. Testing the waters, she asked, "Were the, um, people upstairs happy with how you handled my contract?"

In the midst of dunking a piece of bread in the oil, Jason, paused. "They were, but…" His face pinched. "I didn't plan to talk shop tonight. Did you?"

"Oh?" To give her fidgety hands something to do, Belle toyed with her wineglass. "What else is there?"

"To be perfectly honest, I was hoping to get to know you a little bit better."

That sounded like it had possibilities. "You already know everything there is to know about me," she protested. Trying to act casual, she ticked off the usual items on her fingers. "Pop star before I was thirty. A slew of platinum records. Two-time Grammy winner…"

Jason cupped his hand over hers, shushing

her. "Not that. I read all of that in your bio. Tell me about the real Belle, not the woman behind the mic."

"Hmmm. That's a tough one. There's not much more to me than my music," she admitted.

"I don't believe that for a second." Jason waited a beat. "I know you grew up in Florida. Where'd you live, go to school?"

"Watch out. You don't know what you're asking. I could talk about myself all day." She tempered the warning with a warm smile as a steady stream of memories rushed over her. Not quite sure where to start, she began at the beginning. "I was born and raised in a sleepy little beach town just north of Vero Beach." Thinking of hot summer days and cool winter nights, she relaxed a little. "My grandparents moved to Emerald Beach back in the sixties. Not long after, they opened the Dane Crown Inn. When they passed, my parents and my Aunt Liz and Uncle Paul took it over, and that's where I lived until I left for Juilliard." She glanced at the man across the table. The few men she'd dated had lost interest in her background pretty quickly. Jason, however, studied her with rapt attention. The expression on his face was so unexpected that she lost her train of thought and fell silent.

"Do you have sisters or brothers?" he asked, prompting her to go on after the silence had stretched out a bit.

"Nope. I'm an only child." When sympathy filled Jason's eyes, she hurried to explain. "Before you feel too sorry for me, I definitely never felt lonely. Far from it. Back then, the inn was always bursting at the seams. Plus, my Aunt Liz had three kids—a boy and two girls. Aunt Shirley had two daughters. We all pretty much grew up living and working in the inn together. When us kids weren't busy doing our chores, we swam in the ocean, fished in the river and hunted for buried treasure. Looking back, it was as close to an idyllic childhood as you could ever imagine."

"Did you have any luck finding that treasure?" Jason asked with a grin.

"We're still looking," she admitted. Or they would be if anyone could lay their hands on the map her grandfather had discovered before he built the inn.

"You don't really expect to find anything, do you?" Jason offered her the last piece of bread. When she declined, he helped himself.

"It's not as far-fetched as you might think." She'd grown up listening to the old-timers tell stories of a king's ransom in gold and silver. She gave Jason the CliffsNotes version. "In the 1700s, a fleet loaded with treasure from the New World set sail for Spain. They ran into a hurricane off the coast of Florida. All but one of the ships sank. Millions of dollars' worth of gold, emeralds and rubies spilled into the ocean. Over the centuries, salvagers have recovered most of the cargo, but every once in a while, a shell seeker or someone with a metal detector stumbles on a doubloon or a precious stone. In fact, that's how Emerald Bay got its name."

"So you're telling me that if you hadn't become a superstar, you might have spent your whole life beachcombing?" When she giggled, he leaned a smidge closer. "That sounds like a great childhood," he said, his voice dropping into a deep baritone that raised goose bumps on Belle's arms. "How'd you go from treasure hunting to music?"

"My cousins." The answer was as simple as it was true. "My Aunt Liz was a great cook, but my cousins and I were in charge of cleanup. Practically every night after dinner, the five of us girls worked in the kitchen, washing and drying the dishes. We talked, of course. Oh, my goodness, did we talk. But when we ran out of things to talk about, we sang. Gospel. Hit tunes. You name it. I didn't appreciate it at the time—I mean, who likes doing the dishes?—but that's where I discovered my love for music—singing in the kitchen with my cousins."

"It sounds like you were very close."

"We were. We still are." She would have said more, but their waiter reappeared just then. He whisked the crumbs from their bread service into a miniature dustpan, refilled their water goblets and assured them their order was on its way. In no time, Belle stared down at a half dozen plump shrimp perfectly arranged on a mound of fragrant risotto. Her stomach rumbled. She cast an apologetic look in Jason's direction. "If this is only half as good as it looks and smells, my mouth is going to think I died and went to heaven."

Fanning the air, Jason inhaled the lemony scent of his chicken dish. "This is exactly like I remember it," he said.

For the next few minutes, they were too busy eating to do more than rave about their meals while they ate. Belle waited until she'd made a serious dent in her dish before, curious about his childhood, she turned the tables on Jason.

"So you grew up in Queens, did you?" Promising herself she wouldn't eat any more, she scooped up a final bite of the creamy risotto.

She quickly learned he'd grown up in the music business, the middle son of parents whose names she recognized even though she'd never fully developed an appreciation for hard rock. Both his brothers had joined the band, one as a drummer and one on vocals. Though he'd tried to follow in their footsteps, Jason had recognized early on—far earlier than his parents—that he just didn't have what it took.

"Not enough talent?"

Stretching out his hand, Jason rocked his palm back and forth. "I have a moderate amount, and I still keep up with it. Until I moved to California to take over Noble's operations out there, Donny and I were in a garage band together." His mouth widening into a mock scream, he played air guitar.

She snorted a laugh at his rock-star imitation. "What made you give it up?"

"I didn't have the drive it takes to make it on that side of the mic." Picking up his fork, he swirled pasta and took a bite. After he swallowed, he said, "You know better than most the kind of commitment that life takes. You practice eight, ten hours a day. You spend your nights and weekends at one gig or another. The music has to come first, before everything else. There were other things I wanted more."

"Like what?"

"A home. A family." His expression sobered.

"You're married then? Have kids?" Disappointment filled her chest. Please, she prayed silently, don't let me be on a date with a married man.

"No." He held up his left hand, where not even the slightest trace of a white line circled his third finger. "I tried. Married my high school sweetheart. It only took us two years to figure out that we wanted different things out of life."

"You didn't try again?" On the surface, Jason checked all the right boxes. Power. Prestige. Money—he had it all. Plus, as Gretchen had said, he was certainly easy on the eyes.

But the instant she thought about her personal assistant, Belle froze. She'd enjoyed talking with Jason so much that she'd forgotten everything else. She glanced at the other tables in the restaurant. The diners she'd spied earlier had left. New patrons now filled the tables. How late was it? Slipping her phone from her purse, she checked the clock and gulped. She barely had an hour to make her flight.

"Is something wrong?" Jason, ever attentive, peered closely at her.

"I, um, I'm sorry, but I've lost all track of time. I'm supposed to be on a flight back to Florida tonight. I need to get to the airport. Like, now." But how was she going to get there? By the time her car and driver got here, her plane would be halfway to Orlando. "Do you think Donny could call me a cab?"

"I can't put you in the back seat of some random taxi. We'll take my car." Jason waved a hand, signaling their waiter.

Smiling broadly, the man hurried over. "Did you save room for dessert? The chef simply insists you try the tiramisu. Ours is the very best." He touched his fingers to his mouth and dramatically tossed a chef's kiss into the air.

"We'll have to save that for the next time. I'm afraid we're in a bit of a rush." After pressing several large bills into the waiter's hand, Jason pulled his phone from his pocket and typed quickly. Belle did the same, texting Gretchen to let her know about the change of plans.

While their waiter hovered, Jason said, "Tell Donny thanks. I'll call him later in the week." He sprang from his chair, and without giving the other diners in the restaurant a chance to so much as recognize her, much less ask her to pose for pictures, Belle found herself being guided straight from their table through the door and to the curb just as a long black limo pulled up beside them. Jason didn't wait for the driver but held the door open for her himself.

As she was about to step into the roomy back seat, he glanced around as if he was missing something. "No luggage?" he asked.

She patted the oversize tote that hung from her shoulder. "I'm traveling light. I was just here for the day."

"Okay, then, we're off." Sliding onto the seat beside her, he tapped on the privacy screen. When the driver opened it, Jason told the man to get them to LaGuardia as quickly as possible.

Fortunately, the airport was only a short drive from the restaurant. In less than ten minutes, the car pulled to a stop in front of the VIP terminal where, as promised, Belle's escort waited for her.

She paused before she exited the vehicle. Though the ending had been a bit rushed, she'd enjoyed spending time with Jason far more than she'd expected. She liked that they'd had the chance to get to know each other a little better, and she wanted, needed to let him know it. She took a breath and said, "I, um, I had a really nice time tonight."

Immediately, she felt her cheeks flame. She'd performed before royalty, spoken with kings and presidents, and that—that's the best she could do? *I had a really nice time tonight?* Geez.

But Jason didn't seem to notice her sudden attack of tongue-tiedness. Instead he squeezed her hand, sending another one of those oh-so-pleasant shivers through her.

"I had a good time, too," he murmured, his voice low. "If you're up for it, I'd like to see you again the next time you're in town. You can pick the place. Maybe something that's more velvet ropes and bright lights?" he suggested.

"Georgio's was perfect," she said, putting as much sincerity as she could muster into her words. "I've spent my life in the public eye. Simplicity is the name of the game these days."

"Okay, so we'll stick with Italian." A teasing glint came into his eyes. "But next time, you have to promise to at least try the calamari."

"Um, no thanks." She gave her head an emphatic shake. Her childhood trauma aside, she couldn't imagine anything worse than chewing on a piece of battered and deep-fried rubber. "But I will tell you why you'll never catch me eating it…next time." With that, she leaned forward and pressed her lips to his cheek before she hurried to make her flight.

As the plane taxied onto the runway a short time later, she took a minute to think about the past twenty-four hours. Without realizing it, she'd spent much of the day saying goodbye to her old life. To the Twombly. To her band, her agent. She felt oddly at peace with putting New York in her rearview mirror.

But what about Jason? Where did he fit into all of that?

Granted, seeing him had been a goodbye of sorts—a farewell to the contentious relationship they'd had at Noble Records. But something about having dinner with him had felt more like a beginning than an end. She touched her fingers to her lips, where the kiss she'd given the man lingered.

Yes, she told herself, definitely a beginning.

Eleven

Jen

A loud thunk followed by the unmistakable sound of glass shattering jerked Jen out of a sound sleep. Raised voices filtered through the cardboard-thin walls from the apartment next door. Jen leaped to her feet, barely remembering that she was standing in a dishpan filled with ice in time to catch herself before she fell flat on her face. At least, it had been ice when she drifted off after another endless shift at the Card-A-Val. Now the plastic container held water. Lukewarm water at that.

She groaned and glanced at the worn curtains covering the only window in the one-room efficiency. The relentless desert sun had seeped in around the edges, staining the walls with the rosy glow of morning when she'd walked into her apartment, dumped two bags of ice from the machine in the lobby into the plastic bin she'd set on the floor and plopped down on the chair without bothering to eat or change clothes. She'd meant to soak her tootsies for only fifteen minutes. But she must have drifted off while she waited for the ice to work its magic on feet that had swollen after eight hours of fetching drinks for the gamblers at the seedy casino.

Judging from the searing white glare now creating a halo around the glass and the labored efforts of the small, window air conditioner, she'd slept the day away. She still reeked of cigarettes and sweat. No wonder she felt as stiff as plywood and as cranky as an old goat. While she slept, her stomach must have grown so hungry it decided to eat itself because her whole belly felt like it was on fire. She needed to eat, shower, and take care of the usual, mundane chores before her next shift at the Card-A-Val. And she'd better hurry if she didn't want to be late.

As quickly as it had escalated, the fight next door died down. When the yelling and name-calling gave way to the usual tears and apologetic murmurs, Jen altered her plans. Shower first, then food, she corrected. Her neighbors' makeup sessions were even louder than their disagreements. She'd learned through trial and error that the noise of running water would drown out the sounds that invariably came next.

Padding carefully across the tiled floor on wet, bare feet, she crossed to a dressing area she'd created using a folding screen someone had put to the curb in one of Vegas's wealthier neighborhoods. She stripped off her clothes, tossing the stinky jeans and top into a slightly dented hamper she'd rescued from Goodwill, and cranked the shower on full blast.

Her apartment might not have the best insulation—the ancient window unit couldn't begin to compete with the desert heat—but at least the water pressure was adequate, she reminded herself as she soaped, lathered and rinsed. She had that to be thankful for. And she couldn't complain about the rent, which was even less than she'd been paying at the Rio Villa, the first place she'd stayed when she arrived in Vegas.

In the kitchen she took stock of the meager, day-before-payday offerings. Poking through a bag of spinach that should have been consigned to a compost heap days ago, she salvaged a few green leaves. With the last two eggs in the dorm-size refrigerator, she fixed herself an omelet on a stove that was only slightly larger than a hot plate. At the last minute, she threw a bit of leftover cheese on top. She was scraping the last of the egg onto a chipped plate from the bottom of a battered pan when her cell phone rang. Recognizing the number, she answered with a smile.

"Hey Sally! What's up?"

"Nothing much. I'm just getting off work and thought we could meet up for drinks. The Ghost Donkey at seven?"

Her omelet lost its flavor when she thought of the delicious nachos she'd had at the speakeasy the last time she'd met Sally there. Suddenly hungry for something more substantial than eggs, Jen groaned. "I'm going to have to take a rain check." She didn't bother trying to mask how much she hated to pass up the chance to see the only friend she'd made in Vegas. "I'm working a double shift."

"Oh, how are things at the Card-A-Val?"

"Fine," Jen lied. She wished she could give Sally an honest answer. But the woman wasn't her sister; the two of them hadn't skipped stones across the river or planted a butterfly garden behind the toolshed together. They hadn't grown up playing hide-and-seek together like she had with her cousins. Sally didn't know all her secrets. She was just a friend and a new one at that. Jen couldn't burden her with the truth.

And the truth was, as the oldest "girl" working Card-A-Val's main floor, Jen had been on the receiving end of a barrage of advice on how to earn more tips.

"Move faster!" the manager had coached.

"Be friendlier!" the bartender had suggested.

Sheesh! Like she wasn't doing her best already. From the moment she stepped out of the employee dressing area, she was like a ball on a roulette wheel—constantly circling from the floor to the bar and back again in a never-ending effort to keep the customers well-lubricated.

As for the friendlier part, it hadn't taken her long to figure out that the casino's idea of acceptable behavior and her own were two very different animals. Oh, she never failed to exchange the usual banter with the casino's clientele. And she didn't mind smiling until her jaw ached at the end of every shift—that was simply part of the job. But far too many of the Card-A-Val's customers were under the oh-so-wrong impression that tucking their tips into her cleavage or pinching her bottom was perfectly okay. It wasn't. For the other girls, maybe, but not for her.

As a result, she earned fewer tips than the

other cocktail waitresses. Which meant she had less to share with the bartenders at the end of her shift. Which caused them to fill her orders more slowly. All of which put a vicious circle in motion, one where she had to work extra shifts just to pay her rent.

"It's been eye-opening," she told her friend. She refused to complain. Not to the woman who'd suggested she try her luck at Card-A-Val after all the bigger casinos on the Strip had refused to hire her.

"Hang in there. Once you've worked there another couple of months, you can use this casino as a reference when you look for a job at a better one."

Jen eyed what was left of her scrimpy omelet. She let her gaze drift over the rickety kitchen table the previous tenant had left behind, the stack of cardboard boxes she'd taped together to make a dresser, the lumpy couch that did double duty as her bed. She'd lived in more than her fair share of dumps since striking out on her own at eighteen. This wasn't the absolute worst, but it was close to it.

The low-rent apartment certainly was a far cry from the Dane Crown Inn, where her mother had frequently left her and her sister while she jetted around with her most recent beau of the month. Back then, Jen had resented everything about the inn. She'd chafed under her aunt and uncle's rules, weaseled out of chores when she could, skipped school as much as she'd attended. But even she had to admit it had been better than this. At the inn, she'd never gone to bed hungry. If there was work to do, there'd usually been someone around to share the load. Best of all, surrounded by family, she'd always known she was loved, that someone had her back, that if she fell, someone would pick her up, dust her off and get her back on her feet again.

She eyed the dish tub that still sat in the middle of the floor.

Another couple of months.

Could she last that long?

"Jen." Marge beckoned from behind her desk.

Slowing in her headlong rush to the employee lounge, Jen approached the Personnel Manager's open door.

"Meet me upstairs in the coffee shop after you clock out, will you?"

"I'm on my way to do that right now." Though Jen's head bobbed in agreement, the smile she gave her boss didn't reach her eyes. And with good reason. Dog tired after working back-to-back shifts, she wanted nothing more than to change into her street clothes, cash her paycheck and grab a few groceries on her way back to the apartment.

Another long, drawn-out conversation about her shortcomings at the Card-A-Val was the last thing she needed. Especially when Marge insisted such discussions take place on employees' personal time. Besides, what could the manager possibly have to say to her that she hadn't already repeated ad nauseam?

Not that she'd blown off a single one of Marge's many suggestions. She'd dutifully committed all the shortcuts through the casino to memory like Marge had urged her to do. But the sad fact of the matter was, unless she donned roller skates, she simply couldn't hustle the drinks from the bar to the players at the slot machines any faster than she was already doing.

Although even Marge would have to admit she'd gone the extra mile towards becoming a team player. Hadn't she stuck candles in the day-old cake she'd wheedled from the chef and led the other girls in singing "Happy Birthday" to Camille last week? When she stumbled on Bitsy sneaking out to take an extra smoke break, she hadn't said a word about it, had she? And when she found Ginga crying in the bathroom after a customer got a little too handsy, hadn't she offered the girl only sympathy and not a single I-told-you-so?

Wait a minute, Jen told herself. Maybe that was what Marge wanted to discuss with her. The Personnel Manager must have noticed how much she'd been helping out the younger girls and wanted to reward her for it. Was she about to get a promotion? Maybe something behind a desk? She snapped her fingers. That had to be it.

She held her breath while hope swirled in her chest. Her feet would certainly thank her for snagging a desk job, but was she up to the task? A chortle escaped her lips. Who was she kidding? Though she'd never seen herself as a mother figure, she wouldn't mind helping to oversee the younger staff. As a matter of fact, as long as it put more money in her wallet, she'd take whatever job she was offered.

More than eager now to hear what Marge had to say, Jen hurriedly changed into jeans and a tank top. She started for the door, remembered her tips, and backtracked to the locker where she'd left her uniform. Taking a thin wad of bills from the skirt's hidden pocket, she rubbed her fingers over the money. By working a double, she'd hoped to make enough in tips to treat herself to a nice steak. Judging from the few bucks in her hand, though, it looked like ground chuck was all she could afford this week. Unless Marge offered her a raise.

Certain that's what the woman had in mind, Jen ignored her tired legs and practically skipped up the escalator to the second floor.

"Hey Marge. You wanted to see me?" She took a seat across from her boss in a café so nondescript it could have been in any hotel throughout the United States. Any hotel where water jiggled in the glasses, thanks to a pounding rock beat that came from the casino floor, that is.

Marge motioned to the waitress who hurried over. She closed her menu with a snap. "I don't know why I even look at it. I always get the same thing. Black coffee, two poached eggs and an English muffin." She slid the plastic-coated binder across the table. "Order anything you like. This is going on my expense account."

Tension seeped from Jen's shoulders. A promotion, that had to be the reason Marge had wanted to speak with her. Why else would she spring for a meal? The apparent confirmation melted her worries as quickly as butter melted on a hot biscuit. Wanting to get to the good stuff, she gave the menu a quick scan before she opted for a steak sandwich that cost more than her current, limited budget would allow.

"Thanks for meeting me," Marge said once the waitress had taken their orders and hurried off to get their drinks. "I know you're coming off a double and probably exhausted, so I won't take too much of your time."

"I'm not in a big rush." Jen spread her napkin across her lap. Marge could talk all day as long as she was handing out raises.

"Do you like Vegas?" Marge asked, obviously just killing time while they waited for their food.

"It's all right. I could see myself settling down here. Maybe I'll get a nice little place with one of those xeriscaped yards that are so popular out here." She wouldn't need a big house, not for just one person. As for the yard, rock gardens and cacti didn't require much maintenance, though she'd probably always miss the green grass so common in Florida and the towering oak trees with their dark green leaves.

They chatted for just a few minutes before their waitress slid their orders in front of them. "Oh, that was quick," Jen said.

"I like coming here in the mornings. Gamblers are notorious night owls, so the restaurants are pretty much empty until noonish." Marge pointed her fork at Jen's sandwich. "Dig in."

She didn't need to be told twice. Just one whiff of the meaty aroma wafting up from her plate had been enough to set her taste buds tingling. She took a bite and nearly moaned at the delicious blend of grilled onions, tender steak and melted cheese. Enjoying every bite, she held up her end of the conversation while the two of them polished off their food.

When their plates had been cleared away, Marge swiveled to face Jen. "You've been at Card-A-Val a couple of weeks now, haven't you?"

Jen nodded, but since there didn't seem to be anything else required, she waited.

"It's been tough, hasn't it? Always hustling to keep up with the younger girls? I sympathize. Truly I do. You have to be struggling to make ends meet. Am I right?"

"It's been rough," Jen admitted, curious to see where the conversation was headed. "My salary barely covers the rent. I count on tips to pay for groceries and gas. But it hasn't been enough." She straightened the strap of her tank top, which had slipped off her shoulder. She didn't own a scale. Without one, she couldn't be exactly sure how much weight she'd lost since her move to Vegas, but it was enough that her clothes were beginning to look and feel baggy. She hoped her next position came with a paycheck big enough to let her buy more groceries.

Marge brushed aside Jen's troubles with a dismissive wave. "I'm sure what I have to say next won't make things any easier." Blotting her lips on her napkin, she appeared to center herself. "It's just not working out. You're not keeping pace with the rest of the staff. I think it's time for you to start thinking about another line of work."

Sure she hadn't heard Marge correctly, Jen shook her head. "I'm sorry, what?"

"I'm suggesting you start looking for another job."

Jen gulped. This conversation was not going the way she'd hoped. Not at all. She felt an urge to defend herself and went with it. "I, uh, I've done everything you asked."

After working in the VIP section of the River Delta, she had to admit it had been a bit of a come-down to be responsible for emptying the ashtrays that were strategically placed beside every slot machine. But she'd done it, and she hadn't complained about it. Not even once. She'd memorized the layout of the sprawling casino floor and could quickly and efficiently direct patrons to their favorite nickel, quarter or fifty-cent slot machines. And she was unfailingly polite to the casino's patrons, even while she reminded them to keep their hands to themselves.

"I realize that, but it's not enough. I've also had complaints from the bar staff that you're holding back tips."

"I am not," she said. For emphasis, she reached into the pocket of her jeans, where she pulled out a handful of ones. "Except for the fourteen dollars I put in the tip jar behind the bar, this is everything I made from the time I clocked in yesterday. Count it yourself—you'll see I actually gave the bartenders more than their share."

Marge eyed the small pile of bills. "Which makes my point exactly. If you were any good at this, you'd be taking home hundreds each night, like the rest of the cocktail waitresses." Marge took a breath. Her head swung as she scanned the restaurant for anyone who sat close enough to overhear their conversation. Apparently, she liked what she saw because she asked, "Can we talk off the record? One slightly older woman to another?" She didn't wait for Jen to answer but forged ahead. "I suggested it's time for you to start thinking about a new line of work. Before you get upset, I have a proposition you might want to consider."

Twelve

Kim

"My goodness, you're up bright and early this morning." Carrying a carafe of freshly brewed coffee, Kim smiled at the silver-haired couple who wandered into the dining room. "You have perfect timing. I was just filling the urns."

"I'm so glad! We weren't sure we'd be able to get a cup before we hit the road." Eddie McGruder hurried toward the coffee station.

"You aren't leaving today, are you?" Concern nibbled at the corners of Kim's smile. At the moment, the McGruders were the inn's only guests. She was nearly positive they'd reserved a room through the middle of next week.

"We're taking a day trip, but we'll be back this evening. We're spending the day with Tom's brother and his wife in Kissimmee."

"Rupert and Mildred live in Tampa." A retired Army sergeant major from New Jersey, Tom McGruder held himself ramrod-straight. "We get together for a round or two of golf whenever we're in Florida."

"We're supposed to meet them at nine." Eddie tugged on the banded hem of a pastel top she wore over white crop pants. "I don't want to be late."

Tom checked his watch. "If you don't dawdle, we'll have plenty of time."

"I'm not dawdling." Eddie adjusted the strap of her cross-body bag. "I just asked if we could get a cup of coffee before we left. You know I'm not very good company until I have my morning caffeine."

"Yes, sweetheart. I know." Tom gently placed his hand on Eddie's shoulder.

Listening to the couple's good-natured bickering, Kim felt her smile soften. When she first married Frank, she'd envisioned them spending their lives together. As luck would have it, a marriage for the ages hadn't been in the cards for them. Since then, she hadn't found anyone she cared to spend the rest of her life with, and now that she'd celebrated her fiftieth birthday, it was unlikely she ever would.

Guessing Eddie and Tom had spent a lifetime together, she checked the creamer and sugar bins to make sure they were full before asking, "How long have you two been married?"

"We'll celebrate our second anniversary next month," Eddie said. Standing on her tiptoes, she brushed a kiss on Tom's cheek.

The answer shocked Kim so much, she knocked over the sugar dispenser. A dozen small white packets scattered across the top of the buffet. "Oops. Sorry." She scooped up the tiny envelopes and returned them to the holder while she fought her curiosity. "How'd you two get together?" she asked when her need to know got the best of her.

"When one of our foursome didn't show up for a round of golf, the starter sent Tom over. It was love at first sight." Eddie turned up the wattage on the smile she beamed at her husband.

"By the end of the first nine, it was as if we'd known each other all our lives. We had dinner at the club that night. We've been together ever since." Tom gave his wife a quick squeeze.

"A whirlwind courtship." Kim pressed a hand over her heart. "What'd your family think of that? I hope they were happy for you." She dropped her hand. Would her children support her if she ever remarried? Not that she was even seeing someone. For the briefest of moments she'd thought something might develop between her and Craig, but any hope of that happening had fizzled. The moment she'd told him about Frank, he'd dropped her faster than a hot potato.

"What family?" Tom asked.

"Neither of us had been married before," Eddie nodded. She turned to Kim. "Do you have any travel mugs? I think we'd better take our coffee to go if we're going to make our tee time in Kissimmee."

The McGruders were just full of surprises, weren't they? Marveling that the couple had found each other so late in life, Kim retrieved a plastic sleeve of paper cups with matching lids from a cabinet in the buffet. Moving quickly, she poured coffee for their guests, then stepped aside while they doctored their drinks.

Warmth bubbled through Kim's midsection as she watched Tom and Eddie leave arm in arm a few minutes later. Maybe there was hope for her yet, she told herself. If the McGruders could find true love, maybe finding her own someone special wasn't so far-fetched after all.

Someone who wasn't Craig, that is.

Sighing, Kim returned to the kitchen, where she put a few finishing touches on the breakfast casserole she'd assembled the night before. That done, she slid the dish into the oven, poured herself a cup of coffee and went onto the back deck. Gathering her strength for the busy day ahead, she watched the darkness retreat into pools of shadow beneath the trees while she listened to the distant roar of the ocean. By the time the first of the monk parakeets flitted about searching for their breakfast, the aroma of sausage and eggs drifted in the air. Finished with her coffee, Kim stood and stretched. The rest of the family would be up soon. They'd need a hearty breakfast.

After rinsing her cup in the deep farmer's sink, Kim crossed to the oven, where she checked on the casserole. She stepped aside, dodging the cloud of steam that wafted upward when she opened the door. When the coast was clear, she prodded the egg custard with a fork. Her nose hadn't lied. The breakfast dish was ready to eat.

Once she'd placed the casserole on the warming tray, she switched on the broiler. She hovered, closely watching over the slices of buttered bread she slid beneath the flames. When the circles of melted butter had spread and the edges had browned, she removed the pan from the oven.

As she stacked the toast in a serving basket, a rattle at the back door announced Amy's arrival.

Seconds later, Belle and Margaret emerged from the family quarters. Footsteps sounded on the stairs. Before Margaret made it halfway across the room, the kitchen had filled.

"Wow. Something smells good," Diane declared, walking into the room with Caitlyn trailing behind her. "Good morning, Aunt Margaret. I'm going to fix myself a cup of coffee. Can I get you some?"

"I'd appreciate it, dear," Margaret said. She relied heavily on her cane while she carefully picked her way across the Mexican tiles to her usual seat at the breakfast table. "Caitlyn, you're a sight for sore eyes this morning." She squinted when a ray of sunshine bounced off the sparkly top the teen wore over a cute pair of shorts.

"Good morning, Aunt Margaret." Caitlyn lingered near the doorway.

In faded cutoffs and a man's T-shirt she must have pulled from the Lost and Found box, Diane stopped in her headlong rush to the coffee dispenser long enough to kiss her aunt's cheek. Spying the casserole on the table, she plucked a piece of sausage from the dish and popped it in her mouth. "Is that another one of Mom's recipes?" she asked while she chewed.

"I made a couple of changes, but basically, yes," Kim confirmed. She eyed the casserole with its rich egg filling loaded with thick slices of smoked sausage, chunks of sautéed onion and green pepper and topped with beautifully browned cheese. "Aunt Liz liked to let the flavors blend a bit longer. She poured the egg batter over the meat and veggies and let it sit in the fridge overnight." Kim gave an exaggerated shiver. "I've never been much for letting raw eggs sit for any length time, so I don't add them until I'm ready to put the casserole in the oven. What I lose in flavor I more than make up for in peace of mind."

"Smart." Diane filled two cups, dumped cream and sugar in one, and carried them both to the table.

"Is there any milk? Where's the cereal?" Caitlyn's plaintive request made it clear that she wasn't a fan of the food her aunt had prepared.

"I think I saw a box of corn flakes in the pantry," Kim offered. "Milk's in the fridge. Bowls are in that cupboard." She pointed.

"Don't you have anything good?" Caitlyn's lips turned down. Staring accusation at her mom, she said, "No Cocoa Crunch? Or Honey Brights?"

"'Fraid not," Diane answered.

"Fine. I'll have pancakes." After marching across the room, Caitlyn threw herself into a chair like only an exasperated teenager could do.

Kim chuckled. So the youngster thought this was a full-service kitchen, did she? She'd soon find out differently. Giving what she thought was a credible imitation of their Aunt Liz, Kim propped one hand on her hip and stared at the teen. "Do you see a menu?" she demanded. "Does this look like a fancy restaurant to you?"

"Oh, gosh. You sound just like Mom," Amy declared. She dabbed at her eyes.

"Truth," Diane agreed. Turning to her daughter, she said, "It's corn flakes or egg casserole. Your choice."

"Fine." Caitlyn reached for the serving spoon.

"Hold on a minute. Age before beauty." Amy took the utensil from her niece's hand. Wielding the spoon like the expert she was, she deftly cut a small square of the casserole for her aunt. Then, as if to drive her point home, she fixed a plate for herself before she relinquished the spoon. Sliding onto an empty chair, she said, "I see Max was here yesterday. Did he finish power-washing the cottages?"

Kim nodded. "Not only that, but he fixed the sign out front."

"I wish I could stay and help you paint, but Saturdays are our busiest days at Sweet Cakes."

"You'll have plenty of other opportunities," Kim pointed out. They'd hold several work parties just to paint the cottages. To say nothing of the million and one other repairs they'd need to make. She carried the toast to the table and took a seat.

"The bakery is closed tomorrow. I'll help out then."

"After church," Belle put in from her chair beside Margaret. She pressed her palms together. "Grace?"

They bowed their heads while Margaret led them in giving thanks.

When they'd finished, Caitlyn glared at her mother. "Can I get something to eat now?" she asked, her voice full of huffy indignation.

Diane stopped filling her own plate long enough to make sure everyone else had been served before she slid the dish toward Caitlyn. "Help yourself," she said with a shrug.

While everyone else pretended to ignore the tension between Diane and her daughter, Kim let her gaze shift between the two. After all the teen had put her mother through lately, she thought Diane's frosty attitude toward the child was perfectly understandable. But Caitlyn had to be hurting, too. While she hoped Diane and Tim's problems were only temporary, her own children had reacted with much of the same sullen attitude Caitlyn displayed in the weeks following her breakup with Frank. Hoping to defuse the situation, she cleared her throat.

"You'll never guess who I heard from last night." The strident bleating of her cell phone had woken her out of a sound sleep. Like a mother hen worried about her chicks, she'd answered without checking the caller ID.

"Publishers' Clearing House?" Belle suggested with a teasing laugh. "Did you win ten thousand dollars?"

"I wish." Kim pretended to sigh.

"Josh? Nat?" asked Diane.

"Craig." Amy snapped her fingers as if her guess were a sure thing.

"Nope. You're all wrong," Kim said, although she wouldn't have minded getting a late-night call from a certain tall, darkly handsome someone.

"Do we have to keep guessing? Or are you going to tell us?" Aunt Margaret sipped her coffee.

"Jen."

"It's about time," Amy said. She speared the last bite of her casserole while she fired questions. "Is she okay? Is she still in Biloxi?"

Kim shook her head. Whether her sister was okay or not was something only Jen could answer. "She's in Vegas."

Diane whistled. "I thought she liked it in Mississippi. Wasn't she planning to stay there for a while?"

"That's what I thought, but apparently, things didn't work out for her there. She's been working at a small, off-the-strip casino for a few weeks. She said to tell you she was sorry to hear about your arm, Aunt Margaret. She wants you to know she hopes you're better soon."

"She always did have such a good heart." Margaret nibbled on a piece of toast.

"She does," Kim agreed. Though she'd never cramp her sister's footloose lifestyle, she did miss having her around.

"Did she call just to catch up?" Belle's forehead wrinkled. "Or did she want something in particular?"

"She wanted advice."

Diane drew back. "That's a shocker. Does she ever call to ask your opinion?"

"Never." Kim laughed. "If I hadn't already been in bed, you could have knocked me over with a feather."

"What's she want?"

Kim spared a quick glance at Caitlyn. For all her protests and grumbles, the teen had served herself an enormous portion of the egg dish and seemed intently focused on putting away as much of it as possible. Satisfied that the girl wasn't paying the conversation any attention, Kim nonetheless lowered her voice.

"Apparently the manager at the casino where she's been working wants Jen to give up waitressing and come to work for her as..." Turning away from the girl she loved like a niece, she cupped one hand around her mouth and let her voice drop to a whisper. "As an escort."

"You've got to be kidding!" Amy dropped the knife she'd been using to cut her toast in half. "At her age?" she asked in a tone that contained an equal mix of shock and admiration.

Diane tsked. "I guess anything goes in Vegas."

"Vegas or no Vegas, I think every one of us still has what it takes." Belle cupped her hands beneath her ample chest and giggled.

"Does Aunt Jen *want* to be a call girl?"

In the process of spreading jelly on her toast, Kim froze. Caitlyn had been so quiet, she'd practically forgotten the child was still sitting at the table. She shot Diane a questioning look.

Her cousin waved away her concerns. "It's okay. She knows all about the birds and the bees."

Caitlyn sneered. "Why they call it that when

there's no birds or bees involved, I'll never know."

The comment loosed a round of nervous laughter that wiped a sudden tension from the room.

Her face reddening, Caitlyn asked, "But does she want to…you know?"

"Uh, no." Kim rushed to assure the teen. "Your Aunt Jen has more respect for herself than that. Her motto has always been 'Put a ring on it' before there's any hanky-panky."

"She shouldn't take the job, then." Caitlyn grabbed the spoon and helped herself to a second helping of the casserole.

"I think your Aunt Jen would agree with you." Speaking in a more normal voice, Kim continued. "She turned her boss down flat. But now she doesn't have a job, and she isn't sure how she'll find another one. She wanted some reassurance that she'd done the right thing."

"What'd you tell her?" Amy wanted to know.

"What could I say?" Kim hunched her shoulders and held out her palms. "I told her she ought to think about coming home. That we could use her help and staying here would give her time to figure out what she wants to do next."

"That was good advice, Aunt Kim. I hope she

does what you told her. I'd like to see Aunt Jen again. I haven't seen her since I was little." After giving her final word on the subject, Caitlyn once more focused on her breakfast.

"Do you think she will?" Tense lines outlined Diane's mouth.

Kim shrugged. "I've never been able to predict what Jen will do."

"I know you miss her." Amy reached across the table and gave Kim's hand a warm squeeze. "Next time you talk to her, tell her we all do, too." With that, she pushed her chair away from the table. "Thanks for breakfast, but I've got to get moving before Deborah sends a search party out after me." Looking wistful, she shook her head. "I'd be lost without that woman. She's really kept everything running smoothly at the bakery these last couple of weeks."

"You're going to have to give her a big bonus at Christmas," Diane suggested.

"Don't I know it." Amy rounded the table to the spot where her aunt sat. "You behave yourself today. I don't want to hear any stories about you wielding a paintbrush."

"No problem. I've learned my lesson." Margaret patted the cast that immobilized her broken arm. "I don't plan to do anything more than relax on the deck and supervise."

Smiling warmly, Amy squatted down until she was face-to-face with the older woman. "What would you like for lunch? Chicken salad? Quiche? I'll have whatever you'd like delivered."

"Oh, no need for that, child," Margaret assured her. "Kim's got lunch covered."

At Amy's questioning glance, Kim stopped stacking empty plates on one corner of the table. "Aunt Margaret's right. I bought enough deli meat for sandwiches." Grinning, she added, "With special sauce."

"I hate to miss that," Amy said, sounding like she meant it. She stood and dusted herself off. "I gotta run. Call me if you need anything." With a quick wave, she hustled toward the laundry room. Seconds later, a door snicked shut.

Kim gathered an armload of dishes and headed for the sink. "I'm just going to leave these to soak so we can get started with the painting before it gets too hot out."

"Here, let me help clear the table." Belle sprang into action, gathering cutlery and empty coffee mugs.

Kim squirted liquid soap into the sink and ran the hot water while Belle began scraping bits of leftover egg and toast into a nearby trash can. Behind them, Diane's chair scraped against the tile as she pushed away from the table. "Well, I guess that's our cue." She paused a long second before, in a question that had to be directed at Caitlyn, she asked, "Is that your new Shabby Chic shirt?"

When her daughter mumbled something unintelligible, Diane warned, "That shirt cost a hundred dollars. It'll get ruined if you wear it to paint in."

"I'm not painting." Caitlyn snorted with the air of someone who thought the job was beneath her.

At the teen's haughty response, Kim arched a brow at Belle, whose own expression pronounced the conversation taking place behind them as "interesting." The superstar angled her body so she could watch what was shaping up into a battle between mother and daughter. Kim slowly twisted the spigot and shut off the water. Turning, she pressed her back against the sink and waited.

A deadly calm filled Diane's voice as her attention riveted on her daughter. "What do you mean, you're not painting? We're all painting."

"I'm going to stay in my room. I need to call Sarah. She's probably wondering what happened to me." Caitlyn shot an accusing glance at her mother.

Diane folded her arms across her chest. "You

lost your phone privileges," she reminded the girl.

"That was before you jerked me out of school and brought me here." Caitlyn gestured at the inn like it was the last place on the planet she wanted to be.

"I brought you here so you could get a fresh start." Diane's stiff posture softened, and her tone lightened into the voice of reason. "You and your friends have made some bad choices lately. Think of it as a one-of-a-kind opportunity. This is the first day of the rest of your life, and *you* are going to make it a good one."

But Caitlyn had a fair-size chip on her shoulders, and she wasn't about to let go of it. "It's not fair!" she protested. "You can't move me away from all my friends and not let me even tell them where I am."

"No phone calls," Diane repeated firmly. "You can write Sarah a letter when you have some spare time. Which won't be today, because today, we're painting."

"Uh-uh!" Caitlyn expelled a breath filled with frustration and anger. Shoving her nearly empty plate halfway across the table, she stood. "I'll be in my room," she announced.

"Don't. You. Dare. Walk out of this room, young lady." Diane's voice took on a steely edge that stopped Caitlyn in her tracks. With one finger, Diane drew a circle that included everyone in the room. "Except for Aunt Margaret, who gets a pass because of her broken arm, we are all painting today. That includes you. Now go change your clothes and get back down here. You have five minutes."

Diane stood stock still until a sufficiently cowed Caitlyn trudged up the stairs thirty seconds later. Then, as if every bit of strength had deserted her, she expelled her breath with a whoosh of air and sank onto her chair. "Is it too early in the day for a stiff drink?" she asked no one in particular. "I swear, I never knew parenting could be this hard."

Belle slipped the plate she'd held over the trash can into the soapy water. "You handled that beautifully," she told Diane.

Kim dried her wet hands on a dish towel before she hurried to her cousin's side. As much as she felt bad for Caitlyn, Diane had been right to lay down the law. "She has to know she can't get away with acting like that."

Diane turned an imploring gaze on her aunt. "Do you think I did the right thing?"

"As her mother, it's up to you to enforce the rules," Margaret said without even the slightest bit of hesitation.

"I just never thought I'd be doing it alone." As tears filled her eyes, Diane blinked rapidly.

Kim's breath caught. Caitlyn wasn't the only one who was hurting. Slowly, she asked, "Have you heard from Tim?"

"Not a word." Diane's head shook. "I thought he'd at least call to talk with Caitlyn. But he hasn't even tried to get in touch with her."

"That doesn't mean anything." Belle hurried to offer reassurance. "I've traveled enough to know he won't have cell service unless the ship is in port, and even then, reception can be pretty spotty."

"Or he could have lost his phone or broken it or even dropped it overboard," Kim added.

"Oh! I did that in Barcelona," Belle declared. "After six days at sea, I raced to the bow of the ship so I could make a call the moment we got a signal. There I was, practically hanging over the side of the ship—along with, like, a hundred others—when somebody bumped into me. Sploosh! There went my phone. Maybe Tim did the same thing."

"I guess we'll know for sure soon enough." Diane glanced at the calendar with a mix of trepidation and hope.

Kim squeezed her cousin's shoulder. "Until then, you can count on us to have your back."

"And to remind the lovely young Caitlyn that here at the Dane Crown Inn, if you don't work, you don't eat."

Kim nodded. "That's the way it's always been." Her aunts had repeated the rule so often, she was surprised no one had ever cross-stitched it onto a pillow. From the youngest to the oldest, every family member had chores to do each day.

Margaret struggled to her feet. "Which reminds me, I'd better check the computer if I'm going to earn my supper."

"I think we can make an exception in your case, Aunt Margaret," Kim said with a laugh. She assured her aunt that she'd looked over the reservations this morning. Their next guests wouldn't check in until after the McGruders left. "You're right about one thing, though. We're wasting daylight. We need to get moving if we're going to finish painting Rosario this weekend." They'd chosen to start with that cottage because, other than Regala, currently occupied by Helen March, it needed the fewest repairs.

"Let me get Mama her pills and get her settled, and I'll be ready." Reaching up, Belle tightened the bandanna she'd secured around her red hair.

"I just need a couple of minutes to finish

putting food away and stacking the dishes," Kim said. She'd load whatever she could into the dishwasher and hand-wash the rest when she came in to fix lunch.

"I'll help," Diane offered.

"Great." Between the two of them, they'd get the kitchen sorted out in no time.

"Okay. Let's meet on the deck in ten minutes." Belle handed her mother's cane to Margaret. "Do you want to take a book to read out onto the back porch?" she asked as they shuffled slowly toward the family quarters.

At the sink, Diane and Kim quickly settled into a familiar rhythm of washing and drying the dishes. Kim was applying some elbow grease to a baked-on spot on the casserole pan when she felt her cousin's not-so-gentle jab.

"So what's the story with this guy Amy mentioned? Craig?"

"Nothing," Kim started. Feeling her face warm, she backtracked. "Okay, maybe there was for a minute, but it didn't work out."

"Yeah? Was he a jerk or something?"

"No, Craig's a nice guy." She listed some of his finer qualities. "He's the mayor of Emerald Bay. A widower. His mom and Aunt Margaret are good friends. He was helping me look into putting the inn on the National Registry of

Historic Places, and we talked about the catering business I want to open." She shrugged. "He seemed interested, not just in the business, but in me."

Diane looked up from the dishes she was loading into the dishwasher. "So what happened?"

"I told him about Frank," she answered simply. "I haven't heard from him since."

"Ouch."

Diane grabbed a handful of spoons and forks and dealt them into the silverware compartments that ran along one side of the dishwasher. "You know," she said slowly, "at this stage in our lives, we all have baggage. Some we learn from. Some we just carry with us wherever we go. I think your marriage to Frank has taught you to be even more scrupulous in your business dealings. If Craig can't see that, then maybe it's a good thing you found out now instead of on down the road."

"That's what I've been telling myself, but it's good to hear it from someone else." The door to the family quarters creaked open. The shuffle of footfalls accompanied the soft murmur of Belle's and Aunt Margaret's conversation. From another part of the house came the clatter of another set of footsteps. Finished with the dishes, Kim slung an arm around her cousin's shoulders. "Sounds like this work party is about to get underway. What say we go paint a cottage."

Within an hour, Kim decided their mission was hopeless. Despite wrapping her head in a bandanna the size of a small blanket, it took Belle no more than five minutes to splatter paint in her hair. She'd immediately raced into the house to wash away every trace of the teal blue goo. When she emerged again—this time wearing an enormous straw hat—she lasted mere moments before she abandoned her brush in order to help her mom inside for a nap. Diane's painting skills were more befitting a canvas in an art studio than the cottage's concrete blocks. Working with their smallest brush, she'd spent the better part of the time painstakingly dabbing paint into every tiny crevice in the rough surface of a single block. Caitlyn, meanwhile, had gotten more paint on her than on the house. Kim had to admit she hadn't fared much better. She'd spent most of her time climbing up and down the ladder and very little of it applying the new color. On the ground again, she folded her arms and surveyed their progress. She tsked. At the rate they were going, it would take all winter to paint just one of the six cottages.

The throaty rumble of an engine caught her attention before she climbed back up the ladder. Pulling the brim of her baseball cap low over her eyes, she tracked a pickup truck as it bounced over the rutted coquina driveway. She fought an urge to scratch her head. As far as she knew, they weren't expecting anyone. Had tourists spotted their recently repaired sign and decided to see if a room was available? Or had some of Margaret's friends stopped by for an unplanned visit? She frowned when she lost sight of the vehicle as it traveled past some shrubbery. Less than a minute later, doors slammed and voices— male ones—rose over the ever-present sound of the ocean and the breeze that rattled the palm fronds overhead.

Diane looked up from the lone cement block she'd painted a brilliant teal. "Are we expecting company?"

"I didn't think so." Kim cocked her head. Thanks to an overgrown hedge, she couldn't see their visitors, but she could hear them. Their voices grew louder as they followed the path that led behind the main house to the cottages. One of the men sounded vaguely familiar, and she strained to place him. Before she could, the last person she expected to see stepped from behind the hedge.

What was Craig doing here? Straightening her ball cap, she gave him the once-over. The man wore a stained T-shirt over jeans that had seen better days. Paint trays and rollers poked out of the five-gallon bucket he carried. Not sure whether she was happier to see him or the equipment he'd brought, she hurried toward him with a welcoming, "Craig, what are you doing here?"

"When Toby and I stopped in at Sweet Cakes for coffee and donuts, Amy told us you were painting today. This is Toby, my sister's oldest." Craig hooked a thumb toward a lanky teen who lingered step or two behind him.

"Pleasure to meet you, ma'am." The boy stepped forward, his hand extended.

Kim studied the young man who bore a distinct resemblance to his uncle. She held up hands that were covered in a fine overspray. "I won't shake your hand and get paint all over you, but it's nice to meet you, too, Toby." She cocked her head toward Craig. "So you were just driving around Emerald Bay looking for a project to work on? Do you do that often?"

Craig's laughter rang out. "Toby and I wanted to volunteer at Habitat for Humanity this morning. He needs the community service hours for school, and I came along 'cause I didn't have anything better to do with my Saturday."

"Like we don't spend every Saturday together, Uncle Craig." Toby scuffed one foot through the grass.

"Gotta do it now while I can." Tools rattled, and the handle clanked against the side of the bucket when Craig dropped it to the ground. "You're gonna miss these days when you go off to Gainesville next fall." To Kim, he said, "Toby is headed to the University of Florida on an academic scholarship." Pride shone in Craig's eyes.

"Whoo, congratulations." A full ride to one of the toughest schools in the nation was nothing to sneeze at.

"Anyhow. Habitat had a full crew already. So what do you think?" Craig toed the bucket of tools. "Can you put us to work?"

Kim grinned up at him. "You betcha!" She pointed to the cottage. "As you can see, we could definitely use some help. I was hoping we'd finish painting the exterior of Rosario and maybe even get started on the interior by the time we knocked off today, but we haven't made much progress."

"You don't have a paint sprayer?" Toby

asked. "That would make this go a lot faster."

Kim shook her head. She'd considered renting one, but if Belle could manage to get paint in her hair while opening a can of paint, she could only imagine what damage they'd do with a high-pressure wand.

"No problem," Craig assured her. "Toby's an expert with them. We'll bring one next time. For today, we'll work with what we have."

He beckoned the others over. In no time at all, he and Toby had given everyone a short lesson in painting with rollers and broken them into teams.

"Belle, you and Diane take the back side of the house," Craig directed. "Toby and Caitlyn, you're over there." He pointed to one side. "Kim and I will take the front. The first team to complete their assignment wins. Any questions?"

"What's the prize?" Caitlyn asked.

"It's a surprise. Everybody ready?" When everyone nodded, he grinned encouragingly. "On your marks. Get set. Go!" he called, even though Toby and Caitlyn had already raced around the corner and disappeared.

Shaking her head in wonder, Kim trudged to her assigned spot while Craig circled the little house, checking on everyone else. The man sure had a way about him. The trouble was, she wasn't sure she liked it. Oh, she'd admit they'd been floundering before his arrival. On the other hand, he'd taken charge without so much as a "by your leave." Was he always so bossy?

Seconds later, Craig rounded the corner of the cottage wearing a sheepish expression. "Hey," he said, coming close enough to speak without raising his voice. "I owe you an apology."

Kim frowned. From the way Craig had stepped in and started barking orders, she'd expected him to offer a critique of her painting skills, not an apology. "What for?" she asked.

"I sort of took over there for a minute. I'm sorry about that." His mouth twisted into a wry grimace. "I think I've spent too much time working with the town council. Each of them has their own agenda, so trying to get anything done in our meetings is a little bit like herding cats. I've learned I have to jump right in and take charge if there's something we need to accomplish."

Though the image of Craig trying to wrangle a group of independent felines brought a smile to her lips, she wasn't about to let him off the hook. Not yet, at least. "I would have broken up the teams differently—put you and Diane together and me with Belle." It was obvious that neither of her cousins had handled a paintbrush in thirty-some years.

"We could have done that, but..." Starting with a twinkle in his steel-gray eyes, a grin spread slowly across Craig's face.

"But what?"

"But then I wouldn't get to spend time with you."

"Oh?" A warmth as thick as cane syrup spread through Kim's chest.

"Absolutely." Craig raised his hands in a sign of surrender.

"In that case, you're going to have to tell me about this prize you're giving away."

Craig's easy chuckle drifted between them. "The first team to finish their part gets to paint the remaining wall." He paused. "Unfortunately, Toby is wise to my ways. He and Caitlyn will probably finish dead last."

Kim wasn't so sure about that. "They'd have to do some serious goofing off to go slower than Diane and Belle."

"Trust me. Toby is a master at goofing off."

Kim grinned. "Show me a teen who isn't."

Craig rubbed his hands together. "Are we ready to get started, boss?"

When Kim nodded, he attached a paint tray to the ladder before filling it. "How about if I handle the high work and you focus on the parts you can reach easily?"

"Works for me." Her calves already ached from her earlier trips up and down the ladder. Nor could she deny that, from where she stood, the view was spectacular when Craig stood on the top step and leaned toward the house with the roller in hand. Refusing to get caught staring, she concentrated on smoothly applying paint to one section of the wall. She'd coated a fair-size section before, with a nod toward the corner where the two youngsters worked, she asked, "Do you really spend your Saturdays with Toby?"

Craig dipped his roller into the tray and removed the excess paint before he took another swipe at the wall. "That kid is brilliant, an absolute whiz at math, but he struggled at school after his dad split. Divorce is hard, especially when kids are involved." He shook his head. "Anyway, Toby needed somebody in his corner, and my sister needed a break, so we started hanging out together. It's been good for both of us."

Toby had been lucky to have someone like Craig in his life. She moved closer to the ladder. Pitching her voice so only Craig would hear, she said, "My sister Diane and her husband separated recently. Caitlyn didn't take the news well. Diane brought her here hoping it would help them both get their bearings."

"From what I can tell, she couldn't have made a better choice. With Ms. Margaret and you and your cousins as role models, that kid will turn out all right." Extending his arm, Craig spread fresh paint over a section of the wall using smooth, even strokes. "Speaking of which, have you given any more thought to the catering business? Are you moving forward with it?"

Kim swallowed a laugh. When she wasn't worried about her aunt, the inn's finances or her children, the new business venture was all she thought about. "I've been testing recipes and getting organized. Why? You still think it's a good idea, don't you?" A shiver of nervous energy passed through her at the thought that Craig might have had second thoughts about the business she wanted to start.

Balancing on the rungs, he rubbed his flat stomach. "A man's gotta eat. I'm looking forward to something besides takeout or a box of mac 'n' cheese."

"Ewwww. Spare me," Kim teased despite the wave of relief that passed through her.

"I got back last night, so I haven't had a chance to talk with many people. The ones I did mention it to thought your catering idea was a great one." Finished with the area he'd been painting, Craig climbed down the ladder.

Inclining her head toward his, Kim stopped painting in mid-stroke. "You were out of town?" Was that why she hadn't heard from him?

"Didn't I mention it? The day you stopped by City Hall, I was on my way to a mayors' conference in Tallahassee." While he spoke, Craig repositioned the ladder.

Kim thought back to the day he'd shared his lunch with her on a park bench. "Betty Lauder mentioned something about a ride to the airport. You've been gone since then?" A tiny spark of hope burned in her chest. If Craig had been away on business, it would certainly explain why she hadn't seen him since then. She shook her head. And here she'd been convinced that he'd ghosted her.

"Yeah. After three full days of meetings and workshops, I couldn't wait to get back here."

"Not a fan of North Florida, are you?" Kim concentrated on not staring at him when Craig started working on the new section.

"Don't get me wrong—Tallahassee is a beautiful city. Lots of rolling hills and, unlike here, the leaves actually turn colors in the fall. But it's not Emerald Bay."

Kim smiled. She could relate. Ever since the night she'd stepped off the shuttle bus and Amy had driven her to the inn, she'd felt like she'd come home. Starting her own business would let her put down permanent roots in the town.

"Have you picked a name yet?" Craig frowned at the section he'd just painted. After reloading his roller, he applied another coat to the area.

She hesitated. She'd been thinking long and hard about a name for the catering business, but she hadn't run it by anyone else. Did she want Craig to be the first to hear her idea? She took a breath. "I'm thinking of calling it Royal Meals."

"I like it," Craig said without the slightest bit of hesitation. He held one arm aloft, fingers forming a square as if he were framing a marquee. "I can see it now. 'Royal Meals. We bring food fit for a king to your castle. Catering by Kim at the Dane Crown Inn.' It'll look great on a business card." He grinned down at her.

Wondering if he was serious or joking around, Kim glanced up. The moment their eyes met, she felt an odd shift in her equilibrium. She stared back at him, unable to shift her gaze from his. They froze, neither willing to look away until the scuff of sandals on a nearby paver broke the spell.

"I need to go inside for a little while." Belle rounded the corner and came into view. "It's time for Mama to get up from her nap."

Kim's head snapped away, instantly breaking the connection with Craig. "Um, sure. Is Diane okay by herself?"

"Yeah, she's great. We've made good progress." Belle crossed her arms and scanned the portion of the front of the house that Craig and Kim had painted. "Which is more than I can say for you. Less talking and more painting," she said, dropping her hands and striding in the direction of the main house, but not before Kim spotted her cousin's knowing grin.

Uh-oh. Belle was sure to give her the third degree the next time they were alone together. She picked up her roller. It was time to buckle down and make some progress. Evidently Craig felt the same thing because they spent the next couple of hours bringing new life to the cottage stroke by steady stroke.

"Hey, this soffit's come loose. Grab my hammer and a couple of nails from the bucket and hand it to me, will you?" Craig called from atop the ladder before he started working on the last little bit under the eves.

"You're sure you don't want to leave that for Max to take care of?" After he'd power-washed

331

the cottages, the handyman had agreed to stop by early in the week. Kim already had a long list of jobs for him to tackle.

"Nah. This just needs a nail or two and it'll be good as new. I know my limits." Craig took the tools she placed in his outstretched hand. "The big stuff—we'll leave all of that for Max."

By the time the sun sank into a cloud bank that hung just above the horizon, they were putting the final touches on Rosario's exterior. Kim and Craig had finished the front of the little house and, as the so-called winners of the painting competition, they'd begun working on the remaining side. Diane and Belle had joined them a little later. Proving Craig right, Toby and Caitlyn had finished dead last, but the teens had willingly pitched in to finish the job. Everyone stepped back when, with a final swipe of her roller, Caitlyn covered the last little bit of faded paint with a fresh coat.

"I don't believe we did it." Belle stretched backwards, her hands on her hips.

"We'd never have done it without Craig and Toby," Kim said. "We owe you."

"We're not done yet. Tomorrow, we'll work on the inside." Craig gave a mock bow. "If that's all right with the boss lady."

"That's very much all right." If they could

knock out the interior in a day or two, it would put them ahead of schedule. As for the opportunity to spend more time with Craig, that was a bonus she didn't mind. Not even the least little bit.

"Hey, Caitlyn," Craig called gently to the teen. "Great work today."

"Yes, honey. Great work," Diane echoed. "You did an excellent job."

"Did you see how much she accomplished?" Belle asked. "And how careful she was to cover every bit of the old paint?" Removing her hat, she fanned herself with the brim. "I wish I had half your energy."

Though Caitlyn stared at the ground and dragged one foot through the sandy soil, Kim knew that, beneath the shadow of her baseball cap, the youngster beamed. She nudged Diane. "See? Everything's going to turn out all right."

Diane crossed the first two fingers of her left hand and held them up. "I hope so." Dropping her hand, she rubbed one shoulder. "I hurt in more places than I knew I had places."

"And as a reward, we get to do it all again tomorrow." Kim's dry comment drew groans from everyone who'd gathered on the deck.

Craig clapped his hands on his knees. "Well,

that's it for me tonight." He nodded at his nephew. "You all set to go?"

When the teenager paired a sideways glance at Caitlyn with a noncommittal shrug of one shoulder, Kim hid a smile. Evidently, she and Craig weren't the only two who had enjoyed working together. "Don't you want to stay for supper?" she asked. "I made chili. There's more than enough." The spicy dish had been simmering in the slow cooker and perfuming the air all day.

Craig gave a mournful glance toward the kitchen. "Much as I'd like that, we need to get Toby home before dark or his mama will worry."

"In that case, I'll walk you out," Kim offered.

Craig dug in the pocket of his jeans and pulled out his keys. Handing them to his nephew, he directed, "Stow our gear behind the front seat. I'll be along in a minute."

As they walked side by side down the path toward the parking area a few minutes later, Kim's heart swelled. "For the first time, I feel like we might actually get the place fixed up enough to hold a reunion like Aunt Margaret wants. I meant it when I said we couldn't have done it without you and Toby."

Touching the brim of his baseball hat, Craig

gave a passable imitation of a cowboy. "Shucks, ma'am. T'weren't nothin'.'"

Kim lightly rapped his upper arm with her fist. "Seriously, we wouldn't have finished one wall without you."

"I don't think you're giving yourself near enough credit. You matched me roller for roller. Once we got them started, Diane and Belle turned out to be excellent painters. Even Caitlyn did her share and seemed to enjoy it. Besides, neighbors helping neighbors is kind of our thing in Emerald Bay."

"I've always liked the way people look out for one another here."

"It's one of the best aspects of living in a small town." He kicked a small pebble into the grass. "I'll see you tomorrow?"

"I'm looking forward to it." Probably more than she should. "Will you and Toby stay for supper afterwards?" After all the pair were doing for her family, it seemed only fair to provide a home-cooked meal.

"Can I get a rain check on that?"

"Do you have other plans?" The question hung between them before she even knew she was going to ask it. Not that she should be one bit surprised if Craig was seeing someone else. He was, to use her aunt's words, quite the catch.

It was a wonder that no one else had snapped him up already.

"No, no plans." Craig leaned one hip against the rear fender of his truck. "I just don't think you, or anyone else, should have to spend hours in the kitchen after painting all day. I'll bring fried chicken for lunch instead."

"You fry chicken?" Kim drew back in mock alarm. She eyed him with suspicion. "Have you been holding out on me?"

"No, ma'am." Craig laughed. "I told you, I'm no cook. But I can buy with the best of them, and I happen to know the diner serves the best chicken in town."

"Hmmm. Free help and fried chicken? You sure know the way to a girl's heart." Such generosity deserved a kiss and, at the final bend before the path emerged from the hedge, she rose on her tiptoes and planted a quick one on his lips.

"See you tomorrow." She turned and hurried back the way she'd come, denying herself the urge to kiss him again.

Tomorrow would be another busy day. What with their aunt to watch over, church to attend and an afternoon of painting, she had plenty of things to occupy her mind. Worrying whether Craig Morgan was still standing where she'd left him, watching her walk away, wasn't one of them. All the same, she walked slowly until she was certain she'd moved out of sight. Only then did she pick up her pace as she headed for the house and dinner with her family.

Thirteen

Diane

Margaret sat in the chaise lounge looking lost in thought.

Diane studied her aunt. A pile of pillows propped up her broken arm. A bottle of water and the latest edition of *Southern Inns* sat within easy reach. The wide table umbrella had been angled to provide plenty of shade, assuming the sun ever peeked out from behind the clouds. "Is there anything else I can get for you, Aunt Margaret?" she asked. "A glass of tea? A book to read?"

"No, dear. I'm as fine as I can be." Margaret snapped back from wherever her thoughts had taken her. "I was just sitting here thinking about what the preacher said this morning." While the rest of the family attended church in person,

Belle and her mother had stayed at the inn, where they'd watched the service on Diane's laptop.

"It was a good message, wasn't it?" Without waiting for an answer, Diane said, "I wish Belle could have been there, though. That choir could use a voice like hers." Between a tone-deaf baritone and the faded voices of several elderly sopranos, the robed choir had mangled all three hymn selections.

"Now, child, they meant well," Aunt Margaret chided.

"I know." Diane let her head hang low. "Guess I should have paid more attention to the sermon." *Judge not* had been at the heart of the lesson.

"There *is* one thing you could do for me, if you wouldn't mind." Margaret sat up straighter while she uncrossed and recrossed her legs.

"Anything, Aunt Margaret."

"I haven't even looked at the mail since this happened." Margaret lifted the arm in its heavy cast. "Could you sort through it? Put the junk mail in the recycling and pay the bills?"

"Of course." Handling paperwork was her wheelhouse. "Everything is on your desk in the office?" she asked.

"It should be."

"Okay. I'll run, go get them and work out here. You'll stay put while I'm gone?" The last thing she needed was for her aunt to get hurt on her watch.

"Don't run, dear. You might trip. But yes, I'll behave myself." Margaret uncrossed her legs and relaxed into the cushions.

For the next hour or so, Diane sat at the table while her aunt catnapped on the lounge. She quickly lost herself in the familiar task of separating advertising flyers from important-looking envelopes, entering figures into the spreadsheets she maintained on her laptop and writing checks for the few services that didn't offer online banking. Watching the inn's account balance shrink with every bill caused her throat to tighten, but she forced herself to work her way toward the bottom of the stack. When only a few pieces of mail remained, she eyed the distant cottages. Once they finished refurbishing them and gave the main house a much-needed overhaul, the inn's finances would turn around, wouldn't they?

She didn't have time to reassure herself before she caught sight of Belle striding through the door of Rosario wearing the same paint-splattered clothes she'd worn the day before.

Today, though, her cousin had hidden every inch of her red curls beneath a stylish head wrap.

Talking animatedly, Belle held her phone against one ear. "You've got to be kidding me!" she shouted.

Beside her, Margaret stirred. Diane's eyes narrowed when Belle's excited voice continued to cut through the still afternoon. She trained a questioning look on her aunt. Was this another example of Belle's natural exuberance? Or was something more going on?

Instead of answering, Margaret watched her daughter like a mother hen watched her chick when hawks flew overhead. Holding her breath, Diane monitored the situation until, finally, Belle tucked her phone into her back pocket.

An instant later, the superstar doubled over. Margaret's breath hissed, and she struggled to swing her legs off the chaise lounge. Diane hurried to help her aunt. As she stood, the stack of bills she'd been working on scattered. A couple of envelopes fluttered to the surface of the wooden deck. Diane ignored them in order to focus on her aunt. She'd no sooner reached Margaret's side than a triumphant cry rent the air.

"Yee-ha!" Belle raised both hands above her head and spun in a circle.

"Are you all right?" Diane called. Sensing Belle's happy dance was a good sign, she gentled Margaret's headlong rush.

"What's going on?" Kim's head appeared in the doorway of the cottage where she and Craig, Amy, Caitlyn and Toby had been working.

"Everything's fine! Better than fine." Belle's voice drifted in the still air. She waved to the others. "C'mon. Let's go up to the house. I want Mama to be the first to know, but you'll want to hear this, too."

Belle's sneakered feet fairly skipped over the pavers as she approached the deck where Diane and Margaret waited. Kim followed close at her heels. Caitlyn, Craig and Toby brought up the rear.

"What is it, honey?" Margaret reached for her daughter when Belle had bounded up the steps and onto the deck.

"You'll never believe it. I can scarcely believe it myself." Belle glanced over one shoulder to make sure the others were listening. Once she made certain, she announced, "Someone bought the Twombly."

Diane watched concern deepen the wrinkles around her aunt's lips and eyes.

Margaret's voice strained. "Is that good or bad news?"

"Good. Very good." Belle took her mom's outstretched fingers in her own. "It means someone wanted that painting so badly they made a preemptive bid. They're paying more than I expected to get for it." For emphasis, she added, "And I expected a lot!"

As the others crowded around them, Belle turned to Diane. "Do you know what this means?"

"That you're loaded?" Diane ventured, uncertain. Her cousin had never mentioned the actual value of the painting, but judging from her reaction, it had to be substantial.

"Don't I wish!" Whipping her hair free of its wrap, Belle sank onto the chaise lounge at her mother's knees. "Actually, I am right this minute, but..." She mopped her face with the colorful cloth. "I spent a lot of my own money on the new album and getting ready for the tour. When Noble put both of them on hold, it left me up to my eyeballs in debt. But here's the thing. According to Richard, my financial guy, selling the Twombly will pay off everything I owe."

Diane felt a bit of her excitement wane. While she was happy enough for Belle, selling the pricey piece of art had basically gotten her cousin back to zero. That hardly seemed like an occasion worth celebrating.

"Plus..." Belle held up both hands. Like an actress on stage, she paused for dramatic effect. "Plus, there'll be enough left over to pay for refinishing the floors and getting new carpet for the inn!"

"Why, that is good news!" Margaret declared as all the worry lines faded from her face. She gave her daughter's hand a one-armed squeeze while, on the steps behind Belle, Caitlyn and Kim cheered.

When the hubbub died down, Kim suggested that, since they'd all gathered on the deck anyway, they should officially take a short break. She and Craig went inside. Diane motioned the others to make themselves comfortable and began gathering up the few envelopes she'd dropped in her haste to rush to Margaret's aid. She smiled her thanks at Caitlyn when her daughter retrieved one of the bills from beneath a nearby chair before she sat on the steps, her long legs stretched out in front of her. Diane tucked the bills under one corner of her laptop just as Kim and Craig emerged from the house carrying glasses of sweetened iced tea and a plate of bite-size cheese balls on pretzel sticks.

"What a great idea!" Diane exclaimed, taking one of the treats from the dish. "Where'd you come up with these?"

Kim shrugged. "Couldn't tell you."

Diane popped the cheese in her mouth and nibbled on the stick. Holding up her hands, she said, "No mess."

"And no silverware to wash," Belle pointed out.

Leaning against the railing on the stairs, Toby downed his tea in several quick swallows. "Thank you," he said, crossing the deck to return his glass to the tray. He snagged another couple of pretzels, devoured one and handed the other one to Caitlyn. Nodding toward Craig, he said, "Caitlyn and me, we're almost done with the kitchen. You want us to start on the other bedroom next?"

Craig's head bobbed. "If we get a move on, we'll finish with this cottage before dark."

His words put everyone in motion. Ice cubes clinked while the painters downed the final sips of their drinks and left their glasses on the table. Diane picked up the tray, intending to return the leftovers to the kitchen. She froze when Caitlyn sidled close. The girl had barely spoken to her all day.

"How's the painting coming?" she asked, hiding how much her heart ached behind a neutral tone.

"It's hard work, but Toby and Mr. Craig make it fun." Caitlyn paused long enough to pluck at the hem of her paint-spattered T-shirt. "You were right about making me change clothes yesterday."

"Oh, yeah?" Diane held her breath. It had been a minute since she'd done anything right in Caitlyn's eyes.

"Yeah." Caitlyn leaned close enough that their shoulders brushed.

Before Diane could react, certainly before she had a chance to embrace her daughter in the fierce hug she so wanted to give her, Caitlyn darted down the steps. As she watched the teen rush to join the rest of the painting crew, Diane blinked back tears. Bringing her daughter to Emerald Bay had been the right decision. Whether she and Tim were ever able to resolve their problems, her family would provide plenty of support. Together, they'd help Caitlyn find her bearings.

As for everything else, it was all falling into place. Just like she'd promised she would, Belle had come up with the money they needed for the new flooring. They were moving forward with the plans to fix up the cottages. With any luck, they'd finish renovations on the inn in time to host the family reunion that meant so much to their aunt. She smiled. Sure, some problems still remained. Sooner or later, she'd have to figure out what to do about her job, her marriage, her future. But today, she and Caitlyn had taken the first step. Others would follow.

Feeling better about the future than she had in months, she hefted the tray and carried the empty glasses inside. Returning a few minutes later, she picked up the bills where she'd left off. In the middle of the pile, she found one envelope she hadn't opened. She stared down at the return address for the insurance company that held the inn's policy for everything from hurricane damage to theft to workman's compensation. She frowned. The annual premium wasn't due until spring.

A knot formed in her stomach. Carefully, she slit the envelope open. Her heart sank as she read the official notification that their insurance company was pulling all their business out of the state of Florida. The letter included a warning that Aunt Margaret's policy would be canceled when it came up for renewal in the spring. An attachment provided a list of other companies along with a suggestion that one of them might be willing to provide the necessary coverage for the inn.

Diane quickly ran a finger over the names of

the companies and groaned. In her efforts to keep Aunt Margaret's costs down, she regularly compared insurance rates. The last time she'd checked, all of the ones listed had offered to cover the Dane Crown Inn...for more than double their current payments.

Her knees buckled, and she sank onto the chair. With shaking fingers, she tapped the edge of the letter against the glass tabletop. She did the math quickly, her stomach churning. She'd already earmarked her aunt's meager savings for the renovations. But the higher insurance premiums would deplete those limited funds even faster than anticipated. Unless she found a way to pay this unexpected bill, she'd be forced to shutter the doors of the Dane Crown Inn long before the family reunion. How was she going to tell Aunt Margaret?

Whoa, girl, you're getting way ahead of yourself.

Working to corral her runaway thoughts, Diane took a breath. She squared her shoulders and straightened. Okay, the unexpected bill was bad news. It might even be the worst news she'd gotten all day. However, it didn't mean the world was coming to an end. She wasn't in this alone. She and Amy, Kim and Belle would meet this challenge, just like they'd met the others they'd faced over the last couple of weeks.

There'd been quite a few of them, hadn't there? Less than a month ago, Kim had been drifting along without a purpose. Now, she was starting her own business and had formed a friendship— and maybe, something more—with Emerald Bay's most eligible bachelor. Belle's career had come crashing down around her head, but had she thrown in the towel? No. She was figuring out what came next while she concentrated on the important things, like home and family. As for her own life, it was full of challenges but Diane had no doubt that, with the support of her sister and her cousins, she'd deal with them. And it was already working, wasn't it? Only days ago, she'd feared that a series of bad decisions might ruin her daughter's life. But here, surrounded by women who loved her, Caitlyn was slowly finding her bearings.

So, yeah, the news from the insurance company was disturbing, but she and Belle, Amy and Kim would overcome this obstacle as they'd done all the others so far—together. In the end, they'd find a way to make Aunt Margaret's dream of a family reunion come true.

Behind her, the French doors rattled. The noise startled Diane. She turned to glance over her shoulder and groaned when the last person she'd expected to see stepped out onto the deck.

She tapped the insurance envelope on the table. Just a few minutes ago, she'd been certain her day couldn't get any worse. Apparently, she'd been wrong about that.

Thank you for reading
Treasure Coast Promise!

Want to know what happens next in
Emerald Bay?

Sign up for Leigh's newsletter to get
the latest news about upcoming releases,
excerpts, and more!
https://leighduncan.com/newsletter/

Books by Leigh Duncan

EMERALD BAY SERIES

Treasure Coast Homecoming
Treasure Coast Promise
Treasure Coast Christmas
Treasure Coast Revival
Treasure Coast Discovery
Treasure Coast Legacy

SUGAR SAND BEACH SERIES

The Gift at Sugar Sand Inn
The Secret at Sugar Sand Inn
The Cafe at Sugar Sand Inn
The Reunion at Sugar Sand Inn
Christmas at Sugar Sand Inn

HEART'S LANDING SERIES

A Simple Wedding
A Cottage Wedding
A Waterfront Wedding

ORANGE BLOSSOM SERIES
Butterfly Kisses
Sweet Dreams

Treasure Coast Promise

Hometown Heroes Series

Luke

Brett

Dan

Travis

Colt

Garrett

The Hometown Heroes Collection, A Boxed Set

Single Title Books

A Country Wedding

Journey Back to Christmas

The Growing Season

Pattern of Deceit

Rodeo Daughter

His Favorite Cowgirl

Novellas

The Billionaire's Convenient Secret

A Reason to Remember

Find all Leigh's books at:

leighduncan.com/books

Acknowledgements

Every book takes a team effort.
I want to give special thanks to those who made
Treasure Coast Promise possible.

Cover design
Chris Kridler at
Sky Diary Productions

Editing Services
Chris Kridler at
Sky Diary Productions

Interior formatting
Amy Atwell and Team
Author E.M.S.

About the Author

Leigh Duncan is the award-winning author of more than three dozen novels, novellas and short stories. She sold her very first novel to Harlequin American Romance and was selected as the company's lead author when Hallmark Publishing introduced its new line of romances and cozy mysteries. A National Readers' Choice Award winner and *Publisher's Weekly* National Best-Selling author, Leigh lives on Florida's East Coast where she writes heartwarming women's fiction with a dash of Southern sass. When she isn't busy writing, Leigh enjoys cooking, crocheting and spending time with family and friends.

Want to get in touch with Leigh? She loves to hear from readers and fans. Visit leighduncan.com to send her a note. Join Leigh on Facebook, and don't forget to sign up for her newsletter so you get the latest news about fun giveaways, special offers or her next book!

Made in United States
Orlando, FL
16 January 2024

42586903R00217